THE PRESSURE BUILDS...

The map of Norriya lit up with a bright cursor at the top. Horvath moved the cursor as he spoke. "I toured the entire district—Abibones, Gerumbians, Kaniks, Montayners, and Yuloks. I wore the usual disguises. I talked with the elders and the young people. I sat in on their councils. There is a great restlessness among them. They want—well, they want freedom although the word is in none of their vocabularies. Your peregrini will have to use the new control devices—"

"Horvath, some of those devices—"

"I don't like them either, Shem. But unless we want other, more permanent, solutions..."

"Never," Shem said. "Never!"

"Then we have few alternatives..."

The Gaian Expedient

Part Two of
The Erthring Cycle

Wayland Drew

A Del Rey Book

BALLANTINE BOOKS • **NEW YORK**

FOR PAULA

ACKNOWLEDGMENT

Teperman's last test is an amended version of Douglas Hofstadter's "Luring Lottery," published in *Scientific American*, September 1983. It was suggested by Robert Axelrod's *The Evolution of Cooperation* (Basic Books, 1984).

There was once a madman in us;
the sage has driven him out.

                                    E. M. CIORAN

One of the functions of the intelligence is to take account of
the dangers that come from trusting solely to the intelligence.

                                    LEWIS MUMFORD

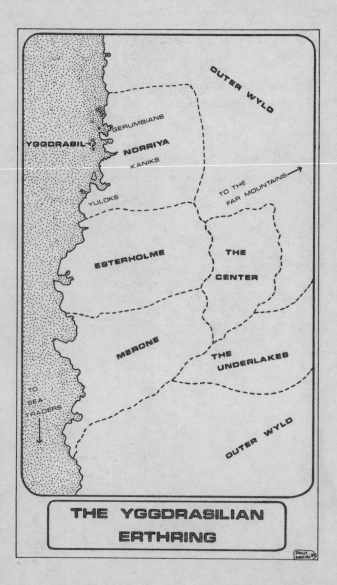

THE YGGDRASILIAN
ERTHRING

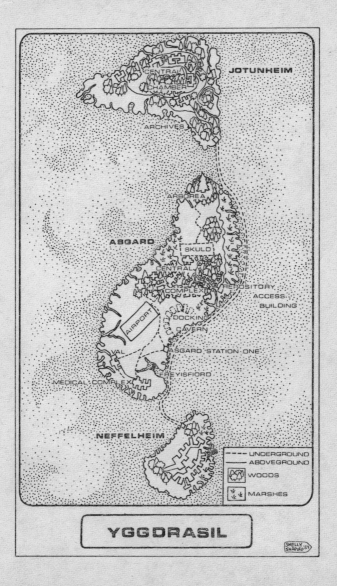

JOTUNHEIM

CENTRAL CHAMBER

ARCHIVES

ARBOREA

ASGARD

SKULD

CENTRAL COMPLEX

REPOSITORY

ACCESS BUILDING

AIRPORT

DOCKING CAVERN

VAL

ASGARD STATION ONE

REYISFIORD

MEDICAL COMPLEX

NEFFELHEIM

- - - - UNDERGROUND
——— ABOVEGROUND
WOODS
MARSHES

YGGDRASIL

SHELLY SHAPIRO '81

PART ONE

THE
OLD
ONES

ONE

ALL DAY A HOT WIND MOVED THROUGH THE RUINS. AT noon it sent shards of glass scraping on concrete sills and twisters of sand swirling along empty boulevards. It moaned and fretted in black cellars and across the doorways of dead rooms. All afternoon flaps of rusted metal creaked and banged in this hot wind.

In a favorite crevasse the lizard drowsed throughout the day. It heard the sounds without listening to them, for all were familiar. During the afternoon, it inched deeper into its lair as the shade slowly angled back like a clock's hand and the sun touched its snout.

At evening, air marbled with the cool breath of the sea spread from the northwest across the ruins.

In the silence, in the long shadows, the lizard heard the first buzzing of the insects. The lizard stirred. The scales on its flanks shivered in anticipation. It tasted the air. Membranes slid off its eyes. It crept forward, dragging its vestigial fifth leg, and with unerring flicks of its tongue began to fill itself with nourishment. The vertical slits of its pupils glowed orange in the twilight.

In front of the lizard's perch the land sloped to a vast desert stretching west. In the distance, a line of hills was an undulating purple ribbon against the sky. Behind it the sun spread and settled, a soft red ball.

In the meager circuitry of its brain, the lizard knew all the sights and sounds that would now occur. The afterglow would light up the undersides of all the clouds with crimson, and yellow, and deep orange, like the glare from a far-off explosion. For a little time the desert would lie still and the walls of the dead city would glimmer with eerie phosphorescence. Then stars would blink on one by one. Perhaps there would be a moon. The hum of the insects would grow louder, and the creatures of the desert would begin to move and make their noises. From the blighted earth would rise a weird chorus of squeaks and moans, and the susurrus of crusted skin scraping across the shale. Occasionally something would howl among the hills. Occasionally something would screech in agony.

All this the lizard knew.

It was therefore instantly alert to an unfamiliar sound. Coming fast was a whine more persistent and more shrill than that of any insect. A thick worm of dust accompanied it. The lizard tensed, crouched, waited . . .

The approaching hovercraft was light and fast, designed for reconnaissance and courier missions. The dusts of distant hills and farther deserts lay thick on its green-tinted windows and on its roof and skirt, almost obscuring the symbol on its flank—a tree with three roots, circled. It was lightly armed. Navigation lights flashed rhythmically on its roof and an air-sensor circled nervously, scooping samples in tiny cups, analyzing, testing. From the swaying antenna flew a two-tone blue pennant with a white *N* in the center.

The vehicle crossed the plateau almost to the base of the hill. It slowed, executed a right-angle turn toward the west with air hissing through its puff-ports, and stopped. The whine of the engine diminished and it settled. For a moment all was still again. Nothing moved except the rooftop sensor whirling, sniffing the atmosphere. Then both cockpit doors opened together and two crewmen dropped to the ground. The driver pulled off his helmet, revealing a thatch of close-cropped orange hair. He linked his fingers behind his neck and swayed forward, working the cramped muscles of his right shoulder, then his left. The navigator-engineer rubbed both fists into the small of his back and stretched. He was shorter than his colleague and more wiry. Instead of a helmet he wore a peaked cap and amber sunglasses. Both wore pale green coveralls. Both were middle-aged. Both carried side arms.

With hardly a glance at the ruins behind them, they moved to the front of their vehicle, talking quietly and nodding toward the red sky in the west. The door of the passengers' cabin opened a crack.

They waited. Soon a deeper and more resonant sound than the whine of the hovercraft came from beyond the hills. In a few moments a small jet swept over the ruined city, banking sharply. The radio in the cockpit of the air-cushion vehicle squawked curtly. The driver reached inside and touched buttons under the dash. A square of orange lights blinked on in the dusk of the plain: a landing pad.

The little plane swept in a wide arc and came to a halt directly over the lights. Its wings swung forward. Its engines tilted vertically, raising clouds of dust. Bright lights flashed on along the lower edges of its wings. Wheels appeared from its belly. The plane descended, touched. The pitch of its engines changed from a whine to a moan, to a growl, to silence. The cabin door opened and a ramp folded down like a delicate arm. For several minutes after it touched the earth, nothing moved on or near the landing pad. The two vehicles waited. The two men waited.

Then, so slowly that it made no sound at all as it fell back against the hovercraft's fuselage, the cabin door swung open all the way and a man stepped out. He was very thin. He bore his long head carefully on sloping shoulders. He walked as if he were carrying something fragile in his belly. He mounted the ramp, taking each step with his right foot, and vanished inside the aircraft. A few moments later, the two crewmen had transferred four light pieces of luggage from their vehicle to the aircraft. They stepped clear, signaled to the pilot. The cabin door closed with a pneumatic pulse. The engines whined up to speed and the little plane leaped clear, banked, and darted westward into the vestiges of afterglow.

After it had gone, the small man in amber sunglasses bent down the aerial of the ACV, removed the pennant bearing the white letter N, swatted it against his knee, and folded it carefully. Then he followed his colleague into the vehicle. The engine started and the craft headed north, leaving the plain and the empty city to their silences.

The lizard relaxed. Its tongue flickered out and plucked a mosquitolike creature out of the twilight.

Far away, something like a cat shrieked in mortal terror.

The Master of Norriya was going home to Yggdrasil, to die.

The time, recorded in the logs of both vehicles, was 1352. The date was 2 June 163 Post Entropies.

TWO

SHE FLOATED TOWARD HIM OUT OF A WHITE WORLD, AND the man who was both watcher and watched held out his arms to embrace her. Her black hair covered his hands, and there was no sound but her laughter and his sobs, which were choked prayers of gratitude to all the gods for bringing her back to him. *Speak*, the watcher said to this weeping man, but he could not speak, could not find even her name in that engulfing joy. He bent close and they danced in their white world. *Speak, tell, say, for it is not a sacrament without the words!* But the dancer danced silent, rejoicing, and then danced apart beguiled by curiosity, careless, so that when he turned toward her again her laughter had been stilled, swept away by interceding winds or tides. Her eyes pleaded, her hands beckoned futilely against these currents that had surged between, currents against which he flailed uselessly until at last, falling to his knees, he saw her borne far beyond his reach. Her hair became the sloping boughs of snow-swept firs and the valleys of far-off mountains, and he who was the watcher moaned *Fool! Fool!* to the supplicant with empty hands. But, in reality, waking, he could no longer separate these two, for he was neither and both.

7

His face was wet with tears, and he had loosed into the world such a sound of grieving that the gods, had they heard it, would have shuddered in the safety of their islands...

THREE

A RAINSQUALL SWEPT ACROSS THE THREE ISLANDS OF the Yggdrasilian archipelago. A brief summer flurry, it arrived without warning out of a clear sky and a tranquil sea. Its onslaught was hardly noticed in the southernmost island of Neffelheim, where parks were few and the blunt buildings housing workshops, repair depots, factories, and laboratories huddled together like a team of nervous horses, their backs to the world. Two or three technicians glanced up indifferently at the slashing of rain across the narrow windows, and then returned to work.

Similarly, the squall was scarcely noted in Jotunheim, the northernmost and highest of the islands, where scholars bent over their work in windowless cubicles or argued in committee rooms. Only a few paused long enough to witness the storm's admonishing energy.

In the central island of Asgard, however, the squall caused a flurry of consternation. Parks emptied swiftly. Mothers with children scurried into their apartments. Old people who had strolled too far from the senarium took shelter in gazebos overlooking the marshes and the sea. Lovers slipped beneath the protective arms of evergreens.

Only one young man made no attempt to avoid the

storm. When the first gusts struck him, he was on a path midway between the Central Complex and the Repository Access Building on the eastern shore. It was a narrow path and very little used. Most researchers preferred to go by the quicker, underground route, using one of the electric carts that were the common means of travel around Asgard and between the islands. Alone on the path, the young man faced the freshening wind so that it swept back his long black hair. He saw the lowering storm clouds. He felt the first spattering of rain across his face above his beard. He smiled. He had been moving with an easy stride that had not been bred on that little island. It came from the mainland wilderness, where the paths of the forests were endless and where a man could run for days on the empty plains. He did not alter this stride, even when the wind whipped low branches across his shoulders and the torrents drenched him.

He wore the green uniform of the Yggdrasilian novice, one of those young people undergoing the arduous five years of basic training before being posted to Neffelheim, to Jotunheim, or to the Gaian Expedient as peregrini. Above the heart was a badge bearing the great tree of Yggdrasil, its boughs stretching to heaven, its three roots held fast in earth. Beneath this was a small bar bearing his name: Asa.

The light shade of the uniform signified that he was not a native Yggdrasilian novice (theirs were dark green), but that he had been brought in from one of the Five Districts of the Erthring for reasons known only to the Masters. He had, in other words, been an aborr, a man who had stepped from the stone age into what was left of the twenty-second century. Into what was left of time.

He moved easily through the storm, lifting his face to the rain. Only his hands sometimes seemed awkward. They clenched and unclenched as if suddenly bereft of tools or weapons they had long been used to carrying. Sometimes they slashed suddenly across the rain. Sometimes they jabbed savagely at the soft branches as he passed.

From inside the Repository Access Building a young woman watched his approach. Like him she wore the green uniform of the novice (dark green, for she was Yggdrasilian) with her name, Yida, emblazoned beneath the tree symbol over her heart. From the low desk at which she sat she looked across a glimmering vestibule, through polished glass doors, and straight down the white stone pathway, now lashed by the storm. She saw him as if at the end of a long tunnel, through veils of rain. She stopped breathing momentarily and caught her lower lip in her teeth. She loved this man. She had loved him for four years, and the reason for her consternation as she watched him approach was that every meeting with him was a kind of torture.

Her love was wholly futile. She knew that. She had known for four years. And yet it persisted despite everything she had done to rid herself of it. It persisted despite even a carefully designed program at Val. For a time after each of her visits there, after each of the meticulous dreaming sessions, she felt little more than kindness when they met; then other yearnings returned.

She had loved him from their first weeks together, in spite of all she knew. Asa's story was well known, for the Alcheringian Solution was part of the recent history of Yggdrasil, part of the training of all novices. She had known that alone of all the tribe Asa had miraculously survived. She had known that he stayed aloof from other novices and resented intrusions on his privacy. She had heard distressing tales of his curtness and incivility. Rumors said that three passions ruled his life; two involved people whose names he sometimes shouted in the night or when one of his spells assailed him. The third was a rage to know.

All this Yida had known, and yet her infatuation had continued through the years of classes, labs, introductory sessions in Neffelheim and Jotunheim, field trips and peregrinus training procedures. She had loved his intensity, his intelligence, his strength, his strange weakness that the doctors now believed they had controlled. Most of all she had loved the quiet mystery at his center, from which all else radiated—his silences, his questions, his tenderness, his rage.

Rage there was. She had learned that the night when,

gathering her courage, she had invited him to stay with her. He had looked at her with wonder, as if she had just suggested a voyage to another planet, and he had accepted and gone with her to her small novice's apartment overlooking the sea.

She would have described what happened there as lovemaking, but she could not speak for him. She would not presume to speak for him. He had acted with the same tentativeness and wonder that he brought to the learning of everything. Then, in the night, in the winter wind, he had murmured a name that was not her name.

Persis, he had said. *Persis*.

She feared then that what she felt for him was hopeless, but not until dawn did she fear for her life. She was awakened by a snarl so bestial she thought at first she was in the Gerumbian wilds and some grotesque had fallen upon their bivouac. Before she had time to move, his hands were on her throat, pinning her to the bed so that she couldn't speak, couldn't scream. His eyes saw her in the dawn, but not her; someone else. His voice was Asa's but not Asa's; some primal breath, some growl from old savannahs, *"Garm! Garm! Garm! You...took...her!"* And his strength was not only Asa's but also the strength of all vengeance, vengeance incarnate. The sound that had finally brought her help was that of her limp body, caught in his fists, banging against the wall. Three friends were not enough. Nor four. It took five to bear him down and free her back into life. Her room was chaos, and those five went hurt and hobbling through the next week's program. "Asa the Mad," they had said to one another.

"Sorry, sorry," he had said to her. And he was.

She had used his remorse to forgive him with a kiss. "Nothing," she had said, smiling. "Aborr craziness."

But she had learned that he was someone else's, heart and soul, body and mind, someone with whom she could never compete for she was a wraith and a memory and utterly insubstantial. Shortly after, on the advice of friends and under the guidance of a sympathetic dream master, she had gone to Val.

But she had not stopped loving him. She had not stopped hurting when they met.

He came out of the rain now in three long strides, up the front steps and through the glass doors, bringing the clean smell of the rain with him. He left wet tracks on the gleaming floor.

"Hel*lo*."

"Yida! I didn't know you were on duty."

An old man glared from a nearby display terminal. "Sh!" he said.

Asa glanced at him and said more softly, "I thought you were off this weekend."

"I am. I mean I was. I'm filling in for Bel. She's sick." Yida turned away from him. She looked at her terminal. He was resting his left fist on the counter, and instead of the watch that regulations required all personnel to wear she had seen encircling his wrist the delicate bracelet of woven black hair and obsidian beads that she knew bound him inextricably to other places, places out of time. "What are you working on?" she asked.

"The Teperman File."

"Teperman!" She looked up in surprise. "But Asa, nobody actually *reads* that file."

"Oh? But it's listed. A prerequisite."

"Yes, but everybody just signs it out to fulfill the requirements, that's all. They don't actually *read* it."

"I think I'll read it," he said, smiling. "I have time."

She ordered it, tapping the call number into her keyboard. "It'll be just a minute." She leaned back and folded her arms. "Do you have a posting?"

"Not yet. You?"

She shook her head.

"There'll be more tests."

"Of course. But if you had your choice, where would you want to work?"

"Jotunheim," he said.

She laughed in surprise.

"Shh!" the old man said, taking off his glasses. "*Sh!*"

"Oh, Asa," she whispered, "with all those *scholars*? Besides, they'd never—" She flushed.

"Say it. They'd never appoint me to Jotunheim because I'm an aborr."

"Well, they've never—"

"I know. Not yet."

A diskette sent from the Repository far below slipped out of the pneumatic slide and into the receptacle on her desk. *Teperman One.* She handed it to him, and he thanked her and crossed the reading room to an unoccupied machine, leaving wet footprints on the floor.

In a moment the forematter of the Teperman File appeared on his screen:

```
FILE: TEPERMAN, J. Y.
TITLE: MEMOIRS/SECTION ONE: FORMATION
OF YGGDRASIL
CALL #: SERIES B59833/PRE-ENTROPIES MSS
COLL
COPY: 132
ACCESS: LIMDIS: ARBOREA/JOTUNHEIM/
NOVITIATE FINAL STAGE.
```

You are alive and I am not, yet we meet. Now.

Yida waited until he was absorbed in his reading, then she turned away and touched buttons on her control console, calling a small maintenance robot from its closet. So quietly and discreetly that neither Asa nor any of the other readers noticed it, the little machine deftly blotted up the wet footprints, buffed the floor to its original sheen, and rolled back into its closet on soft rubber wheels. The door hissed shut.

Yida pretended to work, but surreptitiously she watched Asa. He was engrossed in his reading, his long hair forming a kind of tent at the sides of his head, his hands resting lightly on his thighs. Several times she was on the point of crossing the room to him on some pretext—"I forgot to get your signature in the register . . . I wondered if you'd like me to order ancillary material . . ."—crossing to him, bending to whisper to him, perhaps letting her hair touch his shoulder. But then, she imagined his turning on her as he had that night, out of that other world . . .

With a little sigh she returned to the safety of the extinct language on which she was working. Her specialty was the fragmentation of English into the plethora of tribal dialects after the Entropies, but lately she had discovered the remnants of other languages as well, lying neglected in the vaults of the Repository and in the files of SKULD. It seemed that once there had been something called French, and something else called German, and languages even more beautiful like Spanish and Japanese.

Working one evening shortly before, she had inadvertently accessed a file not listed in any index. Under a strange number the word XTAPLACIAN suddenly appeared on her screen. Probing further, she discovered that this too was a language, a curious amalgam of others. The more she had studied its complex grammar and vocabulary, the more she had read its elliptical literature, the more fascinated she had become. Through it she had begun to piece together a picture of a spirited and beautiful culture.

She could not tell from this random file whether that culture had actually existed or whether it was a fiction.

Neither could she know that one of SKULD's monitors had noted her interest.

FOUR

——Hugin Four Five, are you receiving? Over.

—Affirmative, Yggdrasil.

—Report position, Four Five.

—Rendezvous complete, Yggdrasil. Over Larl at three zero zero. Altitude three hundred. Estimate Yggdrasil fifty-two. Over.

—Fog and visibility zero, Four Five. Surface wind one one zero at fifteen, gusting to twenty-five. Normal ADF approach. Over.

—Request vectors, Yggdrasil.

—Go to nine hundred, Hugin Four Five. Course two six zero. Call entering Neffelheim hold. Over.

—Roger, Yggdrasil. Out.

Garm alone was on his feet when the god came.

Five days earlier he and his small band had ridden west out of the Kanik Mountains. They had forded the Em at dusk on the second day and skirted north of the Middle Wayst by the light of a full moon, moving in single file and in silence, dreading the specter of the gleaming white city far to the south. They had rested the next day in the hilly region out of which the headwaters of the Larl flowed

16

south. They had frolicked like children among the waterfalls, shooting fish and letting their corpses float whitebellied toward the sea.

The next day they had ridden down refreshed upon the Gerumbians who dwelt in the caves west of the Larl. Less deformed than other Gerumbians, these morphs were agile and intelligent, and provided excellent sport in their attempts to defend their mates and their offspring.

They were of course no match for Kanik cunning and Kanik speed. Garm and his followers had ridden and killed until they could kill no more.

They were going home when the god flew across their camp. Sated with rampage, they talked in a desultory manner. They watched their meat cook.

Garm alone was on his feet, halfway to the brush corral they had built to hold the horses.

The god came low above the trees and his roaring terrified the horses. They screamed like birds, thrashing against each other. Garm ran to them under the roaring. The others fell flat, groveling for what cover they could find—bed-boughs, tent flaps, empty packs. Garm alone stayed on his feet. He spun from the terrified horses and jabbed his spear upward, thrusting again and again, leaping, his roar of rage blending with the howl of the swooping god. He screamed. He screamed, consumed by desire to open the belly between the orange eyes and to spill the god's guts in a streaming spume across the hillside.

He was still howling long after the winking eyes and the roar had faded in the west, and his screaming ended in a fit of coughing that drove him to his knees. "Cowards!" he shouted when he could speak again. "You call yourselves *warriors*?"

The others said nothing. One by one they rose warily and brushed themselves off, and when they were sure that the god had vanished for good into the west, they began to gather together the scattered embers of the fire. The youngest shook violently and laughed in a high-pitched monotone until one of the others quieted him.

They were six. All Kanik hunting and raiding parties were the same size, for six was the sacred number. Kanik legends said that somewhere to the west six great gods controlled the host of these lesser deities that sometimes roared across the plains, crossed even the waysts, swooped with avenging thunder, or rose monstrous from the sea, hooting and flashing angry red and green eyes, causing the shamans to mutter over their scapulae and atone for whatever law of the Regulae might have been broken. Legends said that all gods, the Six included, dwelt in the sea, beyond the coasts of the fish-eaters.

Garm calmed the horses. He called to them in the soft sounds that they made sometimes to each other across the evening plains. He spoke their names and reached toward them through the rails so they could smell his scent as they galloped past. Gradually they settled. They snorted, stamped, pranced close to him for reassurance, and he touched them one by one. When their alarm had dwindled to restlessness he returned to the campfire. "I have more respect for them than you," he said to the five men crouched in the dirt.

He spat.

He leaned forward and sliced away a steaming strip of venison. He chewed slowly. He let his eyes fill with the glow of the rekindling embers.

The others did not look at him. They edged close, cut meat, ate.

—Yggdrasil Control, this is Hugin Four Five. Do you read me?

—Go ahead, Four Five.

—Reporting aborr activity, Yggdrasil. Coordinates RFive, MWTwo. Alcheringian Mountains, southeast of Gerumbian boundary.

—Go ahead, Four Five.

—We have a clear infraction, Yggdrasil. Kanik raiders beyond proscribed limits. Master Norriya requests Moran be notifed at once.

—Very good, Four Five. Out.

FIVE

You ARE ALIVE AND I AM NOT, YET WE MEET. Now.

You read, and I am in your thoughts.

You breathe, and I am in the tang of the sea, the scent of evergreen.

You look through a window, and I am in the mist that combs the forest.

You listen, and I am in the laughter of children on the path.

I shall never know you, but in these pages you will come to know me very well. Good. Search every nuance, every subtlety, and every omission, for it is in these that I shall live. Not in the reporting. Not in mere facts. It is not my consciousness which will transport meaning to you across the years. It is my pathetic, fallible, unconscious humanity.

No doubt you are using a standard videoscreen at this moment, similar to the ones to which I have recently been introduced. If our plans succeed, this manuscript—this small stack of paper on which I am writing—will have acquired the patina of an icon by the time you read these words. A relic. It will be sequestered away with others of its sort in the Repository, preserved by the most sensitive archival thermostats and humidistats, and you will be reading a copy. A cold copy. That is a great pity. I wish you could hold this fine rag paper on which I write. I wish you could share the pulpy tang that fills my nostrils, or the mustiness that will, despite all precautions, have invaded it across the gulf between us. I wish you could feel the fine, fibrous texture of it and see how this rich ink flowing amply from my pen seeps into it. I wish you could scrutinize my calligraphy, over which I have taken no precautions whatsoever, and see in it my character laid bare. I wish you could draw from these things some of this very air that I breathe, and so sense the ebbing of my world.

We have engaged historians to chronicle for you precisely what will happen at the end, so far as they are able. If our plans succeed, their accounts should be safe in the vaults of your Repository. You will probably have read them as part of your training. So, by the time you come to this, you will know more than I about how we died. I know only that we will succumb to what we have termed the Kraken Syndrome, a synergistic welter of self-inflicted poisons and abuses of which the violent spasm of unspeakable weaponry will be but the final episode. Long darkness will follow, and desperate cold, before any flesh will walk again in the sun of heaven...

Yes, I admit that I am anticipating it with baleful curiosity. Except for this memoir I have completed my work, and at my age death is less frightening than addlepated senility. Still, there is much I regret leaving. What we have called the simple things, mostly. Crystalline birdsong. Brooks and shaded moss. Woodsmoke. And all extremes of weather, including this wild wind that howls about my eaves as I write, obliterating all other sound.

To work.

Let me begin by properly introducing myself. Facts: My name is Teperman. I am seventy-five years old and in revoltingly good health. I have permitted no photographs to be taken of me for many years, but of course you will be curious about my appearance. Very well. Ask your archivist to show you a photograph of the artist Pablo Picasso. There. C'est moi, Teperman. Except that I am slightly less bald and considerably more quizzical. But my lips are as full, to taste all of life; my ears, frankly animal, are canted forward and oversized to gather all sounds; my eyes bulge, yearning to escape from their sockets and into the world to explore it *from all sides at once. Like his, my skin is walnut-browned from expensive suns.*

Later you may hear a recording of my voice. It is freakishly high, a tenor in a bass chest. All my life others have felt tricked and defensive upon meeting me because of this, and also because of other incongruities carefully nurtured.

The discomfort of others has not prevented my making money. Nothing has prevented my making money. I have always been quite blithe and ruthless about that, and since I have had the necessary acumen, energy, and tunnel vision, I have grown very rich. In fact, disgustingly rich. Such wealth as I have amassed, wealth spawning beyond all talent or need, becomes for some an embarrassment, a prurient secret, a final obscenity. Not for me. For me, there has always been a serenity in such riches. All my life I have perceived a sublime logic in the transmutation of wealth into power, and of power into a transformed world. My companies have changed the face of Earth, cutting, bulldozing, dynamiting, diverting, building, tearing down and building once again. For—answer me this!—how does man define himself except by this domination of nature?

I believed that. There is a part of me that believes it still, as there is a part of all of us. It is that which has made man Earth's cancer.

I was an old man before I understood what we had become and what we had done. The knowledge paralyzed me, choked me with ironies. What, all our ethics, all our Western morality, all designed for man only? As if he were not part of the community of life? As if he did not depend upon the subtle functions of Earth's systems? As if he were not bound by intricacies beyond his comprehension?

The event that brought our dementia home to me may appear trivial to you who have inherited so many more catastrophes. It was the death of the last Grizzly. I had known that we had destroyed one million of the Earth's species. I had known that we were destroying the rest at the rate of three per day. But for some reason the loss of this one species, this one animal, struck me deeply. He was only a decrepit bear trapped in the squalor of some zoo, but as long as he had lived, a kind of hope lived with him, a hope for the broad spaces through which he and his kind had once roamed at will. When he died he took that hope with *him; in his dead eyes, staring from my newspaper, I saw only profound pity!*

The event was an epiphany. I saw that our ethics had been but rationalizations for an appalling selfishness. We had used our vaunted brain not to define what was required, not to control and limit our own evolution, but to prance ever faster in our macabre jigs of death.

So, old but not senile, armed with this modicum of truth, old, but with these yearning eyes, I asked, What can be done to redeem mankind, even now?

The answer was not immediately obvious.

I had learned the truth of Einstein's observation that the knowledge of what is does not open the door directly to what should be.

At length I retired to my lodge, here, in these mountains. With books. For the first time in my life I began to read broadly. I ordered all links severed to the outside world, except those by which I received my supplies, my books and papers. Isolation and a trusted staff guaranteed my privacy. Before long I was engaged in an obsessive quest in which I, Teperman, was dwarfed by the grandeur of the knowledge opening before me. What a wizened life I had led in the cocoon of my megalomania!

The more I read, the more closely I questioned those experts whom I had flown in to elucidate difficult ideas, to amplify knowledge or to compress it or to synthesize it, the more embarrassed I became for my species. Humiliated. Ashamed.

You know very well what I mean. You've read the histories. Look what we inherited. Look what we did to it. Poison, exploitation, and slaughter until we had reduced our majestic seas to cesspools and our green world to lifeless stubble!

Matricide! Suicide!

Hearing the litany of depredation that was human history, I was so mortified and sickened that I wanted to quit my kind. Be a bug. Grow fur, scales, gossamer wings to lift me, shovel paws to let me burrow again. I held my hands at arm's length and cursed my fabled thumbs. I cursed my perverted brain. I cursed my language.

Cursed my cursing.

Cursed.

Went silent.

For weeks I read nothing, said nothing, saw no one. I

went among trees. I watched and listened and smelled. I felt rough bark and the tenderness of petals. I let the clean rain wash through my empty mouth.

In the fullness of time I returned, of course. Returned to reading and questioning. I could not stop thinking. I knew that if I could answer the question, Why was it that this frail and hairless biped, man, after several million years as an integral part of his ecosystem, went suddenly pathological, killing indiscriminately and unable to stop even when he threatened his own survival?—If I could answer that question then we might begin therapy for the pathology.

Nothing I read gave me the answer. No one I consulted could explain. Historians knew the process by which it had occurred very well, and they exulted in providing much dreary detail. But they could not tell me why it was we could not stop. When I asked they fell dumb. They shrugged. They rubbed their noses, pulled their earlobes. They mumbled about speed, momentum, restricted vision, shirked responsibilities. But even I, a mere rich man, could see that much more was involved. Even I refused to fall into that trap of historical determinism which said that because it has been so and was obviously always in the process of becoming, therefore there was no alternative but for events to evolve as they did.

What nonsense!

I laughed at them, and my laughter was shrill and mocking, like a rusty guillotine. Oh no, my dear fellows. Out. Out out! And I brushed them away from me.

But what then? Psychologists and psychiatrists were no help. They were like children watching the fall of random stars, believing that they understood the night. Most medical men glowered and retreated into jargon, although a few honest ones smiled wanly and opened empty hands. Philosophers spoke obfuscations when they were not dissembling, and I perceived in what they said the inadequacies of language. Theologians haggled. Scientists cudgeled each other with hypotheses. Biologists merely chronicled the demise of the living when they were not meddling with the stuff of life itself.

It seemed that in asking this question I was on my own. Not that it had never been asked; indeed, Western mythology and literature were full of its asking, but most hauntingly in fables and myths, in the silence beyond language.

And so, I read the fables.

I had learned that there was no such thing, finally, as scientific method that would assist with such a problem. Method was a term used by teachers and other apologists after the fact, a pretense that logic and reason, dreary reason, played a far greater role than they actually did. I knew the reality was more banal: Discoverers muddled. They immersed themselves in a problem as in a warm bath. They groped. They exulted when they found leads, despaired when they reached dead ends. They got tired. They lived their lives, thought about whether to rake the leaves or see a movie, and went to supermarkets with penciled shopping lists. Then, suddenly, while they were walking, or riding a train, or making love, or turning to take a glass from the cupboard, the answer would be there. *Crystalline. Perfect. A gift.*

For a little time I deluded myself that perhaps I too could be enlightened by such a bold shaft. I too might be inspired. Have a satori. But I had started too late. My bath was much too shallow. What was required was not one lifetime but many. What was required was not one mind but many, a community of scholars. A colloquium. A university at its best, magnified many times.

And it required time. Much time. Time that I did not have. Before such a group could be assembled, civilization would be finished. My experts said five to ten years.

So I had begun too late.

Yet, perhaps not. I had not begun too late to make money, and if time was money then money could be time. No sooner had I thought this than I was granted the revelation I required. I could buy time! Not for myself. Not for "civilization," whatever that might have been, but for man. For the human experiment.

I could create a little island of time in the chaos that was coming. I was stricken dumb with joy at the prospect. I thought: *I am becoming a god!* And then I thought: *I must be careful not to become a god!*

That is why I, Teperman, writing this with my stumpy and ungodlike fingers, quickly tell you the following ungodlike facts:

—my left eye is bloodshot and dribbling;

—I am not entirely continent;

—I need a bath;

—I am profoundly frightened.

You must know that I am merely human. You must reach through time in your imagination and sense whatever warmth emanates from this seamed flesh, now, as our time runs out and yours is about to begin. Yours. The time we bought for you.

Writing this has given me immense pleasure. I wonder if I could have had the same pleasure daily had I kept a journal throughout my life. Probably not. Of course I know what Socrates said about the unexamined life being not worth living, but I have observed that that is simply untrue. Most people have lived quite lustily, irresponsibly, and with some degree of happiness. Not joy, but happiness. Or perhaps there are ways other than writing to examine life—prayer, perhaps, or simply conversation. In any case, most people seem to be quite sure of what they're doing, whereas I have never been sure at the time and even less sure in retrospect.

On reflection I'm relieved that I didn't keep a diary, for I daresay that if I had the courage to open it now it would reveal a callow young man, a complacent middle-aged one, and a cranky old one, all self-centered and terrified and utterly indifferent to the plight of Earth and its creatures. I would be saddened now by such a display of waste. Far better that I should come late to my words, when I know that I shall never reread them to be embarrassed, and when I can see a future (yours!) opening in front of me.

I am tired now. I shall stop writing and go out onto the terrace in the evening. Through the open doors I can see the last of the summer sun on the mountaintops. Bits of ash float in the updrafts: ravens.

Later I shall dine alone with my books. Hushed waiters will come and go. They know as well as I what is happening in the world beyond these mountains—perhaps better, for I have ceased to listen to "the news," whereas they have not. When I ask, they tell me that they keep informed, which means they know which cities have ceased to work, which countrysides have been hopelessly infested with refugees, what are the latest postures of the politicians. They have no desire to venture beyond this sanctuary. They display a touching faith, bordering on the reverent, in my ability to protect them. They call it loyalty. I have made what provision I can for them. And for you. And for myself.

I intend to spend my remaining time here. I shall write as

long as possible. My hope is that I shall be able to complete a full account of what my friends and I have done in these last years, and that this will find its place in the Repository among the others. I hope it can be finished before I see the final aircraft slip through the pass and settle like a fly on the little strip there, below. I hope that before one of the servants interrupts me ("It's time, sir. This is the last flight.") I shall place my manuscript with a few other items into the case that even now sits ready, secure it, watch it carried down the path to the aircraft. I shall watch the plane lift off. And then...

I confess there is gratification in knowing that one will not be outlived by civilization.

So, my friend, my likeness, my postcivilized inheritor, we shall meet next at your convenience and I shall tell you then about the conception of Yggdrasil and the first stages of its creation. Until then, shall I tell you what you must do to be more than civilized? Find the means, against all instinct, to honor mystery.

Asa linked his fingers behind his neck and leaned back from the machine, stretching. The storm had cleared, leaving a calm evening. Somewhere children laughed. He rubbed his eyes with the tips of his fingers. He made a note, the last of several, on the pad beside the terminal.

Yida was watching him. He smiled and held up two fingers. She understood at once and ordered the second installment of the Teperman File.

SIX

THEY WERE GOING TO FAIL.

Horvath knew that. Their failure was already taking shape down there among the restive tribes. He would not see the end, but it would come inexorably, and the work of his life would have been in vain.

He sat in silence. The aircraft's cabin was well insulated against the roar of the engines, and the crewmen did not speak to the Master unless they were spoken to. They exchanged only the muted comments necessary for navigation. Occasionally the radio brought instructions full of numbers from Yggdrasil Control and the pilot replied in a monotone, his microphone touching his lips.

Horvath sat in near darkness. Greenish reflections from the instrument panel shone on his cheek. Faint starlight glimmered on the long and pallid hand resting on his thigh. He leaned close to the window.

The plane banked toward the sea. Behind, beyond the eastern mountains, stretched the unknown lands that lay outside the pale of Norriya. He had often thought that he might one day send scouts into those lands, perhaps units specially trained and equipped. He had thought that he might even go himself, but he knew now that he would

not. Too little time remained. Too much had to be done.
Life must be lived too close to the surface, now.

The Gerumbian Mountains drifted underneath, black
ghosts reaching up purple fingers. Some were tipped with
the last of winter snows. Then quite suddenly they dwindled into foothills and Horvath was given a panorama of
glittering streams coiling south toward the Yulok villages
and the sea. People crouched in those hills, beside those
streams, people who had scattered their campfires at the
first sound of the plane and who now trembled with their
faces against the earth, praying that the god would not
vent his wrath upon them. And here and there in that
darkness, Horvath knew, singular men stood upright
shaking defiant fists.

More mountains loomed ahead. Horvath's thin lips
moved. For him these were still the Mountains of Alcheringia, although no official maps called them that. In
fact, they were no longer called anything at all. Yggdrasil
had renounced all designations, redrafted all charts. Now
there was no such place as Alcheringia and no such people
as Alcheringians except in the memory of SKULD. No one
lived there now, or ever would live there again, and although Yulok hunters and Gerumbians might pass through
the outlying regions, the mouth of the Alcher itself was
shunned by all. Myth-spinners of all tribes had woven
their tales around it, tales altering the destruction of Alcheringia so subtly that even men who had participated
in that massacre had grown uncertain whether they had
been there themselves, or had dreamed that they had been,
or had heard their grandfathers tell the tale, or had muddled the incident with others in their liquid memories.

Afterward, great fires had swept the region.

The jet swept low across the Larl, the sacred river of
the Alcheringians, and Horvath saw the ford near the
Caves of the Dead sparkle briefly in the starlight. Then
they banked into the pass that led through the plateaus
of the Alcheringian Mountains. Small lakes that were the
headwaters of the Alcher gleamed like buffed steel. Then
the land dropped swiftly away toward the sea, and a moment later they were crossing Alcheringia itself.

Horvath had ordered that they pass over the southern

edge of the old encampment, and now he peered close to the window as the aircraft banked right and the Alcher's estuary appeared, a mercurial ribbon ending in the sea. Around it all was blackness, a blackness thicker than any they had flown through that night. It was a palpable blackness, a blackness in which Horvath imagined a stench so pungent that it could almost be tasted. Horvath recoiled from the window. Had either of the crewmen turned at that moment they would have seen the Master sitting rigid and unbreathing. His head was poised as if listening for some distant sound. He did not move again until they were above the forgiving sea. Then he spoke in a whisper to the sea. *"It was necessary,"* he said.

Again the plane banked, rising. Its radio crackled with the dispassionate voice of Yggdrasil Control, and behind that voice Horvath heard the echoes of others in the still night. As the horizon leveled he saw the Yggdrasilian archipelago ahead, a frail question mark of light in the night. They were approaching from the south, from the bottom of the question mark, and the circular island of Neffelheim lay just ahead. It was ablaze. Of the three islands, it was by far the brightest, radiating energy and activity. For a few minutes they circled Neffelheim awaiting clearance to land and Horvath stared balefully at the scene below—factories, workshops, offices, generating stations—the whole man-made crust that was, he knew, only a fraction of the labyrinth underground. Horvath loathed and feared the power of the place and the arrogance it bred in the engineers and technicians who lived and worked there. In recent years that power had grown beyond the General Instructions and was threatening now to grow beyond control by the Arborea. Horvath cursed Yggdrasil's dependency on the place. He dreaded the confrontation he knew was coming.

Clearance arrived. The aircraft completed its final circuit and began its approach to the landing field on Asgard. Larger than Neffelheim, elongated and bulbous at the ends, Asgard curved between its two sister islands. Much of it lay in darkness, but clusters of light marked the nerve centers. At the south end was the medical complex and Val. In the middle, stretching around the island's S-curve, were the residences, the airport, the Central Complex, and various other buildings. Alone at the extreme north end was the dim circlet of lights that marked the meeting place of the Arborea, the governing body of six masters who were responsible for Yggdrasil and the Five Districts on the mainland. Half a mile beyond the northern tip of Asgard lay the craggy island of Jotunheim, the abode of the scholars on whose work everything depended. Horvath could not see it, but he knew it was there, brooding in the darkness.

The aircraft entered a steep glide. In the darkness of the cabin Horvath watched the lights flash beneath him, heard the engines change pitch as the wings moved, felt the soft impact of the landing.

"Home, sir," the pilot said, and the door swung open.

Horvath descended.

The door of the moving corridor leading from the airport to the Central Complex opened as he approached and hissed shut behind him, sealing off almost entirely the whine of other aircraft and the sounds of activities deep in the bowels of Asgard—the hum of turbines, the rumble of submarine gates opening and closing, the purr of elevators and escalators, the resonant throb of tidal generators. Horvath rode down a hundred empty yards of corridor, entered an elevator, and descended three stories. It was only a short walk to his apartment. He had seen no one. Inside, he did not turn on lights. He moved through the soft aquamarine from the skylight and from luminescent dials and clocks. *Like the sea*, he thought, smiling. *At the end, it is fitting for a man to return to the sea.* He imagined himself carried on river currents to those realms, nudged by the creatures of the sea, dispersed into an infinitude of water . . .

Bending with difficulty, he touched buttons that started a warm bath flowing in an adjacent bathroom. He turned toward the sound of the water, beginning to strip off the filthy uniform in which he had been traveling. But then he hesitated and turned back to the monitor to scan messages and the routine reports that had accumulated during his three days' absence. The first of these read, MASTERS: NOTE MEETING ARBOREA 1000 HRS TOMORROW.

Horvath's lips moved. So, they had been busy, Rees, Bret, Moran, Nidor, and the others! They had used his absence to persuade Harrower to call an extraordinary meeting. Tomorrow, then, the last stage of the struggle would begin. It was a struggle he would lose. It was a struggle he would not survive. But he must find the strength to begin.

Slowly he tapped out the instructions that would be read by his executive assistants at 500 hours: LAST ARBOREA MINUTES AT 600. MEET WITH SHEM AND MORAN AT 700.

Other messages waited on his monitor, but Horvath turned the machine off and rose with difficulty. Bent, hesitant, stripped of grace, he moved through the aquamarine twilight toward the bathroom where he would sink deep into the bath that awaited him, surrounded by the recorded sounds of the creatures of the sea—the whisper of tentacles on smooth rocks, the humming of silver shoals, and the fluting songs of the wise whales safe at last in their unfathomable depths.

SEVEN

W$_{HY}$?

How extraordinary that all our science, all our philosophy and literature, all our striving should flower from that small question! How extraordinary that we alone among animals must ask!

Recently, arranging my affairs, I came across a paper I had written as a schoolboy and I was stricken by the title— An Inquiry into the Nature of Inquiry—not because of its presumption but simply because I realized that I had always been obsessed by this question. The paper concluded, "If we destroy ourselves it will be because we persisted in asking that question, Why? If we save ourselves it will be for the same reason." I was moved that I should be returning now to this juvenile concern after the greedy years of my maturity.

As I told you, I had grown to love writing. The fact that I required very little sleep meant that I could indulge myself in this activity while still attending to "serious" business. Had they known that I was writing, my business colleagues would have regarded me with considerable suspicion. In North America any introspection is subversive, and successful businessmen are careful to be merely intelligent, incapable either of that deep curiosity which risks ending in stasis, or of any measurable aesthetic capacity, or even of sufficient altruism for genuine communication.

I wrote under various pseudonyms. In the few years that followed what I shall call my conversion, I published several dozen articles, most dealing with puzzles, paradoxes, dilemmas, and unanswerable questions. Some were merely self-indulgent. My fascination with the problem of infinite regress, the mysterium tremendum, led me, for example, to inquire casually in one article how many terms would be required to reach a sum of 100 in a harmonic series. Most replies gave me simply the upper and lower bounds, but several gave me the precise answer. In other articles I dealt with traditional paradoxes, beginning with Zeno's, proceeding through the various Megarian paradoxes, through the insolubilia of the medieval logicians, through Kant's epistemological antinomies, and so to the modern paradoxes of Burali-Forti, Cantor, Russell, Zermelo-Konig, Grelling, Skolem, and others.

They beguiled me, these dead ends at the outer reaches of language. I saw them not only as failures of language and conceptualization, but as desperate yearnings beyond the limitations of the brain. So, although I toyed with mere mathematical problems, and with diversions in physics like the eleven-dimension extension of the Kaluza-Klein theory, I returned always to paradoxes and dilemmas, for they alone had a human shape. They alone suggested the direction of metamorphosis.

Through these articles I discovered others who felt as I did and who therefore were potential associates in the enterprise I had begun to conceive. Many surfaced. Some used the letters columns of various journals to communicate with me. Some inquired directly, having ferreted out my various addresses and telephone numbers. These were men who had both the interest and the power to discover my identity. I proceeded discreetly, using my own operatives to compile dossiers on all who seemed likely candidates, cautious not to underestimate (although that was difficult!) agencies charged with protecting the commonwealth against people like myself.

Ultimately I published in the international journal Communicado an article entitled "The Natural Perpetuation of the Rational." My argument was that the ultimate act of reason would be to accept the paradox implicit in reason, and thus abandon oneself to natural processes of which reason did not constitute a part. I observed that we lived our lives pinioned like squirming bugs on this reason. For example, our irrational fear of death drove us to thanatoid simplifications of the Earth. Deep in this article I buried the suggestion that, even in the midst of the coming convulsions, it might be possible to preserve a nucleus of sanity by radical, supra-governmental action. The suggestion was phrased and placed in such a way as to escape the attention of all but the most scrupulous of readers.

I received forty inquiries. My operatives informed me that six of these were FBI, MI5, KGB, and CIA plants. Of course I terminated all contacts with these at once, canceling telephones and post-office boxes. To them, I vanished.

The other thirty-two I had scrupulously investigated. I spent over two million dollars on inquiries into them and their lives. I had three criteria: First, minimum annual income of seven million; two, a childlike and anarchic love of play; three, evidence of commitment to posterity. Needless to say, for this last, the fact of having had a family was insufficient.

Twenty names were eliminated from my list at this stage. Some were just too poor. One, though rich enough, was an idiot savant. Brilliant in chess and mathematics, he was dressed, fed, and put to bed by attendants. Senility had crept upon a few like a rising sea while they clung to some isolated peak of their reason. Some revealed hideous deformations of character.

Only twelve met my first two tests. To these I posed the problem I had devised for the third criterion. How does one assess the depth of another's commitment to posterity? Very simply! What is really being tested, of course, is responsibility; that is, the extent to which one is willing to cooperate for the good of all. Those willing to make sacrifices for the present commonwealth would, I reasoned, also do so for a hypothetical commonwealth of the future. I reasoned also that when one sacrifices for posterity one relinquishes control.

I wrote the following letter to my twelve finalists around the world, giving the address of a Swiss bank:

Greetings!
    You are one of twelve recipients of this letter.
    I am in a position to offer one of you an opportunity

to create a perfect society with a good chance of surviving the coming catastrophe.

This is not a joke.

Apply by submitting any number to the address above within three days. The larger the number the greater chance you will have of being selected.

Within the week I had my responses. One of the twelve did not reply at all, either out of a too refined sense of responsibility or on the assumption that he was the victim of a crank. Three submitted the magical number nine. Another, 1,000,000. Another, a googol (10^{100}). Another, a googolplex (10^{googol}).

To these six who had so regrettably revealed themselves as megalomaniacs and defectors, I sent the following gnomic message: BETTER TO TRAVEL HOPEFULLY THAN TO ARRIVE. To them, I vanished. Their mail was returned stamped UNKNOWN. Bank records closed without a whisper when they inquired.

To the remaining five I issued my invitation, for they had demonstrated the kind of suprarationality we would require in our enterprise. One had submitted the number one. The other four had submitted zeros. All had arrived at their decision in precisely the same way: Each had had a twelve-sided die constructed and had rolled it. On eleven facets there was nothing. On one there was the number one.

All had assumed that the others would do the same thing. All had assumed the primacy of cooperation.

During the week agreed upon I retired to my mountain retreat and watched their jets sweep one by one into my valley. By Thursday evening all five had arrived and we enjoyed a drink together on the terrace. We got along exceedingly well from the beginning, as I knew we would. Each came with a well-stocked larder for the sharing, and my crews spent much time carrying goods into the refrigerated rooms.

Thorvald brought fish from the fiords and Chablis clean and cold as a Nordic evening. Michurin brought vodka and caviar and an inexhaustible supply of splendid Russian proverbs. Bornuwalski arrived with Maine lobsters and Yankee wit and astringency. Gonzalez brought anchovies and white wine crisp as Andean snow. And McPhee brought smoked salmon and a whiskey so smooth he swore it had been distilled from heather dew and blessed by the caress of a pibroch at the dawn.

These were last things. We all knew that, although no one said so. We enjoyed.

"Well, Teperman," Thorvald said when we had finished dinner, "this scheme of yours is quite mad. Let us begin at once!"

We swiftly confirmed that we shared the bleak view that humanity was about to bring broadscale destruction upon itself and its world. We agreed furthermore that governments, especially "democratically elected" governments, will be powerless to prevent the coming mayhem and indeed will accelerate the trend. We agreed finally that any vestiges of humanity and civilization will survive because individuals with foresight have taken action.

Our combined wealth made anything possible. For various childish reasons all six of us had retained emotional attachments to the Earth, so there was no foolish talk of spaceships and other planets. We had considerable influence upon, but not control of, the actions of governments, and we therefore knew we could predict neither the nature nor the extent of the coming disaster. We could not know how long we would have to complete our project. Our projections suggested a series of events, each of them terribly destructive but not in itself catastrophic. We assumed that pockets of humanity would survive in ecosystems more or less intact. And we knew that without management these clusters of Homo sapiens would in time grow strong enough to again imperil themselves and the Earth. At least, this was the best that we could hope for.

We broke our project into three tasks:

1. to design a self-sustaining community with an anticipated lifespan of 200 years;
2. to protect surviving ecosystems against man (The Gaian Expedient);
3. to reintegrate man into nature (The Project).

Task One was clearly obtainable provided we had time. Tasks Two and Three we could achieve only by scrupulous planning, by structuring our created community so carefully *that eventually the members would be committed to accomplishing these ends themselves.*

We broke into three committees. Thorvald and I would design the facility, Bornuwalski and Gonzalez would deal with all sociological questions involved in the Expedient, and Michurin and McPhee would address the problem of the reintegration of man. We agreed that we would take no more than five weeks for these tasks. Then would begin the long process of executing our plans.

None of us had so restricted our education as to become an expert. We well understood that strength lay in diversity. Experts were people one paid well. They responded day or night to summonses on computer terminals. They caught quick jets and arrived well briefed. They made sure secrets were kept.

By the end of that first evening we were all infused with a childish enthusiasm that we well knew no art, no woman, no stimulant, no commercial triumph, no entertainment was capable of providing. It was the pointless joy of a kite, or a nonsense poem, or an innocent fantasy. It was the joy of creation.

Together we drank a toast of Glenmorangie in the moonlight.

Thorvald and I set to work at once. My scouts had already identified three potential locations for our community. All were groups of islands, not only for defensive reasons but also for psychological benefits, insularity, which would accrue over time. Part of the mainland, our survivors would also have shared the guilt; islands liberated.

Each of these sites we investigated in turn, but it was not until we reached the last and northernmost that Thorvald's Nordic soul responded. His eyes shone like blue ice as he gazed upon those islands. "Perfect!" he kept repeating. "They are perfect, Teperman! Perfect! Buy them at once."

I agreed. Everything pointed to this choice—location, topography, geological reports, size—everything. I telephoned a brief message to my agents. Then we circled, Thorvald and I, two gnomish deities, gloating in our cloudless sky. I remarked how appropriate it was that the archipelago should form a question mark, but Thorvald saw not a question mark but a magic tree. "Yggdrasil," he exclaimed. "The tree of life! See: bole, trunk, canopy!" He even named the individual islands, quite whimsically, I thought. This roman-

ticism was getting the better of him, clearly. I remarked dryly that if he kept on we would soon see valkyries off the wingtip. I ordered the pilot to take us home.

We agreed subsequently to leave all naming to Thorvald, since it gave him such innocent glee.

Much remained to be done. First, it was necessary to remove the inhabitants. This presented no real difficulties. Our agents simply bought them out and relocated them with handsome profits. Money was really all they cared about.

Secrecy was more important and more troublesome. It was essential, of course, for the five years we estimated we required to complete the project. We paid taciturn contractors well. Very well. Mainland residents, if they thought about our activities at all, assumed that they were bureaucratic and therefore sacrosanct, no doubt having to do with the installation of yet more missiles for their protection. We dealt with governments by buying permits and building a luxury hotel and condominiums on the surface. Bribery helped. Those who were incorruptible met with inexplicable delay, obfuscation, and inertia.

The real work went on beneath the surface, under the islands, under the sea. Excavated materials were barged out to deep water and dumped at night. Construction materials were brought in by renegade freighters from distant ports, freighters whose captains had grown adept at forging manifests in those perilous times. As the global situation deteriorated, port authorities cared less about tramp freighters, and the ever-vigilant military was busy elsewhere. We built. We solved all technical problems one by one; they were, after all, merely technical.

The three islands corresponded roughly to our three tasks. Farthest south, on the circular island that Thorvald had renamed Neffelheim for arcane reasons of his own, we established the technical center of the complex. Geological surveys had indicated a geothermal capacity far beyond the projected energy needs of the three islands, although we ordered several tidal generators designed and built as well, taking fullest advantage of the fiords of Asgard and the heavy currents that swept the southern end of Neffelheim. We made provision for solar and wind generation as well, and each island was given its own desalinization plant. Gasoline and oil were stored in immense quantities deep in the bedrock of Neffelheim. On Neffleheim too were the major workshops, factories, and lab-

oratories dedicated to the functional quotidian operation of Yggdrasil. Here also will be trained the technicians who will maintain all machinery on Yggdrasil. Methods of training were stipulated in the General Instructions for the operation of the islands. We took great pains with these instructions, anxious to avoid the creation of a technical elite.

The center of the Yggdrasilian complex, on the largest of the islands, contained the administrative offices both for Yggdrasil and for the Gaian Expedient, the means of controlling and maintaining whatever mainland population might survive. Everything was initially buried safely beneath sea level, although we knew a day might come when the surface residences might be habitable once again.

Deep in the sea bed between Asgard and Jotunheim, we provided offices and workshops and repositories in which all archival material will be stored and assessed.

All systems have been designed to last for two centuries. That is the time we have given you. It is the maximum, believe me. Of course, a thousand developments will arise that we have been unable to foresee, but we have provided an array of contingency plans which may prove useful. SKULD, the master computer system, has ROM programed to anticipate problems in operational systems and make recommendations.

All this, of course, you know.

All this was part of the grand design that Thorvald and I worked out together. Final details were provided by the small army of architects and engineers who would devote several years of their lives to completing Yggdrasil as you know it.

I have written in the past tense. The five years have flown. All has been accomplished. Time has been compressed in the softening memory of this Old One. But, of course, the structure of Yggdrasil was a mere proposal when Thorvald and I met with the others to describe it.

Evening.

Asa switched off the machine and stretched. All other researchers had left, and he and Yida were alone in the reading room. All was silent except for the occasional hissing of passing electric carts and the laughter of walkers in the warm evening.

He stood up, gathered his notes, and returned the diskette. "Who was Einstein?" he asked.

"Pardon?"

"Einstein. There's a reference to Einstein in Teperman."

Yida shrugged. "No idea. Do you want me to find out?" He nodded.

She tapped the access codes and a question on her keyboard, and they waited while the request sped through circuits deep into the heart of the Urth Repository far below. "You actually *read* that?"

"Yes."

"And understood it?"

"No, but I will." Asa folded the pages of notes and slipped them into his tunic pocket. "You've never read it?"

She smiled. "Years ago. Not recently. It's not *really* important, is it? Not like the General Instructions, or the Injunctions, or any of the other sets of regulations. Perhaps if he had written in Xtapla— Ah, here we are!"

EINSTEIN, A. VIOLINIST AND SCIENCE TEACHER. IN-STRUCTED IN SEVERAL EUROPEAN UNIVERSITIES BE-FORE BECOMING AN AMERICAN CITIZEN IN 1940. NOTED FOR THEORIES OF RELATIVITY (Q.V.). MAJOR WORKS: *ABOUT ZIONISM* (1930), *THE WORLD AS I SEE IT* (1934).

"Is that all?" Asa said.

Yida nodded. "Maybe a friend of Teperman. Who knows?"

Asa frowned at the lines on the screen. "Try a word," he said. "Try *missile*."

She tapped in the inquiry, and in a moment the response arrived:

MISSILE. MI.SIL, FR. LAT. *RES MISSILES*. SWEETS, PER-FUMES, ETC., THROWN BY ROMAN EMPERORS TO THE PEOPLE.

Asa laughed. "Try it again."

She did. Again the answer came.

"But that's nonsense!" He leaned across the counter and brusquely tapped in the request himself, adding his name and aborr number, A8746. "Answer me!"

This time SKULD took a full minute to reply:

REF COLM JOT

"What does *that* mean?" Yida asked.

Asa made a sound of disgust in his throat. "It means that if I want to know more I must go to see the Colm, in Jotunheim."

"Will you?"

For a moment he said nothing, then he laughed the harsh laughter of a man who has just been cheated. "Games!" he said. "Tests!" He struck his fist hard on the counter and strode out of the building, flinging open the glass door with a straight-arm blow.

The night was cool and clear, the sea calm. In front of him the western flank of Asgard sloped down through broad marshes to the sea. Above, the lights of a small, swift aircraft were coming home. On both sides of him, the ranks of cantilevered dwellings and offices swept across the forested hillsides, and here and there in the darkness snakes of light marked the passages of silent carts.

He had intended to go back to his apartment, to bed; but the night was too good to waste. Besides, before sleep he wanted to cleanse his memory. He stretched up toward the froth of stars and then down to the earth, and when afterward he pressed his face, yawning, the shadow of a hand lay across his cheekbone and his eye.

He began to walk rapidly. By the time he had reached the residences on the hillside, he was running, and when he had passed them, leaving behind the serpentine road and crossing the beach to the hard sand at the surf's edge, he had lapsed effortlessly into the loping stride of the Alcheringian warrior.

EIGHT

"About your son," Horvath said. He sat erect at the end of the conference table, his extraordinary long hands flat on his thighs. On the wall to his right, a large clock inexorably sliced time away. Behind him bloomed the emblem of the great tree of Yggdrasil. To his left, windows opened on a warm day. Drapes billowed, and the sea glinted beyond the marshes. Opposite him, to Shem's left, was a relief Master's map of Norriya.

"I asked you to come early so we could speak about your son."

Shem smiled despite the pain that had begun to gnaw early that morning at his crippled foot. His temples were grizzled. Gray streaks fanned out from the corners of his mouth into an abundant red beard. "Just completing his novitiate. He's done well."

Horvath nodded. "I have good reports on his work, bad on his erratic behavior."

"The epilepsy is controlled with Tagonet."

"But other things are not. What does he want to do?"

"To go to Jotunheim. To work directly on the Project."

"I have his request for that. But what else?"

Shem frowned. His heavy brow shadowed his eyes. "To find Persis."

"The Kanik woman?"

"Yes."

"Love? Still?"

Shem nodded. "He says she is his wife. He says that Jared joined them. He says that even if that had not happened..."

"Four years," Horvath said. "Almost five."

"And...he wants revenge."

"On us?"

"Perhaps. Certainly on the Kanik who led the attack on Alcheringia."

A wrinkle appeared in Horvath's forehead. "His name?"

"Garm."

For a few moments there was silence in the room except for the whisper of the drapes and the metallic passing of the seconds.

"Asa has promise," Horvath said quietly. "Great promise. But such promise can evaporate. Like that."

Shem nodded.

"A bad decision."

"Yes."

"Self first."

"Yes."

"A moment's passion."

"I know," said Shem. "I know."

"Gone."

"It's not easy for him," Shem said. "Control..."

Horvath frowned. "Easy? Of course it's not easy! That is why he is exceptional; he insists on making things difficult for himself." Slowly he lifted his saurian hands and placed them on the table, and Shem knew with dread and exultation what he would say next. "I'm going to appoint you his dream master. This will be made official today. Arrange all his *mabinogi*, all the tests which will chart his way to wisdom. Let him have his taste of Jotunheim, if you like, but not for long. Perhaps a few months. And then, Shem, then he must truly be tested."

"Yes, sir."

"His humanity, do you understand?"

"Yes."

"We need that. Above all else, we need the best of that!"

"I know, sir."

"I recommend at least three tests. You and only you will know what they should be as the occasions arise. You've done it often enough before, of course. But this will be the hardest. Your own son. You will be tempted always to minimize dangers for him, to steer him on easy paths. That is why, my dear Shem, *this will also be a test for you*! Devilish, isn't it?"

They sat a moment among the insect sounds of the room, the warm wind in the trees, the distant chatter of helicopters arriving and departing. "Remember," Horvath said, "at least three tests. Journeys, perhaps. The final one the most difficult." He raised an admonishing finger. "Remember."

"Yes," Shem answered. "All right."

Moran was late. He arrived out of breath, sweat gleaming on his bald head and on the fold of flesh below his ear. "Sorry, sorry," he said, wagging his hands to suggest that the fault was not entirely his, that emergencies arose, that underlings were incompetent, that fate and time inexplicably conspired against him. Eyes surprised and contrite rolled behind his glasses. "Peregrinus to the Montayners. Couldn't be helped. Sudden support required. You know the sort of thing, Shem, Horvath. The swamp may look quiet but the demons are playing in it, eh? Aha. Yes. Was I—"

"We were just beginning," Horvath said mildly. "I assume that you received my message?"

"Message?"

"Concerning the Kanik raiding party."

"I—"

"North of the headwaters of the Larl."

"Oh yes! Yes, of course. I meant to—"

"I had no acknowledgment. None in the aircraft, none in my office."

"I beg your pardon, Horvath. An oversight. I did go to work on it right away. Contacted the peregrinus concerned."

"Who is that, now?"

"Aleaha, sir. Still."

"Hm. Time for a change, perhaps."

"She may be eccentric but she's extremely competent, sir. Extremely."

"Is she? This is the third unauthorized Kanik incursion this month. The third we know about."

Moran polished his glasses assiduously, squinting into the sunlight toward Horvath. Shem stood and drew the drapes.

"Well, sir, a tiger can't change his stripes, can he? The Kaniks are a restless and warlike people. That's in their nature. That's encouraged by their Regulae. They're horsemen. Raiders. They must roam. That's, why, that's what they *do*!"

"Who, besides Aleaha, was responsible for this last breach?"

Moran cleared his throat. The sweat that a moment earlier had gleamed on his neck was now soaking his collar. "His name, I believe, is Garm."

"You believe?"

"Garm. You may recall, sir, that he was the Kanik war leader responsible for organizing the attack on Alcheringia."

"Oh yes."

"He was designated a novice candidate, sir. Directive Number N39-467. Four years ago. He was never brought here because of your freeze on the introduction of further aborr novices. If I may suggest, sir—"

"No. I won't rescind that order, Moran. Not yet."

"But the Expedient—"

"Not yet. Now, gentlemen, I have a meeting of the Arborea in thirty-five minutes, and three matters of information to pass on to you before I leave. First, my trip." He touched buttons on a panel at the table's edge and the map of Norriya lit up with a bright cursor ready at the top. Horvath moved this cursor as he spoke. "I toured the entire district—Abibones, Gerumbians, Kaniks, Montayners, and Yuloks. I wore the usual peregrinus disguises. I talked with the elders of the tribes, I talked with the young men and women, I sat in on their councils. I agree that there is a great restiveness among them, particularly among the Yuloks. They want, well, they want freedom, although that word is in none of their vocabularies. It's obvious to me that your peregrini are going to have to make better use of the new control devices that Neffelheim is developing."

Shem looked grim. "Horvath, some of those devices—"

"I don't like them, either. But unless we want other Alcheringian Solutions—"

"Never," Shem said. *"Never!"*

"Then we have few alternatives."

"If we had Clinicians—" Moran began.

"We'll never have them again. We know how to build them, of course, but we lack the materials. No, we must use other means. Those means will differ from tribe to tribe, and that is why I want to meet with you individually this week." Horvath stared for a moment at the illuminated map. "Incidentally, we were attacked twice. Once here, in Gerumbia, and once here, thirty miles inside the eastern boundary. Both times by tribesmen from the Outer Wyld." The cursor swung to the right and zigzagged down the empty space that lay there.

"Second item." The map of Norriya vanished and a map of the Five Districts of the Erthring replaced it. Norriya, immediately east of the Yggdrasilian archipelago, was the northernmost district. To the south, roughly the same size, lay Esterholme, and to the south of that lay Merone. These three all lay along the coast. Inland, bordering both Esterholme and Merone and stretching eastward for a hundred miles, was The Center. Beneath that district, curving in a gentle arc with its middle northernmost and its eastern end probing at least another hundred miles into the dark heart of the Outer Wyld, was the District of Underlakes.

"As you know, all five districts are being plagued by these incursions from the Outer Wylds. The Center and the Underlakes are getting the worst of it. Down there these raids are already destroying the social fabric that the Gaian Expedient was designed to maintain. And they're growing more disruptive by the month. Obviously they

must be stopped. Something must be done. I have reason
to believe that this morning's meeting of the Arborea will
hear a proposal from Bret and Rees on the matter. I am
not naive, gentlemen. I know that you, too, have a good
idea what that proposal will be, whether it comes today
or at a later date. Is there anything you wish me to say
in reply?"

Moran, wiping his face with a handkerchief, shook his
head.

"Let's wait and see what's said," Shem suggested.

"All right." Horvath touched a switch and all maps
vanished. He cleared his throat. "The third and last item
is also a matter of information. The fact is, I'm dying.
Quite swiftly, I understand. Within three months the Arborea will need to appoint a new Master for Norriya."
Quickly he looked from one to the other, noting what he
believed to be shock in Shem's face, anticipation in Moran's. He smiled. "Well," he said quietly. "One day at a
time. One day at a time."

NINE

THE KANIK WOULD DIE NOW, AT LAST. RUNNING, THE
Alcheringian warrior knew that, seeing his enemy coming
along the edge of the sea, passing through curtains of sea
mist. He was balancing a Kanik lance, his enemy, prodding his mount to a gallop, lifting his head in the war
whoop that the Alcheringian, drawing his knife, drowned
in howled rage and exultation. There was neither beach
nor sea nor time nor sound, then, nor feeling except coal-
hot hatred at his center, nor vision except the froth-flecked
horse stretched wild-eyed and the lance slipping snakelike
past his shoulder, too high. He was dropping under it,
under the flashing hooves, slicing an arm's-length of horse
belly, laughing at the beach grit cold on his back and the
sting of the sea and the scream of the animal joining theirs;
laughing at the horse staggering, spilling guts and offal
and caught in sudden yards of intestine, crashing down
with the sand pluming and the man airborne, falling hard.
But then he was up and turning, coming back low and
fast, wolflike on the blood-red beach, low and fast, one
arm dangling and knife in the other, his eyes the wolf's,
his hair pale as birch leaves winter-bleached, low and fast,
lunging, arcs of knife-glint in the sun, stab and miss, slash

and miss, screaming, stab and stab, the Alcheringian himself screaming, jabbing, hitting, knowing something behind the ribbed muscles in the belly of his enemy,
bonescrape and warm juice, and the wolf's eyes rolling
back, down, rolling back, back, back, all gray gone, only
white, only white and red, only red, only red all gouting
from nose and mouth. Alcheringian obsidian vanished in
his throat, through palate, through brain, scraping skull,
and the Alcheringian shouting his name and hers into the
last tremulous life of his enemy so that to the very last,
to the last exquisite moment he should know who had
done this and know why, shouting *PER . . . SIS* shouting
the Alcheringian triumph *eep* his throat raw with screaming *eep* his left arm snagged in the wreckage of the bed
eep and into his pain from somewhere a dutiful voice
*Excuse me, sir, excuse me, you left orders to be wakened
when these dreams recur . . .*

TEN

Hɪs ᴍᴏɴɪᴛᴏʀ ʙᴇᴇᴘᴇᴅ ɢᴇɴᴛʟʏ ᴀɴᴅ ʜɪs ᴀssɪsᴛᴀɴᴛ ʀᴇ-minded him shortly afterward: "You have ten minutes until the Arborea meeting."

Horvath thanked her.

He finished the notes he had been making on his meeting with Moran and Shem, and then he picked up the file that had been prepared for him and went out through the outer office and down the corridor.

For years Horvath had awakened with a little jolt of surprise and satisfaction that he was still alive. He wondered why. Nothing for many years had given him pleasure except astonishment at the peculiarities of his species. *Hope dies, but curiosity remains*, he had written long before in the sparse little book that had served him as a diary. It was one of the last entries he had made, about the same time that he had ended his only love affair and taken the oath of dream master. Since then he had tried to function with crystalline and unemotional precision, like one of the Clinicians when they were at their best, or like one of the most refined of Val's analysts. And in that exactitude, of which his curiosity was a part, he took a baleful joy. Now, dying, he had no intention of giving himself over to the Termination Ward at Val to be borne painlessly out of this world. He had no taste for escapes, and besides, he was curious. He wanted a good look at death as it approached. He imagined it would be rather like a caribou—graceless, bumbling, myopic, apologetic.

Horvath smiled. He waved away the cart waiting for him outside. As long as he could walk with some semblance of dignity, he would.

It was a cloudy and ambivalent day, neither wet nor dry, cold nor warm, the kind of day Horvath loved. Leaf-heavy trees drooped above him. A few had begun prematurely to change their green to crimson, orange, and yellow. Horvath moved alone through their shadows. Occasionally a bird called as he passed. Occasionally a squirrel chattered, but he did not look up. Only a small, surface part of his mind was aware of his surroundings. All his intellect was focused on the imminent meeting.

The Arborea met in the circular conference room at the north end of Yggdrasil. The windows of this room provided a vista of the sea, in the center of which sat Jotunheim, the scholars' island, all green and blue. Through the floor of the council room, through its ceiling, rose the largest of the great firs of Asgard. Its gnarled roots embraced the bedrock and reached beneath the walls of the building into the slightest crevasses, the shallowest depressions where nutrients lay trapped. It was at least three hundred years old, this tree. It had survived the Entropies. Its canopy vastly overshadowed others that huddled close and protected it against the sea winds. It groaned in great storms. In rains its trunk streamed. From the scales of its bark venturing insects found their way into the conference room. All were welcomed, for the council chamber had been built in homage to this pole of life and all that lived upon it.

The room was spacious, full of light, its only furniture chairs, a circular table, and a bank of display screens. Of all the rooms in Yggdrasil, it alone lacked a clock. Here time stopped.

As he approached the chamber, Horvath imagined his five colleagues arriving. Harrower, the Keeper of Yggdrasil, would already have been in his seat for at least ten minutes, quietly using a small terminal to monitor events as they occurred throughout the three islands and to give direction as required. He was an engineer, thoughtful and circumspect. Horvath respected the man, and had often thought that in another time and place, in some spacious and unhurried age before the Entropies, he might have told Harrower of his high regard for him. Now, of course, such a thing was impossible. Urgency was too much with them. Words and actions were too precious. There was too little time at their level of command for any such indulgences. Niceties they knew the Old Ones had observed had simply evaporated. "Whole species of emotions died," someone had said once in his hearing, and the remark had haunted Horvath ever since. Sometimes, in moments of weakness, he wondered what those emotions had been, and if they had been engendered by the profusion of means the Old Ones seemed to have had to express them. But such reflections were fleeting; emotions, he knew, were great wasters of time.

Joell, Master of The Center, would also have arrived and taken the seat with the tree symbol, the chairman's place that they occupied in turn, rotating every six months. Punctilious, sedulous, methodical, Joell would want to review the agenda before they began.

Rees and Bret, the Masters of Underlakes and Merone, would arrive together, for they had cooperated closely over recent years. They rarely differed on any issue and seemed to correspond almost telepathically. More pressingly than the other masters, they faced incursions from the uncontrolled tribes from the Outer Wylds, and it was an open secret in Yggdrasil that they had decided how they wanted the Arborea to respond.

Horvath heard Froele coughing and they met at the door of the conference room. She was the Master of Esterholme, the only woman of the six. She and Horvath smiled at each other and touched hands. She was his only remaining friend, the only person with whom, until that morning, he had shared the secret of his imminent death. They had been lovers once. At least, that is what Horvath thought they had been, for he had never experienced with anyone else what he had with Froele—a feeling that he assumed was what the Old Ones called love in their strange letters, their even stranger poetry.

Both he and Froele had renounced their relationship when they had taken their oaths as dream masters, but there was something still, something despite their age and decrepitude, their awesome responsibilities, something that caused Horvath to hold the door for her with an exaggerated little flourish, something that caused her to touch his arm as she passed through.

Everyone else had arrived. The small visitors' section was filled with scholars from Jotunheim, their umber cassocks glowing like rich earth in a crescent of sunlight.

Horvath and Froele took their places at the round table.

Attendants softly closed the doors.

Joell tapped his gavel and began the meeting with the recitation of the Masters' Oath: I swear to renounce all self. I swear to maintain the Expedient and to further the Project. I swear to act in all things for the good of the Earth. I swear to remember at all times that we can never do only one thing.

"There are only two items on the agenda," Joell said quietly when they had resumed their seats. "The first is a progress report from the Colm. The second is a proposal by Rees and Bret to deal with aborr incursions from the Outer Wyld. First, Colm."

The chairman of the scholars rose, and Horvath's eyes narrowed with interest. Other masters leaned forward. All chief scholars of Jotunheim were called Colm after the first, Colm the Lawgiver, who had presided over the work that had been made possible by the first Opening. This Colm was a retiring philosopher fond of the poetry of the Old Ones, and there had always been some doubt that he was suitable for his taxing administrative post. The masters had not seen him for over three years, for he kept to the scholarly preserves of Jotunheim and the archives that held all secrets to the Old Ones and their world. Five generations of scholars had grown old in those archives, grown thin and dry as the parchment that absorbed their lives. Had they made progress on the Project? For years it was impossible to tell. Then, suddenly, a breakthrough would occur and a small piece of the endless puzzle that preoccupied all their thoughts would be fitted into place, only to be followed by more years of silence.

The Colm had aged. He trembled. His eyes were red and watery behind their thick glasses. The towering forehead that was his most prominent feature had risen even higher as the line of wispy white hair receded. His thin frame was stooped inside his cassock. His voice was querulous and defensive, and he glanced quickly around him as he spoke, as if expecting attacks from all sides.

"Please don't ask me," he said, holding up both hands. "I cannot tell you exactly how close we are to the second Opening. Perhaps a year, perhaps three. The challenge is, as you know, a mere riddle. Hence, implicit in it is the simplicity and randomness against which method is powerless." He rubbed his chin nervously. "Our epigrammists, enigmatists, cryptologists, and paradoxologists have all striven to suggest interpretations, and all have gone as far as they can go. Metaphysicians and linguists have also exhausted themselves. Our historians and psychologists are continuing to attempt to reconstruct the mindset that composed this riddle. All experts have as usual been helpful to some extent, and by pooling knowledge in the usual way we feel we are at last beginning to gain some insight."

Froele's hand moved slightly and the Colm squinted at her, his glasses bobbing on his nose. "Yes? Yes?"

"You say 'in the usual way,'" Froele said, "and yet it seems to me that our previous success resulted from one scholar, Kalevala, transcending logic and method." Her eyebrows lifted in the inquisitive manner that Horvath knew well. She began again to cough.

The Colm nodded. "That is true, true. Yet there can be no insight without knowledge, no inspiration without structure, no creation without discipline and substance. Discoveries lie at the end of what is known. We must have our procedures and our methods of assimilating information, and the utilization of these, all of them, is what I refer to as 'the usual manner.' But you are right, of course. When all is said and done, it is obvious that the Old Ones expected us to take the imaginative leap from

what is known and observable into what is unknown.
Science, always, has done that. So did art. So must we."

The speech cost the Colm a great effort. He was trembling when he finished and sweat gleamed on his upper lip. He wiped it away, drawing a long, shuddering breath behind his hand as he did so.

"We think," he went on, "that in the riddle of the second door, the Old Ones are directing our attention to the quintessential human dilemma: To be human we must subordinate instinct to reason; yet, to survive, we must subordinate reason to mystery. We think that the answer, when we find it, will enable us to proceed beyond this dilemma. How, we don't know." He stopped and looked quickly around the room, like a nervous ferret poised for flight. Outside, above them, wind sighed in the great tree of Yggdrasil. "Questions? Questions?"

Rees raised his hand. Rees was a florid, white-haired man, perpetually worried. "Colm, you are aware of the problems we're having maintaining the Gaian Expedient. These tribes from the Outer Wylds—"

"Of course I'm aware! Of course I know that," the Colm replied testily. "But that's your problem, not ours! The purpose of the Gaian Expedient is to preserve a variety of homeostatic communities for our study."

"Precisely. But the point is, you *aren't* studying them! It's been years since anyone from Jotunheim ventured out into the Districts. With respect, my friend, you scholars are so absorbed with your books and theorizing you simply don't know what's going on in the real world."

"I know," Colm replied, "that if you continue to permit the kind of ferment and interbreeding that's been happening recently, there'll be very little left to study."

The little semicircle of scholars nodded vigorous approval. "Hear, hear! umph," one of the older ones said, making a covert adjustment to his upper teeth.

Rees said, very red, "It isn't a question of what we allow or don't allow. It is a question of what we are powerless to prevent—powerless because we don't have access to the knowledge that you could give us."

The Colm opened his hands. "How can we possibly—"

"By getting that second door opened! It's been twenty-six years, Colm! Whatever's behind that door will help us. We need it!" Rees shook his finger. "And I warn you, there's talk in Neffelheim, even here, here on Asgard, of using force to get it!"

The Colm recoiled, white with shock. "*Force?* Forcing the door? Unthinkable! The Injunctions specifically forbid—"

"Perhaps," Rees said, "the time has come to review the Injunctions!"

Joell stood, raising placating hands. "Masters," he said. "Scholars. Let us not launch again into this unedifying debate about our relative responsibilities. No one, Colm, is seriously suggesting an attempt to force the door. We know that Jotunheim is fully aware of the problems we face in maintaining the Gaian Expedient. We, on the other hand, appreciate that the challenge facing Jotunheim is formidable, so formidable that the societies of the Old Ones chose self-destruction rather than face it. Nothing is to be gained now by recriminations. Therefore, unless there are other questions for Colm..." He looked questioningly around the small circle.

The Colm left the lectern, bowed perfunctorily, and led the group of scholars in single-file from the hall.

Joell waited until the doors had closed behind them. Then he nodded to Bret.

"My friend," Bret said, indicating Rees, "has already alluded to the problem I would like to address, Mr. Chairman." He touched a button on the console under the edge of the conference table, and a map of the Five Districts of the Erthring appeared on a screen that descended silently from the ceiling at Joell's left. "Here," Bret said, running a cursor along the eastern boundary of Merone and the southern boundary of Underlakes, "Rees and I have been having serious difficulties for many years, as you know. Recently, the pressure brought by tribes' raiding from the Outer Wylds has increased. A month ago there was an incident here, at the eastern boundary of the Underlakes, and yesterday there was a serious incursion here, on the northern boundary. We believe it's only a matter of time until large-scale attacks spread northward, up the Center, into Esterholme and Norriya.

As we all know, the tribes within all districts are being seriously disturbed." Bret switched off the projector and the screen withdrew silently back into the ceiling. His voice was calm, his face otherwise composed, but Bret's left eye was twitching spasmodically. "My masters, something must be done. We must act. If we delay much longer, we shall be faced with much more radical solutions."

The six looked at their desks, their hands, and finally at each other. Froele was coughing softly.

"We have been over this ground," Joell said. "As you know, nothing in the General Instructions covers it. Well, Bret, what do you suggest?"

"Force," Bret said. "Drive them back by force. Defoliate a five-mile strip outside the boundary. Patrol more rigorously. Search and destroy. Maintain the integrity of the Erthring."

Rees nodded grimly. "We've consulted Neffelheim," he said. "It can be done. It should be."

For several minutes there was silence. The great tree moaned.

"We're speaking of people," Froele said at last. "People about whom we know nothing."

"Savages," Bret said.

"People," Horvath replied. "And the Earth."

"There is, of course," Rees said, looking closely at his intertwined fingers, "the Alcheringian precedent."

Horvath jerked like a man skewered by sharp pain. "All the more reason for not doing this thing. We must find other means. We must."

"Time," Bret said, "is short."

"Nevertheless—"

"Inaction will destroy us—Expedient, Project, everything."

"Nevertheless."

Bret shook his head resolutely. "I must put it into a formal motion, Mr. Chairman, and ask for a vote."

This was done. The hands rose. For: Rees and Bret. Against: Froele, Horvath, Harrower.

Rees leaned back, puffed out his cheeks, opened his hands.

"There are other options," Joell said. "There must be. Our duty is to find them. Soon. Rees and Bret are quite right; we must act in this matter, my masters, or it will destroy us!"

ELEVEN

I<small>T WAS NOON WHEN</small> T<small>HORVALD AND</small> I <small>FINISHED OUR PRESEN-</small>
*tation to the others. Lively discussion followed through our
meal, which we ate on the lawn looking out on a vista of the
mountains. Secretaries kept notes. We agreed to withhold
all decisions on alterations to our proposal until the other
two groups had reported.*

*Bornuwalski and Gonzalez came next. You will recall that
theirs was the responsibility for making all societal arrangements for Yggdrasil and the portion of the mainland to be
controlled. They and their advisers had begun by considering the problem of the initial peopling of Yggdrasil. Gonzalez sketched out the ethical problems involved. The
question was similar, he noted, to the old lifeboat dilemma.
Food and water for two, but population of three. Who should
go for the good of the others, the navigator, the doctor, or
the carpenter? But, though similar to this dilemma, the problem of peopling Yggdrasil was fundamentally different. Different in kind. Those in the lifeboat were considering only
their own survival. They were dealing in the short term. Presumably, if they selected correctly, the survivors would be
rescued and would reenter the world and society once again.
We, on the other hand, were concerned not only with the*

*survival of a few but with the perpetuation of humanity itself.
Who would contribute most to that endeavor?*

Who indeed? Certainly not those whom conventional wisdom considered important and worth saving—the governors, the militarists and their advisers. Certainly not the scientists with the tunnel vision of their various "disciplines." Certainly not the leaders of the mass religions, those great soporifics, those great guarantors of docility and happiness. Certainly not...

One by one Gonzalez eliminated them, all those who were flawed by their education, by their experience, by their knowledge and assumptions.

In the end, Gonzalez and Bornuwalski chose ignorance. And innocence. Most of the first inhabitants of Yggdrasil, they announced, would be children. And most of the adults who must necessarily accompany them would be mere technicians, skilled and highly specialized, although those with certain types of knowledge would be judiciously excluded, as the knowledge itself would be edited out of all Repository records. The leaders would be women. Women, furthermore, who were young.

Gonzalez had appended a brief detailing selection and transportation procedures. The presentation was meticulously prepared. Every eventuality had been considered.

Bornuwalski rose to speak, but I requested a brief recess. I went to the window to gaze down through the valleys of my mountains.

My reflection in the glass was water-eyed. Shall I tell you what had moved me? It was no nostalgic memory, as you might expect. Rather, it was an image of the future, a vision of those children emerging from the catacombs we were preparing for them. Children white-faced who had known nothing else but the artificial light of the labyrinth deep beneath Yggdrasil. Emerging for the first time. Their faces warmed by the sun. The taste of the sea in the air they breathed. Birds, perhaps.

I cleared my throat. I returned to the table mumbling apologies.

Bornuwalski began to speak.

He was, he said, going to proceed on the assumption that our precautions had been effective, that Yggdrasil had survived, and with it an intelligent population. Formidable difficulties yet remained to be addressed. Questions of *breeding, for example. Questions of the division of duties, succession, training, and so forth. All of these would need to be set out clearly in policy papers and orders. The difficulties would be compounded by the fact that it was impossible to predict the extent of the coming simplification. However, Bornuwalski believed that these matters could be prepared for in such a way as to allow for alterations by those who would be involved. We should set the policies, he said, and leave the establishment of regulations to others.*

Yggdrasil, as Bornuwalski understood it, would have three responsibilities: first, to sustain itself for two hundred years by scrupulous use of the resources allocated to it; second, to direct all available energy into what he called "The Project," which, as I understood it, was the determination by scholars of the means for man to maintain a homeostatic presence in nature; third, to salvage and conserve as large a gene pool as possible on the mainland.

Bornuwalski elaborated on this third point, describing what he and Gonzalez called "The Gaian Expedient."

They had assumed that the coming disaster would not be total, that although the damage would be severe, the Earth would survive. It would be radically simplified. It would be blighted by radioactivity and mutations. But it would be Earth still, and with luck and time the effects of what we had done would diminish. Some normalcy might return. Some areas might even remain intact, their ecological fabric untorn. There would be men and women still. Life would go on.

"But"—Bornuwalski peered at us above his half-lenses, tufts of Yankee white hair flaring like small wings from his temples—"but it will be a very different kind of life. It will effectively be life returned to the tribal state. To the neolithic. To the stone age. Is this bad? But I must remind you that out of the bad, paradoxically, comes good! For the hunting-and-gathering way of life is the most successful of man's adaptations to date!" He smiled beatifically around the table. "A way of life that continued successfully for millennia, until the spread of agriculture, until the advent of mining and iron-mongery.

"To Gonalez and me, to the sociologists, anthropologists, ethnographers, and psychologists we have consulted on this matter, it is clear that those who survive in Yggdrasil will have, if they survive at all, a ready-made laboratory on the mainland in which to study the relationship between man

and nature at firsthand, in nearly ideal conditions. Of course, not all retribalization will occur along identical lines. There will be regional variations dictated by topography, availability of game, size of population, and so forth. We think that these variations are absolutely essential to the work of the Project, and that they should not be allowed to evolve past a certain point for the duration of the Yggdrasilian enterprise. That point will vary from tribe to tribe, but we will ensure that scholars in Yggdrasil will recognize it. It will, in every case, be the beginning of a descent into civilization.

"If"—Bornuwalski raised an admonishing finger—"if we fail, if the work of Yggdrasil fails, then the decline into civilization will surely begin again. Therefore, we must be sure to give our inheritors the best means of control that we can devise in the time remaining. That array of controls we have called the Gaian Expedient. This brief will outline the range of devices we have in mind."

We took a few minutes to scan what they had prepared. Several control devices dealt with memory manipulation and memory elimination. They ranged from simple language alteration (the eradication of history, the invention of new nouns and proper names to break continuity, the radical narrowing or destruction of connotation, and so forth), to more sophisticated proposals for the invention of selective mythologies, and even to certain repugnant computerized robots capable of a range of operations.

"Of course," Bornuwalski continued, "we must also develop the ethos to control the controls. Whatever we do, we must eliminate change and randomness, while keeping alive man's invaluable natural curiosity. Perhaps, for a time, we must plan to restrain the application of knowledge by limiting knowledge itself. Hence the word expedient. But if we are careful, man will eventually become self-regulating in that regard. The best option seems to us to devise careful games to induce man to play with knowledge without applying it."

Bornuwalski beamed at us, his glasses glittering. "Questions?"

Thorvald raised his hand. "This installation outlined on page fifty-one. Part of the hospital facility you propose for Asgard—"

"Oh yes, yes! Splendid, isn't it? A good example of what we are capable of, even now. It will eliminate all the messiness of 'Art,' you see. In brief, it is possible to satisfy with great precision those personal yearnings that what we call Art has addressed in a hit-and-miss manner. Individual needs (notice that I say needs, not wants) can be systematically analyzed with the aid of computers, measured, and wholly satisfied with custom-designed dreams. Electrically induced dreams. Programed dreams. The system can be so refined that no other artificial devices will be required in Yggdrasil for this purpose—no alcohol, no drugs, no painting, no music, no other forms of debased Art. We can achieve a fine-tuning of individuals with no sacrifice of 'individuality,' free choice, or creative energy. The evils of repression will simply cease to be."

"Valhalla," Thorvald said.

Bornuwalski smiled. "Better, for there will be no need to die."

Later that evening we had our third and last report, from Michurin and McPhee. They had undertaken the most formidable of our three tasks, and their solution was so elegant that when they presented it to us we rose as one man and applauded them there in the frail sun. Less imaginative people would have proposed the simple depositing of what knowledge we could assemble in the vaults Thorvald and I had proposed, deep in the bedrock beneath the sea. Men who were merely conscientious would have preoccupied themselves with details of assembling the collection, obtaining classified information, microfilming millions of volumes, and so forth. Michurin and McPhee, and those they had chosen to advise them, provided for such things to be done, of course; but then, men of genius, they pressed forward to the real problem: To leave a mass of undifferentiated information would be no kindness. Even with the most sophisticated of retrieval systems. Something like a course of study must be created to accompany it, and our survivors had to be led through it and tested like students, despite the fact that their teachers had long since passed from the face of the Earth. The ultimate objective must be kept clearly in sight, but there must also be closer objectives. And so the notion of a separate depository in the heart of Jotunheim was born, a depository cunningly designed to contain essential information, essential both to the operation of Yggdrasil and to the release of further information.

You, reader, who know already of the existence of the Central Chamber, may well ask why it was necessary, why *our cadaverous applause echoed when Michurin and McPhee announced what they had done and what they proposed. Why, you might ask, were we so presumptuous as to restrict that information to which you had initial access? Why did we keep back what we did?*

We hope you will find the answer to that question.

All we can tell you now is that it lies in the distinction between knowledge and wisdom. Knowledge is inert, raw material. Wisdom is the correct use of knowledge.

And what, you ask, is correct?

Ha! That, you see, is what makes necessary the Central Chamber. When you have begun to deduce the answer, doors will open. Until then, they stay sealed against abuse. Yes, against power. So, if you rely on power you will be weakened. If you use force against the doors—I warn you!— you will lose all!

Softly, softly, dry hands clapping, we applauded the elegant symmetry of failsafe devices that Michurin and McPhee had laid before us: the Colloquy of Scholars, and the arduous training necessary to enter into it; the methods of directing research within the realms of truth; the selective release of knowledge; the design of the questions that will determine heuristic progress...

Dusk filled our valleys. The mountains faded. Unobtrusive attendants provided light, brought drinks. We walked together out upon the lawn and raised our glasses, six tired but exhilarated old men silent in the encroaching night.

This first stage of our work had been done as well as we could do it, and although we would continue to supervise, and although messages would pass among us from then until the end of our world, never again would we look each other in the face so easily and yield to that divine laughter which stole upon us from the peaks. We laughed together the wheezing laughter of old men, and when the paroxysm had passed and we were wiping unaccustomed moisture from the corners of our eyes, I raised my glass westward to that point on the horizon, all roseate and gold-shot, behind which our tiny new world lay in its cool sea. "To Yggdrasil!" Thorvald said, raising his glass as well.

"To humanity," said McPhee.

"And memory," said Michurin.

"And wonder," said Bornuwalski.

"And our next world," Gonzalez said.

"And . . . mystery," I said.

We drank to all those as the last of our sun faded.

Mystery, yes. Remember: You must find the means, against all instinct, to honor mystery.

TWELVE

ASA RAN.

On paths little used, skirting the salt marshes, he ran toward the north end of Asgard, toward Jotunheim. Aloof, misty in the twilight, the scholars' island rose into sight as he crested the last rise and began to descend the long curve that would take him beneath the Arboreum and back down the west coast of Asgard. Probably he would be in time for his meeting with Shem, but if not— Asa shrugged. He wore a light bracelet of stone beads where others wore a watch. He abhorred time. "Why," he said of time when he had first been brought to Yggdrasil and been told about it, "it is just another way of killing!"

To his right, the sea browsed languidly along the salt marsh. Gulls spiraled. A fast pack of mergansers broke cover and scooted north toward Jotunheim, so low their bellies brushed the surface. Beyond them, across the broad strait, he could see the jagged line that was the Gerumbian Hills.

To his left, pools of sunset lay like blood in the windows of the Central Complex. Running, Asa knew he was being watched from behind those windows. One by one, passing through screens of shrubbery, he examined them but was able to see little through the red glare except, in the northernmost, the subtlest and most surreptitious movement, the flicker of a tunic's hem or a sleeve brushing out of darkness and back again.

Horvath's apartment.

Running, Asa watched that window, glancing away only when the ground got rough, then back again, watching that window until, finally, it passed beyond a fir copse and was gone.

Horvath.

Only once had Asa met the Master. Shem had arranged the meeting at Asa's insistence after his first year in Yggdrasil, after he had learned that the final decision to obliterate Alcheringia had been Horvath's. At first he had decided quite simply to kill Horvath as he would one day kill Garm. Seeing that, Shem had said, "We are all responsible. Will you kill us all?" And Asa had roared inarticulate rage and frustration into Shem's white face.

In time, Shem had arranged the meeting.

It had occurred at night. Asa had entered an office that was dark except for the eerie glimmering of greenish lights from various dials and instruments. For a moment he had glimpsed the silhouette of Horvath's elongated head against the western window, and as his eyes grew accustomed to the darkness he saw that Horvath had silently crossed the room and was sitting near him, within reach, and that Horvath's long soft hands moved like pale fish in the green phosphorescence. They gestured toward a chair.

Asa sat.

"I am told you have questions," Horvath had said. "I am told that you are a young man with many questions. Tell me, what is your greatest question?"

Asa had feared that his voice would tremble at this moment, or that hot rage would well up to choke him, or that he might even weep with fury. None of these had happened. When he spoke his voice was cool and level. *"How does it feel to kill a people?"*

"You disappoint me," Horvath had replied after a moment. "Severely. I expected a better question. A question about prevention. Or causality. Or irony. Or the Project. To ask an administrator a question about *feelings* is to waste a question. Still, I promised to answer you: To kill a people involves no feeling and almost no effort. Why? Because it is an infinitesimal step in a *process*, no more important than scrawling one's initials once more, for the hundredth time that day."

"You could refuse."

"When?" The question had come even before Asa had finished speaking. "*When* should you refuse? When you are a novice? When you learn first that ideals cause suffering, cause death and horror? Or later, when you take your oath as a peregrinus? Or when you act first, in the name of the Expedient, to alter someone's life? *When* should you refuse?"

Asa was silent.

Horvath leaned forward slightly to show Asa a face of absolute impassivity. "Perhaps you should refuse before you begin. Hm?"

"But then you don't *know*," Asa had said.

"Exactly. And by the time you know, you are in the belly of the fish, going where the fish swims." Horvath had leaned back gently into the depths of his chair, and Asa had heard a soft, hissing intake of breath as he did so. "*That* is what administration means. So. Please. Spare me your naive righteousness. We share ideals now, you and I. Share objectives. Someday you will have to make such decisions as I have made. I tell you, it is less difficult to order the destruction of a people than to crush a man's skull with your war ax in some midnight skirmish!"

Asa had flushed. So they knew even that! "I have done the one," he said. "I shall never do the other. Never."

"Never?" Horvath's laughter was like the scraping of rusted metal. "Never? That is a long time." The laughter had ended in a fit of coughing. One of the hands had moved languidly in the green light, waving him away.

Asa had stood and turned to leave, but Horvath spoke again, spoke in a harsh whisper. "Asa! Make no mistake. You have two choices. Only two. If you would go to her, go now. If you wait, you will be drawn into knowledge."

In the years following, Asa had made no conscious choice. Rather, he had been beguiled by what he was being shown by his Yggdrasilian teachers, by the strange problems and paradoxes of the Old Ones, and above all, by what the Old Ones had held back, kept secret. Always, beyond that, lay the Project itself: Jotunheim, the rediscovery of man.

He had thought: Only a little longer.

He had thought: Soon I shall tire of this and I shall go back then. I shall go for her then.

But he had not tired. He had kept asking, asking, and the answers, enticingly incomplete, had drawn him ever further into the slow dance of knowledge as Horvath had predicted, until now he had completed his novice training and the time had come for an appointment.

He knew what this meeting with Shem would be about. He knew what Shem would ask. He had decided what his answer would be. Shem would ask him to take a posting within the Gaian Expedient, perhaps as a messenger, a peregrinus-in-training. He would say no. No. He would say, "I'm going to the mainland. I'm going to look for Persis. No."

In the dusk he rounded the end of the island where the great tree of Yggdrasil rose through the conference room and high above the copse surrounding it. Little by little he turned his back on Jotunheim and let it fade into the darkness behind him. He ran the last two miles on the hard sand at the water's edge, jubilant. In the morning he would arrange transport to the mainland, and he would go east as far as the patrols could take him. Then he would go on alone, past the Kanik Mountains, past the place where he had fallen to his knees in exhaustion and stabbed Garm's arrow—a promise—into the earth. If necessary, he would even go into the Outer Wylds.

He would find Persis.

Then all time would end, and they would go together into fresh, new winters...

Night filled all the windows in the corridor leading to Shem's office, and Asa was accompanied the whole way by mocking copies of himself. Wind buffeted the panes. Leaves scratched against the sills.

Shem's chief assistant was still at her desk. She glanced up, smiled, nodded. "Just go in. He's expecting you."

He tapped on the door, opened it, and entered a room filled with the music that was Shem's atavism.

"Congratulations," Shem said, watching him closely. "You've got what you wanted. A posting to Jotunheim."

Asa heard himself asking, "For how long?"

"A few weeks," Shem said, his face grave, pitying, waiting. And when Asa did not reply he asked, "Well, can you start tomorrow?"

THIRTEEN

Late at night, Moran made two calls. The first
went to Nidor, Head of the Biological Unit at Neffelheim.
Moran's voice when he spoke to Nidor was coolly cour-
teous. He listened to his reply and then said, "Very well,
I'll come there. Thirty minutes?"

His second call went to the chief of the hoverport serv-
ing the Central Complex.

He could, of course, have gone through the subterranean tunnel that connected all three islands, taking one
of the electrical carts. But the night was cool and blustery,
and a low moon slipped from one cloud to the next like
a stalking warrior. Moran loved such nights. He exulted
in them. He loved all weathers that involved movement—
wind and rain and wild snow—restive moods that chafed
his torpid spirit into action, into the illusion that he was
in touch with ultimate realities. Also, such nights conjured
memories for him of those long-ago days when he had
been a messenger and then a peregrinus among the tribes.
Skin days, he called them. Free. Innocent. Full of movement and excitement. He was not troubled then by the
worries that had since weighed him down. He had brimmed
with vitality and faith. Through many such nights as this,

in vehicles and out of them, he had traveled far. And sometimes, now, after the days of tension, compromise, abuse, uncertainty, and intrigue, after days in the Central Complex with its artificial wind sounds and birdsongs and surf, it was good to be reminded that such things were still real, and that beyond the beaches and fiords of Asgard, nature still moved with its majestic unpredictability.

So, having decided to go to Neffelheim by sea, he descended in a swift elevator through the levels of the Complex and emerged into the weather. A large, lumbering figure, he walked a hundred yards on a gravel path, spoke jovially to the driver waiting at the landing, and ducked into the cabin of the hovercraft. Moments later the engine roared alive and the ACV was turned out of the harbor toward the sea. The green light on the end of the pier faded behind. They passed the red signals that marked the perimeter of a small phalanx of contour rafts rocking gently in the swells, delivering their bit of energy into the Yggdrasilian grid. They rounded the last point where the automatic beacon winked, and then suddenly the wind whipped spray across their windshield and the chop drummed on the heavy rubber of the skirt.

They sped up. On the lee side, Moran kept his face close to the open window, inhaling the tang of salt and iodine. Soon they passed the tidal dam across the mouth of Freyisfiord, and in another minute they had rounded the south cape and saw Neffelheim ahead, a glowing hive in the dark and fretful sea. Moran imagined he could hear the thrumming of Neffelheim's activity even above the engine of his craft.

Moran disliked Neffelheim intensely—its noise, its crassness, its efficiency. He disliked and feared its power, that awesome power symbolized by the profligate brilliance of the place.

The energy for that light, and for much of the rest of Yggdrasil, was sucked from deep in the earth. Huge turbines were spun by steam, steam generated in holes sunk by the Old Ones into the Earth's hot mantle. Poured down one of these shafts, cold water struck the magma, vaporized, and rose through a second shaft, a man-made fumarole. Inexhaustible, that power source was beautiful

in its simplicity, but Moran nevertheless saw those shafts
as an insult to Earth herself, a violation. Whenever he
was in Neffelheim and felt the incessant tremor caused
by the rising of the steam, Moran would think fleetingly
of tribal explanations for such phenomena. All shared a
common theme: Earth had been violated. Earth was shuddering in pain. Earth would retaliate. Soon.

Moran was troubled not only by the power itself, but
also by the potential for its misuse by those who governed
it. Although the scientists and technicians of Neffelheim
were nominally the servants of Yggdrasil, although they
like all others had taken the oath of obedience and ser-
vitude, Moran knew that they were the real masters of
Yggdrasil and the Five Districts of the Erthring, and that
they could impose their mastery at any time. They had
such latitude, and such awesome autonomy!

Yet, though he feared it, Moran himself could not resist
that power. He had to be near it. He had to smell it and
hear it and see its results and rub shoulders with those
who controlled it. That, he knew, was his great weakness.
Power, he said to himself. *The recognition of necessity*.
Power was attracting him now, to Nidor.

He sighed heavily as the ACV curved into Neffelheim's
harbor. He pushed the window shut as the lights of the
pier loomed close. Well, perhaps it was true that he must
compensate in this manner for some deficiency, but he
was still Dream Master of West Norriya and he was still
dedicated to the Expedient. *The best*, he reminded himself
resolutely as he disembarked, *is the enemy of the good*.

Nidor himself had not come to meet him, but a cart
and driver waited. The pier trembled like the skin of a
stretching animal. From far beneath, Moran heard the
rumble of turbines and centrifugal separators. He heard
the squawk of a distant alarm like the cry of a metal bird.
He smelled electricity. He smelled synthetic astringency
drifting down on the salt air from the banks of laboratories. He smelled power.

"Beautiful night," he said to the squat driver, and got
only a sullen grunt in reply.

They rolled swiftly down a nearby ramp and into the
subterranean labyrinth that connected the buildings of

Neffelheim. Nidor's office in the Biological Wing was on the far side of the island. It took only minutes to reach it through one of the deep express tunnels. The driver dropped him at the elevator, nodded crisply, and was gone, accelerating off into the maze of lights.

Moran ascended.

Nidor's office was four levels underground. Unlike the buildings on Asgard, which had cautiously crept into the sun as the years had passed and the air grew safer, most of the Neffelheim complex had remained subterranean. This was partly because the core of Neffelheim—the workshops and laboratories—predated the Entropies, and partly because those who worked in those areas preferred stable environments. Controllable environments. So Neffelheimers had less daily contact than other Yggdrasilians with the passing of the days and the seasons, and some even claimed to be indifferent to nature. "Nature," Nidor had said once, scornfully, in Moran's hearing, "is what I produce in my laboratories."

Moran had smiled to himself. He knew Nidor did not believe what he was saying. Years earlier, doing routine work at Val, Moran had discovered a file bearing Nidor's code number. Surprised that Nidor, who appeared so self-sufficient, would have any need to resort to Val, Moran had ordered Nidor's dreams run for his viewing. This was against Val policy; Nidor was not his subordinate. But Moran had not regretted his decision. The dreams astonished him. All had been dreams of wilderness! In them, across plains of swaying grass, through soft forests, moved wild creatures—not morphs, but animals as well formed and graceful as they had been before the Entropies. With them ran men. One of these men, naked in the sun, was Nidor. "So," Moran had breathed when the viewing concluded. "Even him!"

He had never mentioned his discovery to Nidor. That would have spoiled the pleasure. *You are not invulnerable*, he would think when faced with Nidor's overbearing arrogance. *I know your deficiency!*

Nidor leaned back from his desk as Moran knocked and entered his office. He did not stand, but his eyebrows lifted expectantly and his lips pursed in a wry and condescending smile. He was a lean man in his early thirties, with the prominent blue eyes and elongated face of a bird of prey. He wore the crisp, blue and yellow, high-necked tunic of the Biological Unit.

"I have news," Moran said.

"Yes?"

"News of considerable importance."

Nidor said nothing.

"The fact is, Horvath is dying."

Nidor's gaze dropped to a paper on his desk. "Men die," he said quietly. "In any case, this is not news. I have known it for some time."

"But his death will raise the question of succession."

"Obviously."

"Under the circumstances, it seemed to me that some, uh, preparation might be in order. Thatch your roof before the rain begins, eh?"

Nidor's thin nose wrinkled.

"When you go into the labyrinth, take a ball of string."

"Speak plainly, man. In other words, you want my help."

"Quite. Give me fire and I'll give you a light. A symbiotic relationship, Nidor my friend."

"Is there any other kind? Symbiotic and . . . beneficial to our endeavor."

"Quite."

Both men smiled quick smiles.

"As we know," Moran went on, "we need only one more vote in the Arborea. As Master of Norriya I could provide that vote. I would also be in a better position to protect Neffelheim's autonomy to continue—I beg your pardon—*conduct* experiments that so far the Arborea has refused to sanction."

Nidor blinked innocently. "And which experiments are those?"

"Oh, I don't think I need to be specific, do I? I believe that there are certain . . . explorations in both physics and biology that you would like to pursue, are there not? Explorations that can be carried only so far in secret. Admit it, my friend, you're going to need help."

"I admit nothing of the sort," Nidor said. "Perhaps we

shall be prepared to assist you in your ambitions, perhaps not."

"Keep in mind your experiments," Moran said, nodding slowly. "Keep them in mind. *I* shall."

"Is that all?"

"No. I have a further request. There is a certain young man. An aborr. Bring him to Neffelheim as an apprentice. Train him."

"Impossible. We have no provision for aborrs here. This is a community of experts. Busy experts."

Moran leaned forward eagerly. "He learns quickly, and he has other qualities that would be an asset in your work. Permit me." He unzipped his portfolio and drew out several large photographs and a video diskette. The photographs he passed across the desk to Nidor. They were pictures of Garm taken over the past year, surreptitiously, by the Kanik peregrinus Aleaha. Garm speaking in a council. Garm directing a hunt or a raid. Garm alone, musing. In all, sardonic gray eyes stared past the camera at a world that was less, infinitely less, than it should have been.

Nidor smiled as he looked at these pictures, stacking them one by one with the tips of his fingers. "His mother," he said, looking keenly at Moran, "must have been a very interesting woman."

Busy preparing the machine, Moran apparently did not hear. A moment later the VDT came alive and an image moved across it: Garm, recognizable even in the poor light of evening and despite foreshortening and movement. Garm moving in a fluid run toward a makeshift corral where horses reared in terror, and then twisting around to scream hatred and defiance at the intruding god, leaping to plunge the tip of his lance into its belly. Nidor heard his cry of rage pierce even through the silence of the film.

"A berserk aborr," he said when Moran had shut off the machine. "What would we do with someone like that? We need precision here, not passion." But his eyes were thoughtful.

"Do not underestimate that passion. It can be directed."

"Perhaps."

"Believe me. If our plans succeed we shall need men like that on whom we can rely completely. Leaders. Among other things, of course, we shall need an independent force on the ground."

Nidor's eyes closed. The tips of his index fingers touched his lips. He considered. He thought of the devices the Old Ones had left for the Arborea to use if necessary in the management of aborr populations—psychological, chemical, and mechanical. He thought too of the array of control mechanisms that had been developed since the Entropies and that now lay at the disposal of the Biological Unit in Neffelheim; mechanisms the Old Ones could not have imagined; mechanisms so subtle that neither the subject nor those about him would ever detect; mechanisms lying in readiness, having been well tested on aborrs captured by Neffelheim's unofficial operatives on the mainland. He thought finally of the wilderness in which this young man Garm had spent his life, and of the wildness he would bring to Neffelheim... "It might be interesting," he said at last.

"After he has been trained here, he could enter the regular novice program. He could be, perhaps, the first of many."

Nidor nodded slowly. "Agreed," he said. "There are advantages."

When he arrived back in his rooms later that evening, Moran sent the last of the day's messages. It went to his peregrinus among the Kaniks, Aleaha.

FOURTEEN

No HOVERCRAFT RAN TO JOTUNHEIM. NO HELICOPTERS
landed there. No electric carts moved down its wooded
paths. Nothing mechanical disturbed the tranquility of the
island's green hills, or the deliberations of its scholars.

Asa went at the appointed time, alone, taking a cart
to the Jotunheim station and continuing on foot along a
half mile of corridor. At the end was a checkpoint where
a persondat machine took a few seconds to scan his pass,
confirm his identity from the palm he laid on its surface,
and open the barrier with a hiss of escaping air.

A few yards beyond, he stepped into the Jotunheim
elevator and the doors closed behind him. With a trembling that was barely discernible, the elevator rose.

A voice spoke from concealed speakers, an old man's
voice, querulous, harried, petulant. "This is the Colm
speaking. Greetings, Asa. Welcome to Jotunheim. I have
received the questions you asked the SKULD database
concerning the Teperman File. You shall have answers
here. Throughout your training you have asked such questions. Sometimes you have received answers, sometimes
not. We believe that you understand that answers are

sometimes less important than the questions which follow them.

"We have only two rules in Jotunheim. The first is the rule of silence, which applies everywhere, constantly, except in the conference rooms and designated conversation areas. Of course, the need for such a rule is obvious. The second is the rule of candor. In theory, all research within Jotunheim is public when it occurs. Of course, this second rule is broken constantly, unintentionally, by subconscious activities that we do not fully understand. However, we do attempt to keep it. Jotunheim could not function otherwise. There would be no community of scholars. Any information you require while you are among us will be given to you as fully as possible.

"The mentor I have assigned to you is Egon. He will assist you with all work here. He has been informed of your arrival and will no doubt meet you when this elevator arrives at the vestibule of the reading room. He will orient you. After that, your research may begin.

"Good luck, Asa."

The elevator door opened.

Ahead was a large, glassy room filled with sunlight and noise. The sunlight came through skylights and through the windows of the reading room that lay beyond, overlooking the sea, a room reached only by an intermediate chamber designed to filter out the noise. The noise came from the scholars. They argued. Standing face to face, or sprawled on couches, or gripping each other's elbows earnestly while making points, they argued. At least a dozen conversations proceeded simultaneously in the anteroom, most at top volume.

Out of this cacophony emerged a tall, dark-haired man of thirty-nine or forty. His earth-colored caftan flowed around a very thin frame, suspended from stooped shoulders. Quizzical, alert, amused, his eyes peered at Asa from behind owlish glasses.

"I'm Egon," he said over the din. "Come. We'll go out where we can talk." And he led the way through a door and onto a patio among the trees. "I should say first of all," Egon said when they were outside, "how delighted I am that you've come. You see, I know a great deal

about you already, and about your people. It was my task
to complete the SKULD memoir when the Arborea . . . when
they decided . . . Well." He opened his hands. "I'm an
ethnohistorian with a special interest in the linguistic analysis of myth. But of course I do many other things, as
we all do here." His smile was crooked and congenial,
revealing teeth carelessly arranged. "So, you see, you can
help me. But the more important question is: How can I
help you? I think I know part of the answer. We'll have
a tour first. Then we'll begin to go to work."

They began with a short stroll to a lookout that emerged
from the surrounding trees to provide an astonishing panorama—a northern view of the entire strait from the mainland to Yggdrasil. Far below, made miniature by height,
Asgard lay curled on itself like a small, sleeping animal.
Beyond it, a plume of steam rose from Neffelheim and
drifted south. Hazy in the east lay the mainland, the mouths
of the great rivers, and the coastal mountains beyond
which, invisible in the mist, the Middle Wayst stretched
away to the Kanik hills.

Egon followed Asa's gaze. He smiled. "You would
almost rather be there than here," he said. "Almost but
not quite. You see, I know that, too. Come. Let's walk."

For the remainder of that first day they walked together
on the paths of Jotunheim, and Egon showed Asa the
living quarters of the scholars, and the committee rooms,
and the reading rooms of the various departments. All the
buildings were low and unassuming, none higher than one
storey.

About two hundred scholars worked there on various
facets of the Project. Some were department heads, dis-
tinguished by saffron gowns. Some were initiates, as Asa
was, assigned for a limited period to test and be tested.
Most were men and women freed of all responsibilities
and (so far as possible) all personal concerns. They lived
only for ideas, and for the delicate blending of those ideas.
"What is a scholar?" Asa had asked Shem once, soon
after his arrival in Yggdrasil, and Shem had replied,
"Someone whose mind watches itself."

They had been walking in a gentle spiral that circled
the island and took them down almost to sea level before

curving back into the trees and down through spacious and well-lit tunnels into the heart of the island. Warm air sent from Neffelheim under pressure wafted around them. "As you know," Egon said as they walked, "our ancestors survived the effects of the Entropies by living here, in this labyrinth provided by the Old Ones, for ten years. They had everything they needed. For that decade, the work of understanding the Yggdrasilian operating manuals occupied the scholars almost completely. Only later, when they had begun to emerge, only after the boundaries of the Erthring had been defined and the extent of the damage to the Earth assessed, did they begin to turn their attention inward. When they started serious work on the Project, when they began to act for posterity, the secret of the Central Chamber revealed itself."

"What is infinite is minuscule," Asa said, remembering the old challenge that all novices learned early in their training. *"What lies in your palm contains you."*

Egon nodded. "Exactly. The Paradox of the First Door. We know now, of course, that the Old Ones had designed the door so that it could be opened only when our ancestors had attained a certain level of understanding and, perhaps, humility. Only then would they find the key. For some, the quest became obsessive, the equivalent of a quest for power, and they destroyed themselves in it. No one interested in mere power made progress. In fact, no one made progress until—"

"Kalevala," Asa said.

"Kalevala. A man utterly selfless. Utterly disinterested. A scholar who had grown old in the service of the Project and who had come to perceive a profound irony through that work: Man's existence was insignificant; his responsibility was inestimable.

"After the event, Kalevala characteristically denied any special insight. He claimed that all he ever knew for certain was that life was a network of mysteries. One night, alone, he walked down this corridor that we are now descending, entered the Central Chamber, and offered his solution. The story is that others working nearby heard him laugh. On the waiting console he spelled out two words: INFINITE REGRESS.

"And the door opened.

"Behind it was a little vault. Inside lay a repository of new knowledge—books, manuscripts, diagrams, maps, films, computer disks, tapes, and so forth—knowledge of which we had previously had only the slightest inklings in obscure journals and manuscripts imperfectly censored by the last group of the Old Ones' editors to work on them. There were all the personal papers left by the Old Ones, including Teperman. There were the complete plans for the Gaian Expedient. There were technical data essential for the long-term maintenance of Yggdrasil, including information on the manufacturing of materials that would be required for repair and expansion. There were many bodies of knowledge that we now know have been invaluable to the Project but which, had we discovered them earlier, beset by fear as we had been and lacking the humility and sense of stasis that characterizes true play, we would have exploited and transformed into mere power.

"If it seems absurd to you that so obvious a fact took over forty years to rediscover, remember that the survivors of the Entropies were the inheritors of the deistic and anthropocentric philosophies of the Old Ones, with all their residual biases. Elemental simplicities were not the forte of our great-great-grandparents. They had to relearn much.

"In fact, when the door swung back it was obvious that in the Old Ones' opinion they still had some distance to go, for beyond the stacks of new material another door identical to the first stood waiting."

As Egon had been talking they had arrived at the Central Chamber and passed through it to stop in front of the first door. The large room they stood in was a semicircle, surrounding what appeared to be a wall of solid granite. The first door opened into this wall, and on the far side of the vault Asa saw the second door waiting. They were too far away to read the inscription, but Asa recited it. *"Circling, I am not a circle. Flat, I am not straight. I give strength though I have none. Progressing, I end where I begin. Single, I start life; double, I stand in life's core;*

triple, I link life to life. Through me knowledge becomes wisdom. Through me time returns."

"Yes," Egon said. "A riddle. A child's riddle. Any ideas?" He nodded toward the alphabetical panel waiting at the side of the door. "You're welcome to try."

Asa shook his head. "Not yet."

Each morning during his weeks in Jotunheim Asa woke in the tiny, sparsely furnished cell built into the hillside, looking out over the sea. In silence he ate breakfast with the scholars. In silence he walked to his desk in the reading room reserved for visitors. In silence he read through the day, often looking up to watch the calm sea sparkling far below through the screen of evergreens. All the records of Jotunheim were open to him, everything that had been preserved from the days of the Old Ones and everything that had been accomplished since. He read as a hungry man eats, avidly, devouring history, and science, and the haunting poetry of the Old Ones. Biology fascinated him, and he spent several weeks following the meandering lives of cells and feeling the awesome complexity of life, mystery opening into mystery.

His request for information on missiles brought a full dossier of detailed technical descriptions, but the synopsis that introduced it told him that although much was known about these curious devices of the Old Ones, what was not known was *why they were built*. All explanations had been excised by the last censors to have worked on the documents before the Entropies. References to the word *payload* ended in etymological tangles, for it was impossible to tell who was being paid, and for what. Similarly, although Jotunheim had information on Einstein, whom Teperman had apparently so much admired, again the censors had been at work and nothing remained to indicate why he had been especially admirable. So far as Asa could tell, he had been quite an ordinary teacher. Other scientists less admired by the Old Ones seemed to Asa much more interesting—Heisenberg, for example, and Bohr, and Gödel—all of whose work placed surprising limits on what could be known by the brain alone and, thus, questioned the authenticity of merely scientific ways of knowing.

Even more interesting were the paradoxes and dilemmas that Teperman had grown so fond of toward the end. Asa made a point of tracing them all and examining them, beginning with Zeno as Teperman had done. Among them he began to sense what he believed Teperman had felt, that they represented man's groping attempts to surpass the best of himself, and Asa began to see that the brain alone was inadequate for this psychic mutation that must occur, for the brain functions by limiting, by focusing attention precisely. It is an organ of defense. But what was required for the *salto mortale* that the Project demanded was not increased protectiveness but increased risk and vulnerability. Asa thought that perhaps it was this that Teperman's beloved Einstein intuited when he said, "The most beautiful experience we can have is the mysterious. It is the fundamental emotion that stands at the cradle of true art and true science. Whoever does not know it is as good as dead, and his eyes are dimmed."

In those long days, Asa came to realize that man before the Entropies had been not so much a flawed species as one that had made a small misstep in evolution. He must go back. He must evolve a conscience large enough to enfold the Earth that contained his animal self. That was the work of the Project. And when Asa thought of this he thought again of the old story of Orphus and Urdci that he had been told as a child on the banks of the Alcher, and he knew that the meaning of the story was that man must go deep into the unknown recesses of himself, and there claim his bride, and be whole . . .

"Yes," Egon said, when Asa told him how he had been thinking. "Our scholars too are moving in that direction, but it is very slow, very slow."

Most evenings after they had eaten, he and Asa would meet and talk. Sometimes they would stay in one of the areas designated for that purpose, and if there were other scholars present Asa was content to listen to their conversation, watching ideas crystallize like diamonds under the pressures built by questions and counterquestions, thesis and antithesis. Sometimes Egon and Asa would walk alone along the paths, and Egon would listen patiently to Asa's excited summary of what he had learned that day, gently guiding his thought, opening doors.

They walked together on Asa's last night in Jotunheim. "Ah." Egon smiled when Asa began to talk confidently about the nature of man and the ease with which, it seemed to him, the Project might be completed. "Do you know what I think? That man is an abyss. For thirty years I have been staring down into that abyss without ever once having seen the bottom. All that has happened is that I have grown dizzier!" He stopped walking and held Asa by the shoulder. "You have been here only a few months. That is not time enough even to make a beginning, is it? However, it is time enough for me to know that you should return. Sooner or later you *must* return. You are like us. Ideas nourish you. You must have them as other men need comfort, or action."

Asa said nothing.

Egon asked, "Persis?"

He nodded.

"The Arborea won't let you go," Egon said quietly. "You know that."

"They have no means of stopping me."

"Oh yes they have."

"Not against my will. I can refuse to take the Oath of the Peregrinus."

Egon laughed. "My dear Asa, you believe that you want to leave on your quest for Persis, but isn't it true that part of you wants to stay here, in Jotunheim? And that another part of you knows that time is running out for Yggdrasil and wants to help? Of course! They will *use* that schism in you, use it so subtly that perhaps you won't even realize. So"—he offered his hand—"I won't say good-bye to you because I know that we shall meet again. I think we might share some great adventure, you and I. Farewell, Asa. Go carefully."

After Egon had gone Asa stood for a little while on the lookout where they had walked on his first day. The sea was so calm and the night so still that not only could he see Neffelheim but he could hear the rumble of its technic life across the whole length of Asgard and the intervening straits. It was a sinister, glowing beetle in the darkness.

Asa turned from it toward the east and made a promise: The next morning he would leave Yggdrasil. He would leave time. He would go in search of Persis. He would meet with Shem and then he would go. And nothing that Shem said would stop him.

Smiling, he walked alone back to his cell. He slept.

Light gleams on the arrow shaft sliding along his thumb, on the tautening bow. Light glints off the war point coming back, back until it nicks his hand, until the feathers touch his cheek and his fingers quiver waiting, waiting until Garm comes into light, and sees him on one knee in the path, and knows he is entering the last moment of his life. He . . . lets . . . go . . . And Garm moving left fast toward the shadows is suddenly clumsy, suddenly contorted, an Alcheringian shaft in his thigh, his soundless mouth open, still wondrously on his feet and even drawing his dagger before the next shaft comes like a lover's whisper from the quiver, down, back, launched in that flat parabola that ends in the Kanik's gut, and the next, so beautiful, in his breastbone and the next and last in his throat, so fast that he has not had time to drag a step forward but stands impaled while the last of life drains out. Watcher, watched, Asa looses the shriek of Alcheringian triumph into his eyes, screaming until blood comes, choking, saying *What? What? What?* Somewhere a matins bell is ringing, and the scholar in the next cell has opened an anxious door, saying, "You dreamed. You screamed. Are you all right? Can I help you?"

FIFTEEN

SHEM'S FACE WAS THE COLOR OF CLAY, OR OF SILT AFTER floodwaters have drained away. A tuft of beard on his lower lip twitched. Strands of white glimmered among the red. His eyes receded as if seeking refuge under the broad brow, and he massaged them gently with the tips of his fingers. Softly, around Shem and Asa, measured music moved, and the powdered ghosts of the Old Ones bowed through their quadrilles.

"Tomorrow," Asa said when Shem had not spoken for several seconds, "I want—"

Shem raised a hand. "Please. I know what you want."

"In that case—"

"I need you," Shem said. His head leaned back. His eyes closed.

Asa thought, *This is what his death will look like*. He felt pity, and he saw the power of that pity to entrap him. He was afraid. "No," he said quietly.

"Yes. I need you to go on a mission. A very special mission." Shem's eyes opened. "In fact, only you can accomplish it. If you don't do it, it won't be done. I need it done."

"What—what is it?"

"I want you to find Alva."

"Alva!" Asa stood up and crossed Shem's office to the windows, gasping. Something had struck him between the shoulder blades. For a moment the room tilted up and began to recede, and he feared that he might float into a spell. But then things steadied. The pain diminished. His breathing became regular.

He had thought of Alva often—how she had brought him to Yggdrasil after the death of Jared; how she had saved him at the risk of her own life, and how by doing so she had prevented a final encounter with Garm. He had never forgiven her; he could never repay her. She alone, of all the Norriyan peregrini, had recoiled in horror from the decision to destroy Alcheringia and its people. She had sent her curt message of disgust to Yggdrasil, broken her oath, and vanished.

Alva! Squat, tough, honorable Alva with that grotesque bear-paw hand!

"How do you know she's even alive?"

"We've had reports from peregrini. Vague reports, but substantial enough. She's alive. Deep in Gerumbia. Reaching her will be very dangerous. If you attempt it, you will have the best ACV crew I can give you—Horvath's own crew, Fenris and Vogh."

"Why do you want her?"

Shem stood with difficulty. The cartilaginous mass of his foot was stiffening with age, and the stiffness rose through the once-silken ligaments of the calf, toward the knee. "Because Horvath is dying. He has no more than five months. Six at most. When he is gone the Arborea will appoint either Moran or myself Master of Norriya. If I am chosen I will need her."

Asa stared incredulously. "Alva? A dream master?"

Shem nodded.

"But she would never accept. Even if I find her and bring her back, she would never accept that."

"Perhaps not."

"She rejected the Project, the Expedient, Yggdrasil—everything!"

"But, you see, she did not reject *you*." Shem smiled regretfully.

"So. That is how you would use me."

"Of course."

"Her decision was a matter of principle."

"Principle," Shem said. "That is a word I haven't heard for a long time. Moran used to say that a principle was anything not needed for survival. Teperman uses the word, I think."

"Yes."

"I would have said that her decision was almost purely emotional. That it was a decision for life. We need that. We need it very badly. Well, will you go?"

"How long?"

"I don't know. Perhaps a few weeks, perhaps longer."

"And after?"

"Then look for Persis. I'll help you, then. But first, this task. Well?"

Asa opened his hands. "All right."

"Good. This will be a test for you, of course. You will have to deal with the Gerumbians and perhaps with others who participated in the Alcheringian affair."

"Say slaughter."

"Slaughter. All right. The Alcheringian slaughter. You'll meet those who were responsible."

"No. I *have* met those who were responsible. Now I'll meet some who were there."

Shem closed his eyes wearily. "In any case, it will be a test. A submarine will be ready when you want it. Let Operations know a day in advance."

Asa nodded.

"Of course we'll have a full briefing when you're ready. The sooner the better. Where do you want to be taken?"

Asa remembered his first journey with Alva, when she had brought him to Yggdrasil. They had gone north, north past the singing harps and the mummified bear's head, past a dead city full of sorrowing shades, to a great beach. "Gerumbia," he said to Shem. "The north beach."

Three days later, he left. He boarded the submarine swiftly and went directly below. He did not look back.

Deckhands sealed the hatches. The captain and navigator welcomed him perfunctorily and turned their attention to the tasks of launching. The craft submerged and slipped through the open gates and out to sea, where it surfaced again for the run to the mainland.

They passed through a calm night, beneath a canopy of stars. Behind the phosphorescence of the wake, the lights of Neffelheim blazed, and dim orange pools glowed among the hills of the other islands. Ahead, all was darkness. Clouds massed above the hills. There would be storms later.

The little boat rocked gently, and Asa let himself be carried by the rhythm and the undulant throb of the engine. From the storerooms of Asgard he had selected a Yulok tunic, breeches, and moccasins. It was a good disguise. He could have passed for a Yulok warrior. Over his shoulder was slung a skin pouch containing a weapon, a radio, food, and other devices. Feet braced on the deck, he breathed deeply and watched the dark line of the mainland draw closer.

When they were about halfway across the strait, the lights of another surface-running submarine blinked on ahead of them. The helmsmen of both craft had obviously been in radio contact, and the ships passed each other to starboard at a safe distance but close enough for Asa to see a man standing on the deck, in the shadow of the superstructure. Despite darkness and distance, he saw that the man was clad like himself, in skins. An aborr. A candidate novice being taken to Yggdrasil for assessment. Asa was on the point of raising his hand in greeting when something made him hesitate, something made him lean forward and peer hard into the darkness as the craft passed. It was traveling fast, and in another moment the figure on its deck was scarcely recognizable as human, but Asa sensed that he too had been watched as the distance between them widened, watched until they had passed from each other's view and into their separate nights.

Troubled, he turned again toward the mainland. Fifteen minutes later the south cape of the great bay of Gerumbia curved out of the darkness, a beckoning finger.

SIXTEEN

ON THE NIGHT HE DIED, HORVATH LEFT HIS ROOMS AND made his way slowly to the closest exit, where a cart waited. With great difficulty he settled himself behind the wheel and drove slowly to that part of the Complex where Froele's apartment adjoined her offices. When he arrived in the small parking area he sat a few minutes before making his way inside. He walked very slowly. "If this is dying," he said to the empty night, "I don't think much of it!"

Froele met him at her door. "Man," she said, slipping her arm around his waist and helping him inside and onto a couch.

"Contemptible," he said. "Contemptible." But she was not sure whether he meant his illness or her solicitation. She did not ask.

"Horvath, there are drugs."

He shook his head. "I have a question."

She sat beside him and held his hand in both of hers.

"Do you remember when we were both young, before we took our oaths?"

"Of course."

"Were we then...in love, you and I?"

"I think," she said, smiling, "that we were."

"What do you remember?"

"That I would have gone with you anywhere. That I would rather have done that than take the oath. What do you remember?"

"That I believed I might do some good that no one else had done. That I could forward the Project some way, in some special way. But I remember, too, that I would rather have gone with you. On the sea."

Her arms slipped around him and she held him tightly, her face pressed against his shoulder. "It seems," she said, "that we made a serious mistake..."

Horvath's drowned body was found at the edge of the salt marsh that spread below his window, to the sea. Somehow he had dragged himself across it, over the muskeg and through the tangled shrubbery, until at last he could hold the incoming tide in his outstretched hands.

PART TWO

THE
OPENING

ONE

"VOICES," SAID THE NIGHT OPERATOR.

He sat very still watching his radar screen, the fingers of his right hand touching his earphones. His face was green, underlit by instruments. His eye sockets were pools of pensive blackness.

The controller had been turning away from him, about to leave the tower, but now she paused. "Voices, of course." She smiled. "What would you expect?"

"Not patrols. Not missions," said the operator. "Something else..."

The controller touched the loudspeaker switch, permitting the ghostly sounds of the Yggdrasilian night to slip into the room. They came from air, land, and sea patrols the length and breadth of the Erthring, and from peregrini in all five districts, and from special missions returning, asking instructions from the Asgard tower. All these occurred every night in a soft cacophony of mixed tedium and urgency. But tonight, underneath them and filling the pauses between them, there was something else: an undulant ribbon of melody. Swiftly and skilfully, while the operator returned to his work of answering those other voices, the controller found the channel on which this

95

sound was clearest. She isolated it, fine-tuning the antenna. It came from somewhere to the south, beyond Merone and the Underlakes.

She knew at once what it was, for she had been well trained in radio emissions of all kinds and had spent the required hours in the archives listening to the liquid sounds of the Old Ones. They had always moved her strangely, so beautiful had they been, so gallant and poignant, like fires defiant in the growing night.

Now, after all this time, here were these sounds again! Alive! She knew at once what they were. They were music.

TWO

No record existed of the trip of the submarine that brought Garm to Yggdrasil. Moran and Nidor were careful to see that the daily report bore no mention of it, that the craft's log showed it had lain at its berth all night, and that the crew enjoyed an unexpected leave in Val, from which they emerged with clouded memories of the previous two days.

Their journey had ended at the docking facility of Neffelheim. Here Garm and Aleaha disembarked. Here they were met and transported to Nidor's office.

Everything was ready. The assessment techniques Nidor had arranged included the deployment of cameras that allowed Nidor to watch Garm's progress across the island. What he saw confirmed his impression from Moran's tapes and photographs that this was no ordinary aborr. Everything about Garm suggested vast reserves of intelligence and energy. Nidor felt a qualm of mingled pity and remorse, which he suppressed immediately.

He entered the room and stood still, giving time to allow himself to be examined. Then he raised a hand in the Kanik salute. Garm nodded warily, but did not return the gesture.

"Cold, cold," Aleaha said, huddling in her grimy clothes. "Is there no warmth? Is there no nourishment? And why here, to this godforsaken place? Why to Neffelheim? Why not to—"

Nidor turned to her. "Be quiet, please," he said.

She tried to straighten herself, but her voice was wheedling still. "And who *are* you? You aren't my dream master. I've served—"

Nidor crossed to the door and opened it. "I think," he said, "it would be best if you left. Please report to your dream master." How he hated them, these aborr peregrini! These seamed people stinking of meat and smoke, puffed up with their own importances! What disgusting anachronisms! "A driver is waiting outside."

Aleaha recoiled. Her nostrils dilated. A claw emerged from some orifice in her clothing and began a series of obscene gestures, the overture to a curse.

Nidor said so quietly that the word was scarcely more than a movement of his lips. *"Now!"*

She left, muttering.

Neither of them watched her leave. They were looking at each other.

"My name is Nidor. You are here because we understand that you are hungry to know. Because you believe that knowing brings strength." He spoke in the Kanik dialect he had learned for this purpose. "If that is not true, tell me now and we shall take you back to the Kanik hills with many gifts, with many dreams."

"It is true," Garm said.

"Then you are willing to learn?"

"Of course."

"Good. Come." Smiling, Nidor led the way to the laboratories where the subtlest of all teaching programs lay ready, awaiting its first test.

THREE

Tʜᴀᴛ ꜰɪʀꜱᴛ ɴɪɢʜᴛ ᴛʜᴇ ꜱᴜʙᴍᴀʀɪɴᴇ ʜᴀᴅ ᴛᴀᴋᴇɴ Aꜱᴀ ᴀꜱ close as possible to the great northern beach of Gerumbia.

No one had seen him land.

No one had seen the nervous sailor row him in and hurry back out into the fog. No one had watched Asa run across the beach, bound up the long slope behind it, and crouch for a few moments at the edge of the fractured highway that had once run into the dead city. No one had seen him stare hard at that city, seeing its buildings like rotted teeth on the horizon, hearing wind moan among the boulevards and through the emptied dwellings.

At dawn he made his rendezvous with Fenris and Vogh. Shem had promised that he would have a seasoned crew at his disposal. They were. The corps of drivers and nav-engineers whose job it was to run dangerous missions on land were the toughest and most cynical of all Yggdra-silian units, but even they had their elite. They called them Wylders. These were the few men and women who had grown to know intimately the labyrinthine routes through the Five Districts of the Erthring, routes pro-tected by the carefully constructed myths of Jotunheim's

ethnographers and by constant use. They had been beguiled by these routes, and by the lands they traversed,
and by the tensions and harrowing dangers of their job.
They lived their lives on a knife edge, yet they rarely took
leaves, and never resorted to Val, unlike the submariners
and the flight crews. The Wylders were content in and
with the wild. Even their vehicles acquired with time a
dusky patina of the wilderness, almost as if they belonged,
like strange fungi. They were the most reliable of a hard
lot, these Wylders. They lived for speed and action, and
they took a gritty pride in their work.

Asa saw at a glance that Fenris and Vogh were two
such men. Men who could be trusted absolutely in all
physical crises. Men for whom the saddened world offered few surprises. Rumors said that the Wylders were
not too concerned with keeping the standing order against
killing, and that they would as soon use their hovercrafts'
lasers as the relatively harmless lachrymators, nauseators,
and piezosonic oscillators with which the machines were
also equipped.

The ACV waiting at the rendezvous was a standard
SCAT IV, turbocharged for fast work in rugged terrain.
Photovoltaic cells lined its roof.

"Morning," Fenris said, rising as Asa approached. He
was a lean man with close-cropped orange hair. His eyes
were wary, his smile noncommittal, revealing crooked
teeth. "A hot place with no shade," he said thinly.

"There is shade under the tree," Asa answered.

Vogh emerged then from behind the vehicle, amber
sunglasses glinting, and Asa knew from the purposeful
tension of the man's movements that if the password had
not been correct he, Asa, would have died. Vogh nodded.
The peak of his cloth cap bobbed.

Neither man offered to shake hands. Their hands remained on the hips of their tight green coveralls.

"Where to, sir?" Fenris asked.

Asa unfolded a map and showed him. "Here."

Vogh grunted. "No need to stop there unless you want
to. We can run you anywhere inside Gerumbia. Drop you
there, you'll have quite a hike, won't you?"

Fenris agreed. "Why not let us run you right in?"

"Orders," Asa said. "I have to go on foot. I have to make contact with Gerumbians. My mission depends on it."

Fenris shrugged. "You're the boss."

An hour later they deposited him at the edge of a stunted forest.

Vogh shouted through the open door above the screaming of the engine. "How're you getting back?"

"Probably helicopter," Asa said.

Fenris leaned across to him. "Listen! Listen, mate. If you have any trouble in there, I mean *any* trouble, you call us in, y'hear? I don't care whether it's in your orders or not. Do it! And that goes for when you want to come out, too. If those fly-boys let you down, call us. Give us your position. We'll be there. Got it?"

"Got it!" Asa smiled. "Thanks."

They gave him a thumbs-up and roared back down the valley.

When they had gone, he pushed cautiously into a tangle of warped bushes and misshapen trees, hearing the groaning and shrieking of Gerumbian wind harps like a chorus of demented souls, passing the grisly totems mounted to warn off all wanderers—the heads of bears and stags and indescribable beasts that were the grotesque results of sifting poisons and ruined genes. "Keep away!" they said. "Keep far off! If you are innocent and well formed this is no place for you. Flee!"

To say that Gerumbia was blighted was a ludicrous understatement. Gerumbia was horror incarnate, its inhabitants hideous grotesques. Fate had been far kinder to those slain at once by the Entropies—incinerated, suffocated, broiled, flayed, poisoned, starved, mangled, and mutilated beyond all hope—infinitely kinder to them than to those that lived bearing chaos in their genes, loosing it into the tissues of Earth. Almost everything in Gerumbia was a morph, a freak, a rank travesty. Flowers that should have been five inches tall grew to five feet. Huge, soft blossoms swaying on carbuncled stalks were torn by bizarre insects. In stunted trees, weird birds yammered and growled, and beneath them crept animals hissing with the agony of pustulating skins. The very landscape was strangely discolored, and the soil chafed and friable, but restive, as if perverted nutrients might suddenly leap full-blown into macabre new life. Biological anarchy prevailed in that place. From the other districts, even from Waysts far to the south, morphs crept there hoping that amid the weird burgeoning might be some creature sufficiently like them to permit communication or even affection before Death, disgusted, swept them into blackness.

Asa knew he had been watched from the moment he passed through the first fringe of forest. He had glimpsed humanoid creatures flitting in the shadows at the edge of a clearing, and loping along a distant ridge, and bobbing up in the pools of a purplish river. But he did not expect the attack to come when it did.

It came out of the Earth.

He was stepping across what he took to be a moss-covered and decaying log when suddenly it rose. It was alive. It lunged upward in thrashing dust and crumbling leaves. On one end was a sort of head, a shapeless mass out of which red eyes peered. On the other end were bent and scrabbling legs. Flaps of skin like wings hung from its wrists to its ankles down the length of its body. It looked like a scabrous bat or a diseased flying squirrel, yet it was five feet long and it was human, just barely human.

It leaped on Asa, and before he could move it had wrapped him in the ghastly cocoon of itself, pressing his face into the furry stench of its flesh, filling his ears with his own gagging and its loathsome wheezing.

He twisted, lurched back, got his knife and lifted it to plunge into the thing's heart, to stab and keep stabbing until it fell away from him. That was his first impulse, and he very nearly carried it out. The blade was already descending when he diverted it, slashing to his right and through the leathery membrane that enfolded him, right, left, drawing great gouts of air as he fell free and the thing scrabbled away, squealing.

He forced himself to fall on it and crush it to the ground.

He forced himself to fling it onto its back and stare into the red, lidless eyes, and grasp its throat, and endure the rank breath rasping out its pleas for mercy: "Pease, pease, no hurt, no hurt!"

He brought the point of the knife up under its lower jaw. "Can you understand me?"

The head wiggled.

"Good. You have a choice. You can die now or you can go ahead of me, there, over the hills, and tell all you meet that I am coming. Say I want talk. Say that they who attack me will die. Do you understand?"

Again the head wiggled.

"Go, then," Asa said, standing.

Mewing, the thing scuttled away and vanished, trailing ribbons of itself, speckling blood across the stony hillside.

Asa dropped to his knees, retching.

Then he went on. He knew that word of his coming would spread like pestilence now. He knew he would not go much farther before Gerumbian leaders met him. He was right. An hour later he sensed a quickening of activity around him. He paused in the middle of a large clearing, set down his pack, and made preparations. Then he sat and waited.

The woods moved.

Something flew, creaking, overhead.

A huge Gerumbian, grinning, detached himself from the undergrowth a hundred yards in front, and Asa knew that there would be others close behind, inching forward with their hungers, their clubs and hammerstones. He touched the little control panel inside his pack. Behind him and to the sides, phosphor capsules hissed and blossomed, showering sparks and puffing smoke high above the trees. At the same moment he drew his weapon and selected a pine stump fifty yards away. The muzzle gouted red. Red engulfed the stump. Blooms of red and yellow rose to heaven, and in seconds the stump had crumbled to smoldering ashes. The other fireworks sputtered out to liquid circles in the grass.

When the smoke cleared, the Gerumbian in front of him had fallen prostrate and was grinding his forehead into the dirt. The others lay at the fringes of the forest. Asa gestured with both arms, summoning them all, watching with pity and loathing as they gathered, these warped creatures, into an abject knot in front of him. One who could speak said, "God, what would you have us do?"

"Come closer," Asa said. "Be my guests." He gestured to a space where he had distributed meaty joints brought for this purpose, and when they had crept forward, when they had consumed the meat in the ravenous Gerumbian manner, Asa singled out one who had come reluctantly from behind him and who had begun once again to watch him with a predatory interest. He was hairless. Spread thickly across his scalp and down his cheeks and chin, scattered over his arms and the rest of his body, was a loathsome, suppurating crust as if the stuff of hair had liquefied in each small follicle and dribbled out. "Your name?" Asa asked, pointing.

"Drynak."

Asa held his gaze levelly. Wind scooped their odor to him. "Drynak, you think you know what it is to suffer?"

The crusted lips parted in a raw laugh.

"No, you do not know, Drynak. You think you do, but you will not know unless you try again to kill me. If you do, then you will learn what suffering truly is. You and the others also."

Drynak's gaze faltered. He glanced at the others, and then at the ground. "What do you want, O God?"

"Runch."

A tremor ran through them like a breeze through fragile leaves. One chewed his knuckles, moaning. One suddenly hammered the ground. One shrieked gibberish. "Runch is gone," Drynak said. "He is dead, maybe."

"Where?"

Drynak jerked his head backward, to the southeast.

"How far?"

"Far. Two, maybe three days."

"How long ago?"

Drynak shook his head. "Long."

"After—after Alcheringia?"

The man's obscene head tipped back and he uttered a

crowing laugh that set the others into paroxysms of delight.
"Ah, the Alcheringians! The pretty ones! Their riches!
Their smooth bodies! How we gave it to them! We, Gerumbians, first over their parapet! And their women! Ahhh!
Women without a scar, without a blemish! Women with
hair streaming like fire! Do you remember what we did
with them, old sons?"

Waves of recollection sent them groaning, swaying,
beating the earth.

Asa reached for his weapon. He was ice. He was a
man of ice, and something was devouring his guts. That
instant he wanted nothing more than to draw the gun and
liquefy them where they sat yowling and chortling. He
wanted nothing more than to reduce the lot of them to a
puddle of scum. He endured that instant. And the next.
And the next. And then, he did want something more.
He asked, "Runch left after that?"

"After," Drynak grunted.

"Alone?"

Drynak wiped away from his eyes a yellowish fluid
that had dribbled down his forehead. He shook his head.

"Who went with him?"

"A woman. Hairy. A Wanderer. A Gerumbian." His
face brightened. "She had a hand—" He held up his left
hand and made a close-fingered, pawlike gesture.

"Alva," Asa said.

"Yes." Drynak nodded, remembering. "Alva."

"Draw a map, Drynak." Asa watched as the man
scratched in the dirt. He watched the others huddle close,
grunting, erase portions, redraw them. "Go now," he said
when they had finished and a sort of map lay before him.
"Come here tomorrow morning and there shall be food
for you. Food, knives, arrow points. Do you understand?"

Their faces lit with wonder and anticipation.

"Go now."

They went, backing into their tangled forest, bowing
to him until they faded from his sight. Last to leave was
a pale, fair, smiling man whom Asa had not noticed in
the tension of the encounter. This man paused momentarily in the deep shadows at the edge of the clearing, and

looked back. Asa rose. *"Kenet!"* he whispered. But the man raised his hand in the old Alcheringian gesture of greeting and farewell, and shook his head, and was gone into the depths of the forest.

Asa sank slowly to the ground and sat still for a while. Then he spoke into the small black panel he had drawn from his pack. When he had done that, and copied the map, Asa moved.

For two days he was aware of furtive life in the countryside through which he traveled. Gerumbians peered at him from the mouths of caves and fissures, gazed down on him from surrounding ridges, sometimes kept pace with him at a safe distance across the open spaces. Only those whose bodies were unwarped and untrammeled by extra limbs could keep up with him.

On the third day he reached the region where Drynak had said he would find Runch and Alva. Compared to the rest of Gerumbia this area was almost attractive. It had escaped the worst of the Entropies. Fresh streams tumbled out of its hills. It was more green than purple, and a larger proportion of its animals and birds seemed normal. It was a region tabooed in Gerumbian lore.

He had hunted as he went, using arrows, and each evening he stopped early to cook his catch and show his position clearly to anyone who cared to find him. Pure food in Gerumbia was not easily acquired, and several times he had to discard morphs whose anomalies had not been obvious before the kill. By evening, however, he usually had something fit to cook.

On the third night he camped beside a small river, far enough downstream from the waterfall to hear movement in the surrounding forest. He had slain a clean rabbit and spitted it over a good bed of coals. Just at dusk he sensed he was being watched. He felt it on his neck, on the insides of his thighs. He left his gun in his pack. He drew his bow closer; he slid two arrows out of his quiver.

The man who appeared in silence out of the twilight turned empty hands toward the fire and stood waiting to be recognized.

Asa motioned him to sit.

He was no fighter anymore, this man. His left shoulder was contorted as if it had been slammed between giant fists. From it dangled a useless twig of an arm, a flaccid thing with vestigial fingers splayed at its end like little sausages. Framed by gray hair, his face was monstrous with growths and scabrous scales, the eyes lidless, the jowls lipless, the gums strips of toothless cartilage. It was a face such as might have risen from a protean sea bed a million years before.

"You are looking for Runch." His voice was a rasping whisper.

"Yes."

"You wear the clothes of a Yulok. Your weapons are Yulok. Like them you smell of the sea. But you are not Yulok." He raised his chin at the knapsack near Asa's hand. "You carry the weapons of the gods."

Asa said nothing.

"What do you want with Runch?"

"Talk."

"And behind the talk?"

"Knowledge."

"About?"

"Two women."

Runch stared for a long moment, and then he nodded. "Ask."

"You took part in the killing at Alcheringia. You led your people there."

"Yes," Runch said. His face remained impassive. Plated and scaled, it was no more capable of expressing emotion now than the face of a carp.

"There was one woman—"

"There were many women. Some died, some lived. Some who lived wished that they had died."

"She was the fairest," Asa said, his voice taut.

"And did she have a name, this fair one?"

"Persis," Asa whispered.

Runch nodded. "I saw her, yes. The dancer. She danced amid the slaughter. When we moved to take her like the others Garm struck us back."

"Garm."

"She was Garm's prize," Runch said. "His alone. She went with him"—his head moved slowly—"to the east."

"Since then, have you seen Garm?"

"We have met twice."

"And the woman, was she—"

"The first time, the spring after the death of Alcheringia, she was with him. The second time she was not."

Asa looked at his hands. Sharp dread struck through him. "Did he . . . did he speak of her?"

"Garm does not make idle talk. To him, one woman is much like another. He is interested in other things, Garm."

In the silence Asa was aware of Runch's steady gaze on him. He was thankful for the draft that shrouded him in smoke. He bent, toyed with the cooked rabbit. "We'll eat now."

"Women?"

"What?"

"You said two women. You have asked about only one."

Asa slid the rabbit off the spit, broke it, and passed half to Runch. "The name of the other is Alva."

Runch ate.

"A woman as ugly as the other is fair."

Runch turned a rabbit bone, regarded it thoughtfully, and tossed it into the fire.

"Her left hand is the paw of a bear."

Runch finished his meal slowly and wiped his hands on the grass. "In Gerumbia," he said, still chewing, "we are not interested in appearances. You have not yet described a woman I know."

"Intelligence. Grace. Humor. Diligence. Integrity. Above all, compassion."

The hideous face stared long at Asa. "I do know such a woman," Runch said.

"She is alive?"

"Yes."

"Near?"

"Quite near." Runch sat still. "You have come to take her away?"

Asa nodded.

"Why?"

"She is needed elsewhere," Asa said.

"She is needed here. I need her." Runch began to gasp, and Asa realized he was hearing the laughter of a man who had no muscles in his face. "Do you think I have so much that I can spare her?"

"No."

"Do you think I feel less pain than you because I have this face that is scales and plates, with no way to show my pain?"

"No," Asa said.

"And yet you expect me to *take* you to her?"

"Yes," Asa said.

"Why?"

"Because we are old friends. Because I have a message for her alone. It is important that she know my message. She herself will then decide whether to stay or go. I have no power to make her do either."

"And if I refuse?"

"I shall keep looking for her."

"And if I kill you?"

"Then another will come. Messengers change; the message remains the same."

Runch nodded slowly. "You are right. The choice is hers. Come, then."

They had less than two miles to go. For part of the distance they followed the bank of the river, and then left it and ascended a gentle slope. At last Runch stopped before the low entrance to a cave and drew aside the screen of brush that partly covered it. Asa bent, and entered.

Inside, all was warm and dry. A vent somewhere in the ceiling drew away the smoke from the central fire that lit the whole area. The place gleamed with sleek furs and polished wood.

Alva sat cross-legged on the sleeping platform, facing the door. When Asa entered, she rose and embraced him. "Asa," she said, holding him tight. "Asa. Of course. Who else would they send?"

She had aged well. Her body was less bulky than he remembered it, and her neat dress gave her an illusion of height, although her head came only to the center of his chest. The black hair that had once framed her face in disheveled clumps had grayed and was longer now, drawn back and tied so that it revealed her face entirely. It was gaunter, that face. Its suffering had drawn its curves and hollows into taut angles, and her eyes seemed larger, more luminous than Asa remembered. She had lost nothing of her strength, however. When she embraced him he felt again the extraordinary power of her arms and shoulders.

"You lived," she said. She drew back to arm's length and her paw flicked his deerskin jacket. "Yulok? No. Oh, no. I know a Yggdrasilian messenger when I see one. Come, Asa. Come here and sit beside me and tell me why you went to those who destroyed your people. Tell me what they have done to you through these years."

And so Asa told her all he could remember: How he had set fires to sear away the final horror of Alcheringia; how afterward he had pursued Garm eastward until he had lost the track of his horses in October snows; how he had sworn to return one day and take Persis back; how, after that, he had wandered far to the north; how he could remember little of what had happened then, although he believed the spirits of the dead had protected him, had fed him and kept him warm through the long winter of his delirium, for he remembered an endless dance of the dead on the walls of his cave. He told her also how in the spring, emerging, he had made a choice and sent the signal to Shem that he was ready then to go to Yggdrasil.

"Why?" Alva interrupted at this point, her paw gripping his elbow. *"Why?"*

"Because I wanted to know. And besides—"

"Besides, you thought it would be for only a little while." He nodded.

"Yes." Alva sighed. "That is what we all think when we begin. That it will be for just a little time. And Persis?" He shook his head.

"You haven't gone in search of her? No, of course you haven't. The years have passed, haven't they, and you've been busy. They've kept you busy, training you to be a peregrinus, convincing you that the Gaian Expedient is necessary."

"Yes."

"Training you to be a messenger. To move among the tribes."

Asa nodded.

She folded her hands in her lap. "And what message have they sent to me, Asa? To this lapsed peregrinus?"

"Shem has sent me. Only Shem. He wants you to go back. He asked me to tell you that Horvath is dying, and that if Shem replaces him he will need your help. He says that he will need it very badly. Things are changing in Yggdrasil. Some masters want to abandon the Project and make the Expedient into something the Old Ones never intended. That movement is getting stronger. If it prevails, then the destruction of Alcheringia will be just the prelude to something infinitely worse. That is what Shem asked me to tell you. Now you know."

Alva sat unmoving. "I renounced them forever. Because of what they did to Alcheringia. Because they betrayed all the best, last hopes of the Old Ones."

"I know."

"And yet you, you of all people, come here now and bring me this message. This obscene message. Why? Have you forgiven them for what they did to your people? To Persis? To you?"

"No. I will never forgive."

"Why, then?"

"To stop it happening again. Because *I can prevent*. If I do not, then I am as responsible as those who do the killing. That is why I am here."

Alva sat in silence for a long time, looking into the fire. "Yes," she said finally, drawing a shuddering breath, "yes, that is what knowing means."

"It's in the past," Asa said. "It's done. I will never forgive, never forget, but the future is what matters now."

Alva swept her paw back behind her as if to rid herself of a clutter of memories. "Oh," she said, "all of *that*!" Then, heaving another heavy sigh, she stood up.

Runch had been sitting to one side as they talked, listening impassively. No gesture betrayed his emotions.

Alva crossed to him now and stood behind him, reaching down to caress his abominable face and to hold his good shoulder with her paw. His left hand rose and took her right one. "My dear man," she said softly, "is the time here?"

"Yes," he said. "It is."

"We are one."

"Yes, and we have had good years. Now you must do for others what you have done for me."

"I must. You know that. You have always known."

Runch's baleful gaze fixed Asa across the fire, through the wraiths of smoke. "Even gods err," he said. "But they do not cease to be gods. They do not cease to create the world. They cannot. What is important is that it be done so that never again will there be any like me." Alva's face was pressed against his neck and shoulder. She was weeping. "So," Runch said to her very softly. "There are no surprises. We have always known. It is a thing you must do for all who will come after, for all who are not yet born."

Asa left them together and went out alone into the night. A great moon had risen and by its light he could see the length of the somber valley. Something far off cried almost like a wolf. It was answered with a guttural shriek, choked off—perhaps a great cat.

He felt empty, and cold, and dirty. The certainty that he had done the right thing was only a pinpoint of light in the abyss of himself. *So*, he thought. *This is what expediency means.*

Alva emerged. "I'm ready," she said.

"It needn't be so soon," Asa said. "Tomorrow—"

"No. Now. It's best now."

In the valley were several clearings large enough to receive a helicopter. Alva had followed his gaze, and she touched his arm as he began to take the radio out of his pack. "No," she said. "Don't bring them in here. We'll go by sea."

So Asa summoned Fenris and Vogh and arranged a rendezvous a few miles to the north, on the boundary of the Northern Wayst. By dawn, he and Alva were climbing into the cabin of the Wylders' ACV. By late afternoon, they had reached the sea again and were crossing the great beach with the sepulchral city of the Old Ones gleaming in the distance.

At dusk, the submarine came.

FOUR

Moran lowered himself gently into his bath and leaned back, sighing. Beyond the skylight a panoply of stars spread itself for his enjoyment. Around him in the muted light the water undulated and settled. On the far side of the room a digital wall clock spun tenths of seconds into the void, but Moran did not look at it. In his office the monitor beeped occasionally, announcing developments throughout the Erthring—Aboreal decisions, policy changes, deaths, appointments, and so forth. But Moran did not wish to hear it; he was slipping out of time. Exhaling, he sank until the water covered his ears, covered his chest and arms and legs, covered all but his nose, his eyes, his bulbous belly.

Moran gazed at the stars. He wallowed. He dreamed.

Sometime in the next few days the Arborea would announce that he had been appointed the new Master of Norriya, and Moran had begun to plan how he would consolidate and use that power. Changes would be made. The foolishness of trying to maintain the Gaian Expedient was becoming increasingly clear with every day as fuel shortages grew more acute, equipment broke

114

down irreparably, and incursions from the Outer Wylds
grew ever more serious. He knew precisely what should
be done. He and the other reformers—Rees, Bret, Nidor,
and the rest—had clear objectives, but the strategies for
reaching those objectives had yet to be designed.

Deep in his bath, Moran thought strategy.

He thought about Garm's place in that strategy. When
he had finished his clandestine training in Neffelheim, it
would be necessary for him to complete his novitiate—
Rees would sponsor him, or Bret—and then...

Moran considered. Rocking gently, looking at the stars,
he set up currents that surged softly against his belly.

Despite all the injunctions against it, despite all his
training, power excited Moran. Power had a sweet taste.
He pitied men who did not want power.

He pitied Shem.

Poor Shem: vulnerable, unsure, perpetually beset by
doubts, betrayed by his emotions into irrationalities, and
crippled besides. Probably he would have to be replaced,
but with whom? Garm was not ready. Not yet. But there
were others, young peregrini who were indebted to him
in various ways and who shared the views of the reformers...

Moran considered.

After a time, puffing in the steam, he rose and toweled
dry his ample body. Rosy parts of him rolled and trembled
in several directions. He glanced at the clock now. In the
other room, his office, a cedar fire crackled and shadows
moved like furtive warriors on the walls, among the sou-
venirs of Moran's skin days with the tribes. The monitor
beeped.

Toweling, Moran strolled out into that other room. He
dropped more gnarled cedar on the fire. He glanced through
the window toward the mainland and saw the running
lights of a Munin patrol coming home. He glanced at the
scanner. A decision of the Arborea was being announced
at precisely that moment:

2300 HRS 2 APRIL 164 P.E.
APPOINTMENTS/ARBOREA: SHEM/MASTER NORRIYA.

Moran uttered a sound like a surprised small animal. He sat down slowly beside the fire that had begun to feast exuberantly on the cedar.

"So," he said.

"Well," he said after a while, "to lose is to learn."

Much, much later, drifting to sleep at last, he thought: *The wise man doesn't climb the mountain. He walks around it.*

FIVE

"The general instructions ordered us to keep that frequency clear," Harrower said, leading the way into the tower elevator and holding the door open for Shem. "We've never known why. We've never used it or even monitored it. Probably we've been receiving these signals for some time and the operators simply haven't noticed."

The elevator lofted them silently into the island of green light that was the control room. Controllers murmured into their microphones. In the darkness beyond them, aircraft lights rose and settled. The supervisor nodded as Shem and Harrower arrived, and handed them head-phones. "There it is," he said.

Shem's eyes widened in astonishment. What he heard very faintly, distorted with extreme distance, was, un-mistakably, music. Music! He recognized it at once—the larghetto of Mozart's last piano concerto. He turned away from Harrower and the supervisor, turned toward the starry night over the sea so that he could listen to this most wanly joyful of all the master's melodies, the passage in which he acknowledged that he was living in the last springtime of his life...

Shem wept.

"Yes," he said, turning back to Harrower after a few minutes. "There's no question about it. Music. It's the music of the Old Ones." He turned to the controller. "Is it always the same?"

The man's brow furrowed. "Something the same, sir. I can't tell exactly. Different, too. Different from night to night. If you'd like, sir, we'll call when it comes again and you can hear it for yourself."

"Please," Shem said. "Have that done."

"Who?" Harrower asked as they rode back together toward their offices.

Shem shook his head.

"And where? And how? It's coming from far beyond the range of anything we have. How're they doing it?"

Again Shem shook his head. He was marveling at a world that had suddenly expanded incalculably, a world in which that concerto could lift sublimely across time and space, bearing Mozart's serene laughter into the teeth of brutality, hideous waste, and even death.

Shem smiled.

SIX

SHE DANCED AND RECEDED, DANCING. SHE REACHED imploringly, and when he did not go to her she receded, and sometimes people interposed themselves, and sometimes a burgeoning forest, and sometimes swirling fog, and sometimes only distance. His feet would not move. He was dumb. He wanted to compress his love into a gesture, but his arms were stone. Stronger than his will, other forces drew her away ... Sometimes she was laughing, running toward him through brilliant winter, but when he reached to hold her she was gone ... Sometimes her face filled his world, weeping, entreating, her mouth helpless with passion ... And sometimes she was leading a child away from him, and no matter how desperately he called, layers of time passed between them and in the end he was left alone with silence ... But, sometimes, at the end of his journey, there was a fire in the lodge, and food cooking, and furs, and she was waiting. Persis was waiting ...

In the morning sun they walked a hundred yards down the gravel path, Asa smoothly and soundlessly, Shem leaning heavily on his cane. They stopped at a stone bench, set facing the mainland.

"This was Jared's place," Shem said. "He couldn't stand the debriefing rooms. Most peregrini have trouble with claustrophobia when they come back, but Jared couldn't be inside at all. So we'd come here to talk, rain or shine." Shem lowered himself carefully to the bench and Asa sat beside him. For a moment, neither spoke; both were enrapt by the dusky strait and the mainland beyond. "You did well to bring Alva back."

Asa looked at his hands. "I know I did well," he said. "I'm less sure I did good."

"You did." Shem cleared his throat. "I have good news for you. It's this: We have reason to believe that Persis is beyond the Kanik Mountains, in the Outer Wyld."

Asa stood up slowly. "What reason?"

"Moran has had a report from Aleaha. She has spoken to captives, raiders from the Outer Wyld. Of course we can't be—"

"Tell me. Please."

"A woman fitting Persis' description was traded to those tribes by Garm over three years ago. Subsequently she was traded farther east, so the trail grows faint."

"What else?"

"She was pregnant. According to the report she has had a son. They're alive. Together. Living in a place far to the east of the frontier of the Erthring."

"Does it have a name, that place?"

"No one knows. Aleaha says that they fell silent when she asked. She insisted. They spoke in obscure mythic images. They said it is a place of men who are more than men. High among mountains. That could mean anything, of course. You realize that this is rumor and hearsay. There may be no truth at all. As soon as we find out more—"

"I'll find out more," Asa said. "I'm going."

Shem massaged his thigh and knee.

"Shem. You promised. A vehicle and crew."

"I said I would consider it. Didn't I say I would consider it?"

Asa stood. "I'll go alone, then."

"Don't be a fool. Who knows what that terrain is like? Who knows what tribes live there? You wouldn't have a chance in a thousand of reaching her alive. Sit down and listen to me. Please."

Asa stepped back.

"Hear what I have to say. Afterward, make your decision. If you decide to go east, to Persis, then you shall have the vehicle and a crew. Fenris and Vogh, if you like. I promise."

"I'm learning what your promise is worth."

"On my oath," Shem said, lifting his hand.

"Speak, then."

"I've learned that the situation here is much worse than I had thought. There's a strong movement to do away with the Project entirely, to redirect the energies of the scholars, and to transform the Gaian Expedient into something else, something horrible."

"You knew that."

"What I didn't know before I became Master is how far advanced that plan is, and how rapidly it's gaining strength."

Asa swept his hands back and forth, as if clearing off a table. "*You'll* have to deal with it, Shem! You and the Arborea. It's your problem."

"No, it's *our* problem."

"I can't help."

"Yes you can."

"I—"

"You can become peregrinus to the Yuloks. You can persuade the Yuloks to keep their law."

A hawk slipped from its aerie in the Asgardian hills and rode through the morning down through the gentle layers of warmed air above the marshes. They both watched it check suddenly, fold its wings, and plummet behind a screen of marsh grass, lift away again with a limp rodent dangling from its talons, and swoop back into the hills. Across the distance they heard its thin, sad scream of triumph.

"There are many peregrini," Asa said.

"But only one Alcheringian. Only you can do this. If you choose not to do it, it will not be done."

"And then?"

Shem was silent.

"And then, Shem?"

"It's serious. The Yuloks are in grave danger. They've fallen under the control of seafarers from the south, from beyond the Erthring. Their culture is crumbling. They've gone from discontent to insubordination to open defiance of Yggdrasil, all within the last ten months. I've sent three peregrini; they've all failed. The situation's critical."

"What must they do?"

"Repel the traders and their seductive goods. Respect their laws again."

"And if they don't?"

Shem looked at his hands. "The Arborea...has... taken an interest. Given me an ultimatum."

"So," Asa said, sitting down slowly. "They're going to do it again!"

"Perhaps. It's very close."

"*Kill* them! Like us! Like the Alcheringians!"

"Yes."

"And you, once again, will permit it!"

Shem rose. The fatigue, the age, the pain, the defeats and compromises, all fell away, and for an instant Asa saw the proud young warrior his mother had once watched wading out of the sea in moonlight. "*You* speak to *me*? *You* tell *me* about responsibility? You, who urged your people to break their Tabuly? Despite all warnings? Despite all Jared's pleading, and Alva's?" He slashed his cane across the bench. "You, who now want to bargain your petty personal concerns against the work of the Project, against the death of a people? You dare to tell *me* what responsibility is?"

"I've learned—"

"*What* have you learned? Tell me!"

Asa turned toward the darkness and the mainland.

"What?"

"I've learned that man must—must make amends to Earth."

"What else?"

"And that the future must be earned."

"*That*," Shem said, driving his fist toward the mainland, "is what you must show the Yuloks!" He sank back onto the bench.

"Why not strike against the traders?"

"That too might be necessary," Shem said. "It depends on you."

"I'm not a peregrinus," Asa said after a moment. "I haven't taken the oath."

Shem said, "Tomorrow morning." He drew a long, shuddering breath. He smiled. "One more thing. As a peregrinus you will have the usual autonomy in the field. You will have a vehicle at your disposal. You'll have a crew, probably Wylders. They will have taken journeys not recorded in their logs, these men. Perhaps they have even gone beyond the eastern frontier." Shem paused. "There will be nothing to stop you from giving them the order to take you east, in search of Persis. You will not be explicitly forbidden to do that, because only you and I know that the temptation will exist, always there." Shem looked up.

"A test."

"Yes. One that you will face every day."

Asa stood with his hands locked behind his back, not looking at Shem, or at the sea, or at the distant darkness where the mainland lay. For a moment he looked at an empty place on the gravel path, then he walked away.

"Go," Egon told him finally, when Asa found him in Jotunheim later that night. "Shem's right. There's little you can do for us here, Asa. But perhaps in the wildness..." Egon smiled and opened his hands in a gesture that suggested both futility and an infinite capacity for hope. They embraced and the older man turned back to the meeting from which Asa's arrival had drawn him. Briefly, as the door opened and closed, Asa heard the voices of scholars raised in argument.

"Please, don't ask me," Alva said. "Only you can decide this. You were sure for me; now you must be sure for yourself."

* * *

The following morning, before Shem, Moran, and Alva, the new Dream Master of West Norriya, Asa took the Oath of the Peregrini: I believe man can be a sane animal again. I believe in the Project and in the Gaian Expedient. If required, I shall give my life for the Expedient, and the Earth.

Shem presented him with his peregrinus staff, carved from a limb of the Great Tree, and topped with the three-rooted symbol of Yggdrasil.

The brief ceremony was flawed only slightly. Alva wept.

SEVEN

THE SQUEAKING OF THE CART'S TIRES, LOUDER THAN the purr of its electric motor, echoed in the empty tunnel. Ahead, at the end of the long upward grade, both men could hear the grumbling of Neffelheim.

Moran drove. Garm sat erect beside him, his hands resting lightly on his thighs.

Moran was sweating. His hands moved restively on the steering wheel. The tour of Yggdrasil had not gone as he had expected. Since Garm's arrival in Neffelheim, Moran had looked forward to the message from Nidor that would tell him that Garm's preliminary training (programing, Nidor called it) was complete, and that the proper attitude (mindset, Nidor called it) for entry into the Novice Program had been acquired. He had thought that this call would mark the beginning of his friendship with Garm, and when it had come the previous evening it was in a mood of cheerful expectancy that he had arranged for the falsification of manifests to show that Garm had arrived in Yggdrasil that very day. "Blood is thicker than water," he said to himself. "We are members of one another." This day spent with Garm would be marked by shared warmth, joviality, perhaps even affection. From watching the hours of videotape he had ordered taken of Garm in Neffelheim over the previous months, Moran believed he knew him and that they would share interests from the start.

He had miscalculated badly.

From the time they had met in Neffelheim that morning Garm had been aloof, his gray eyes coolly assessing Moran and (Moran realized with a chill like a needle in his belly) dismissing him. Nothing all day had changed that.

At the Central Repository, Garm had been restive after only a few minutes and had finally interrupted Urtha with a sweep of his hand as she was describing the retrieval system. "Nidor has explained this to me," he said. "Besides, all this is of little consequence. It is the future that matters." Not even the films of the Old Ones' world interested him. He had walked out of the viewing room.

"So," Moran said, smiling, coming out behind him, "happy is the country that has no history, eh?"

Garm turned, curious, as if a frog had spoken to him. "Exactly. Besides"—he waved toward the archives—"all this so-called history can be summarized in a sentence. We know how the Old Ones failed."

"So? How?"

"They lost control," Garm said.

In the Operations Center he showed even less patience with the activities presided over by Verthandi, and even when she took time to suggest to him some of the exigencies of her job—the day-to-day problems of meeting the demands of all three islands and of compiling accurate records of all missions and transactions—Garm smiled and shook his head. "Again, Nidor has explained this process to me. This waste in running what you call the Gaian Expedient. Obviously, the sooner the whole thing is rationalized, the better."

"I agree," Moran said, watching him closely. "Less is more."

"Nonsense! Less is just less."

Val was mildly interesting to him, and he asked several questions there about the methods of analysis and the schemata used for the classification of dream scenarios. But he was fascinated by SKULD. He had brought a program that he asked to have run, and he laughed softly at the speed with which the computer assimilated his assumptions and extrapolated from them. He had many questions, and it was clear to Moran, listening, that Nidor had carefully prepared him to use the vast artificial intelligence of the machine.

"This is the center of Yggdrasil," Garm said as their cart emerged into the sunlight from the SKULD complex.

"Some would say," Moran suggested, pointing to the misty hills of Jotunheim ahead, "that *that* is the center, and that SKULD is useful only as directed by the scholars."

Garm grunted and dismissed Jotunheim with a toss of his head. "Old men. Old ideas from a world that destroyed itself. Garbage in, garbage out."

When they arrived on the western side of Asgard and Garm saw the beaches stretching before him, steaming in the afternoon sun, he told Moran to stop. In an instant he had shed all his clothes except his shorts, had left the cart behind, and was running across the beach to the water's edge. Then he turned south, running parallel to the sea in the long and easy stride of the Kanik warrior, and Moran, left to trundle behind in the cart, could hear his laughter and, twice, his shout of joy (or his challenge to some imaginary foe, Moran could not be sure). "So," Moran said to himself, riding along, "no matter how much you feed a wolf, he will always return to the forest."

"Did you enjoy?" he asked when Garm returned.

"Only two things would make it better," Garm had said. "A horse and an enemy."

Now, at the end of their tour, the cart proceeded up the last tunnel and emerged into the cool sunlight of Neffelheim, filtered through clouds of steam from the geothermal generators. "Tomorrow you enter the Novice Program," Moran said as Garm stepped out. "I assume Nidor has briefed you on what will be involved."

Garm smiled. "Mainly dissembling. Pretending that I have just arrived in Yggdrasil. Pretending to be interested in the facile battery of tests I will be given. Pretending that I don't know what must be done to bring some order to this place." He shrugged. "Pretending."

Again Moran felt that cold needle of fear. "I hope you

realize that there might be something left to be learned. After all, when you've finished this training you'll have some responsibility. You'll make decisions that affect us all. Nothing is more terrible than ignorance in action."

"Nothing is more pathetic than useless knowledge," Garm said. "I intend to learn what I can use."

Moran laughed, but his laughter was empty. "Well, remember that the starting point is the realization that we are all, in some degree, mad."

Garm looked at him for a long moment with the steam clouds rising behind like baleful mushrooms. Then he walked away without further comment. Moran started the cart and turned it back into the mouth of the tunnel that would return him safely to Asgard. He rode with his gaze fixed. He was afraid for himself, and for Garm, and for the new direction in which he and the others planned to take Yggdrasil. He was afraid because that last calm look of Garm's had been full of scorn. He was afraid because he had often seen such expressions in Neffelheim—the terrifying sureness of men who had no questions about their sanity.

EIGHT

Asa heard the ACV long before he saw it. At first its whine was inseparable from the droning of bugs about his ears; but then it grew stronger, fading briefly as the vehicle dipped into hollows and behind hills. At last it became the unmistakable throbbing of machinery.

Heat lay on Asa like a blanket. Heat shimmered across the opening of the crevasse where he lay and distorted the slope before him, and the plain reaching to the east, and the distant hills. Heat pressed on the concrete slab over his head, and sizzled on the wings of dragonflies skimming the arid slope. Heat squeezed sweat out of him and rolled it into his eyes and beard.

Through this heat, thick as wool, the ACV whined toward him, along the narrow valley. Out of the mountains it came, sunlight glinting off its flank. Asa watched it skim across the plain, swing around in a graceful arc, and stop. He watched it settle in its own dust. He listened to the engines sink from a scream, to a whine, to a growl, to a moan. He watched the doors of the craft pop open and Fenris and Vogh emerge.

Asa rose and dusted himself off. He cupped his hands

to his mouth. "Where there are no trees there can be no sanity," he said. His voice clattered and rang on the shale.

"Therefore we shall go to a place of trees—" Fenris called back.

"—to a forest," Asa finished, "and in its coolness consider what might be done for the good of man."

They came forward, offering their hands.

"How are you, sir?"

"I'm well, Fenris. Vogh."

"A peregrinus now," Vogh said, nodding at the staff. "Congratulations." He shaded his eyes with both hands and looked across to the white city of the Old Ones shimmering in the heat like a ghastly dream.

"Yuloks, sir. Correct?" Fenris squinted into the sun.

"That's right."

"Too bad." He picked up one of Asa's aluminum cases and Vogh took the other, leaving Asa only the small parfleche and the staff. "My opinion, oughta push those damn Yuloks into the sea. Just push 'em all in. Let 'em drown."

"They're people," Asa said.

Fenris grunted. "Maybe, but they're a damn nuisance, if you ask me. Be a lot simpler if we just got rid of 'em. Word is, the trouble's as bad there as it was in Alcheringia. Worse, maybe. You're the third peregrinus we've taken out in six months. You want to know how many we've brought back?" Fenris made a circle with his thumb and forefinger and held it up for Asa to see clearly. "You want *my* opinion?" He slashed his free hand horizontally, waist high. "Snuff 'em!"

"Easily done," Vogh said, squinting at the sun. "They're isolated. Contained. One little strike..."

Asa had trouble breathing. He stopped walking. The sun reeled. Smiling gods edged close, and he said to them, *No! Not now!* and forced the world to come back, back to details like the small crease of concern above Vogh's glasses, to the double reflection of himself, to the trickle of sweat in front of Fenris' ear.

"Gentlemen," Asa said, planting his staff firmly, "I think we shall work better together if we understand each other. I am a peregrinus. It is my duty to preserve life at all costs. To prevent killing. That is what the Gaian

Expedient was designed to do. That is what I will do in Yulok."

Vogh stroked his chin. Fenris glanced at him and cleared his throat. "Sir, ideals are all very well, but we all know that the Expedient—"

"That's not an ideal. That's a practical objective."

Fenris peered at him. "You—you *believe* that, sir? That one person..."

"Yes. I believe that. And your job is to help me do it." Asa picked up the case and stepped up into the cabin of the hovercraft. "What are your orders from Yggdrasil?"

"We're to take you to the crest of the Yulok Hills and return within radio range every day at twenty-one hundred hours. Do you want to change those orders, sir?"

"No. Let them stand."

Fenris secured the cabin door. He and Vogh climbed into the cockpit and started the engines. Cool air hissed into the cabin. Outside, a great distance beyond the tightly soundproofed windows, the whine of the engines mounted to a scream. The vehicle lifted, tipped forward, and sped across the plain toward the foothills of the southern range.

Asa gazed at the slopes and copses as they flashed by. Once he saw a terrified face peering back at him from behind a screen of bushes, a truth-seeker as he and Kenet and Rusl had once been, creeping down into the forbidden zone against the direst of injunctions, against all tribal myths and incantations, risking his life to glimpse the gods.

"Aborr! Aborr!" Vogh shouted, pointing. "You see him there, sir? Two o'clock. Up in the bushes."

"I saw him."

"Shall we swing 'round and neutralize him, sir?" Fenris' voice was perfectly flat. His hands grasped the stick to make the maneuver. Vogh readied his weapon, clicking gunsights up.

"Leave him," Asa said.

"Leave— But sir, he's at least seven miles into a forbidden zone. If he gets back—"

"Then he'll have nightmares." Asa remembered: Rani screaming; himself erect and snarling; the pitying, comprehending stare of a gunner in the waist of a helicopter; and the guns, all silent . . .

"But *sir*, standing orders—" Vogh had half turned, his mouth bitter with disappointment.

"That standing order," Asa said softly, "has just been overridden by this peregrinus."

Vogh turned back, snapped down the sight, and returned the gun to its resting position. "Yes, sir."

They rode in silence.

Asa leaned back into the cool shadows of the cabin and watched the blighted contours of the Wayst slip by. Stunted forests swept past. Strange lizards grinned. Hairy shapes started up when the vehicle was almost upon them and fled through curtains of heat. Twice the vehicle passed through swarms of insects thick as smoke. In all that vast area, no birds flew.

He had at least an hour before they reached the Yulok Hills. He switched on the reading lamp and broke the seal of the file Shem had handed him as he left Yggdrasil. He knew it would contain a succinct SKULD summary of the briefings he had received during the previous two weeks.

On top was the standard map of Norriya in orthomorphic projection. Asa studiously avoided looking at the blank space around the mouth of the Alcher where Alcheringia had once been, and followed the coastline forty miles to the south, where a large oblong island stood at the mouth of a huge bay. This region, island and bay, was Yulok. Attached to the map were a number of appendices giving detailed topographical information, depository locations, compass bearings, and so forth.

Next came a copy of the Yulok Codex. Like all the codices devised for the tribes, this was very simple. In fact, it consisted of only four laws:

1. Yulok is the sacred center of the world. It is bounded on the north by the River Larl, on the south by the second bay past the Great Promontory, and on the east by the crests of the Yulok Hills. The fourth boundary lies in the sea, and runs south from North Cape to the tip of Eyul, to the second bay past the Great Promontory. These boundaries are

ordained by the gods and you shall not transgress them.

2. The Great Bay and the land between the hills and the sea will supply all the needs of Yulok—all food, all clothing, all knowledge, and you shall take no more than your needs.

3. Yulok shall have four villages, one on Eyul and three on the mainland, and each shall have no more than two hundred people.

4. Yuloks shall have no commerce with other tribes.

Several appendices followed this statement. One summarized the mythology that had been created to support the law. Another, an ethnohistorical report, listed the deviations from it made both with peregrinus consent and without. A third presented the crux of the present problem: Sea traders had disrupted the previously stable Yulok economy. Recent generations of young Yuloks had not driven them away as their ancestors had done, and, once the fourth law had been broken, the others quickly came under pressure also. The wondrous tools of the sea traders speeded up the slaying of deer and sea mammals, forcing the Yuloks to go beyond their boundaries. Soon the composition of the villages had begun to change; the Eyul community shrank, the three on the mainland grew.

A detailed summary of the effects of these changes followed, but Asa just scanned it. He already knew too well what had transpired.

The next item summarized the reports of the last three peregrini who had attempted Yulok reform. All had failed dismally, and Asa flipped through these sad pages as quickly as possible, going on to the profiles of the principal Yulok chieftains and myth-spinners as they were last known to Yggdrasil. These he reread carefully.

Next came a technical summary prepared by Neffelheim. It set out once again (as a cool technician had done for him three days earlier) communications procedures, weapons use, and the array of techniques and devices provided to assist him with his work of pacification. Asa loathed all these devices and had been revolted by the technician's delight in their sophistication. The worn-out Clinicians may have been destroyed, but Neffelheim's laboratories had labored hard and long to replace them with more portable instruments. Now peregrini going into the field carried as part of their standard equipment an elegant array of chemical and mechanical tools to snip the connectors of memory, to crush the first shoots of curiosity. "Painless, painless." The technician had smiled. "At least, for the most part. Merely injections to interfere chemically with the neurotransmitters I have described to you and to leave the biological unit modified but otherwise intact, capable of breeding and of participating almost normally in the life of the tribe."

Asa had thought of his friends, Kenet and Rusl, those "biological units," sitting stolidly side by side, watching the sea. He had made a solemn promise to himself that he would never, ever, use such methods. Peregrini regulations might require him to carry the vials and syringes; the trepanning auger; the tiny YAG microprobe laser; the doses of sodium amytal, stramonium, eidetics, psychogens, and phantasticants; all would stay in the bottom of his pack, unused. With the Yuloks he would use reason alone, and he would succeed.

He closed the file and looked through the window. They had been following a winding valley between tall peaks, and were now entering a narrow pass. Snow lay close above them on the north slopes, but lower, wherever soil had lodged among the fallen rock, the hills glowed with the red, orange, and vivid yellow of tiny arctic flowers.

When the pass began to descend toward the north and Yulok lay before them, Asa ordered a stop. He stepped out to look. There was the Larl, a silver snake on their left, branching into three streams as it flowed through its delta into the sea. There was the Great Bay of Yulok, with placid smoke rising from the three villages around it. And there was Eyul, the somber island, with the smaller fourth village on its southern tip. Far out, he saw a speck of white on the sea, and when he investigated with Vogh's binoculars he saw one of the ships of the sea traders outward bound.

Fenris and Vogh took him another six miles, into a little clearing behind the broad band of forest that circled the Yulok settlements. The motors whined down; the craft settled on its rubber bumpers.

"This is R One, sir," Fenris said, peeling off his gloves. "It's the rendezvous point marked on your map. At twenty-one hundred hours every day we'll either be here or very close by." He unloaded Asa's two cases of equipment and he and Vogh carried them to the edge of the clearing. Fenris pressed buttons on a small control panel he had brought with him from the vehicle. Before them, a two-foot square of earth trembled and began to rise. For an instant, Asa's loins went cold. He remembered too clearly the creature that he had seen rise three times from such a lair, once to attack Rusl, once at Jared's bidding to lay its tiny pads on Kenet's temples, and once more when he, Asa, had done battle with the thing and destroyed it. He half expected to see one of these rise again, all sensors alert, and come scampering off its platform toward him. But instead the hatch revealed only a metal compartment underneath, insulated against the damp of the Earth. "Your depository," Fenris said. "You have the combination. You can leave your heavy equipment here, as well as any messages for us or material that you want to send to Yggdrasil. Also, your radio."

They tested their communications link and wished him luck. Then the hovercraft's turbines whined up to speed and the vehicle roared away toward the west.

Once more, Asa was alone in the wilderness.

He breathed deeply, and listened. The musk of the forest shrouded him: dark mushrooms pushing out of their mulch; pine resin fragrant as perfume; the cold breath of a cascade from the snowfields above the dark firs. A circling hawk called once, sliding off the edge of an updraft.

Asa turned toward the sea.

In two hours he had reached the south bank of the Larl and followed it down to the great beach of Yulok. Above the first settlement he forded the river and angled north, so that he could approach along the beach in clear view.

It was a calm evening. Smoke from Yulok fires hung like a canopy over the bay. A startled clutch of mergansers scampered away across the water as Asa appeared. Far up the shore he could hear the cries and laughter of children playing in the pools of the Larl. He walked barefoot, passing in and out of the gentle sheets of water that smoothed the sand and left fringes of froth upon it. Some of his footprints were extinguished at once; for a little time, some remained. The tip of his staff touched the sand beside his left foot.

He had gone only a little way before the Yulok dogs caught his scent. First one and then a dozen pelted toward him, alerting the whole bay with their yelping. Children dashed out to look at him and then ran back behind the dunes, into the lodges. Villagers emerged and stood in small groups, unmoving, their chief and councillors at the front, waiting for Asa to come to them.

They were a large people, the Yuloks, not tall but heavy with the easy living they drew from the sea and the surrounding hills. They alone, of all the tribes of Norriya, had developed a monumental art. Carvings and paintings embellished the doorposts and transoms of their lodges. Lofty carved poles brooded between their dwellings and the sea. Their dead were borne away to their funeral poles in coffins intricately carved, and the prows of their sea canoes bore the figures of the creatures of the depths. Their paddles, too, were carved and painted, and their clothing was elaborately fashioned both to protect them from the dampness of their climate and to proclaim their status.

The chief of the first village came forward to greet him. Asa recognized the chief's headdress, the honorary shawl, the rain canopy that the four bearers held scrupulously overhead, although the evening was clear and mild. Hazel eyes assessed Asa coolly, moving from his face down the length of his body, and back to the Yggdrasilian symbol carved in the gnarled head of his staff. The chief seemed younger than the dossier had indicated.

"My name is Asa. I seek Alexis. I seek the peace of the Yuloks." He bowed in the Yulok manner.

The chief inclined her head, smiling. "I am Alexis. You are welcome to this place," she said.

NINE

THE PRINTER BEHIND NIDOR SUDDENLY BUZZED INSIS-
tently, alerting him to the arrival of a top-priority message.
Keys sputtered. A tongue of paper emerged. He reached
back and tore the message out of the machine.

30/5/165
1600 HRS.
EYES ONLY: NIDOR/BIOSEC/NEFFELHEIM
FROM: HARROWER/KEEPER YGGDRASIL

MONITORS HAVE BROUGHT UNAUTHORIZED
DATA TO MY ATTENTION.

NOTE SECTION 13 SUBSECTION 47F GENERAL
INSTRUCTIONS. NO, REPEAT NO, EXPERIMENTS ON
HUMAN SUBJECTS TO BE CONDUCTED WITHOUT AR-
BOREA APPROVAL THROUGH THIS OFFICE.

ANY SUCH EXPERIMENTS NOW IN PROGRESS TO
BE TERMINATED FORTHWITH.

FULL REPORTS OF SUCH EXPERIMENTS TO BE
SUBMITTED STAT.

ALL, REPEAT ALL, MAINLAND SORTIES TO BE
AUTHORIZED BY YGGDRASIL CONTROL ONLY.

ACKNOWLEDGE.

"Fools," Nidor muttered, biting his lip. "Meddling fools!" He pressed a microphone button and dictated an answer that the computer instantly relayed:

30/5/165
1603 HOURS
EYES ONLY: HARROWER ETC
FROM: NIDOR ETC
    THIS SECTION CONDUCTS NO EXPERIMENTS INCONSISTENT WITH THE EXPEDIENT.
    THIS SECTION AUTHORIZES NO MAINLAND SORTIES.

Nidor waited several minutes for a reply, hands flat on his desk. When none came, he grunted in satisfaction and spoke into his intercom. "Send Garm in," he said.

Together, silent in the darkened room, the two men watched a tape of Asa. It was a montage assembled over the previous five years, beginning with clouded footage of a very pale, very thin young man in skins stepping from a helicopter, and ending with the same man, dressed as a Yulok, entering another helicopter. In between was footage of Asa studying, Asa running along the very beach where Garm had run, Asa with other novices, reserved, on the fringe of the group, watching.

"When?" Garm asked. "When do I meet him?"

"This is just part of the dossier," Nidor said, switching off the machine. "You may—"

"When?"

Nidor let a silence grow on the desk between them. Then he said, "When it is in our interests. When you have learned restraint."

"He shamed me!"

"I know."

"I intend to return that shame to him."

"What you intend and what you will do—"

"Have been the same thing," Garm said quietly. "Always."

"Until now. You were not brought here to pursue some aborr vendetta."

"I will—"

"You will do nothing," Nidor hissed, his voice like a thread of steel. "Nothing! Unless I tell you."

Garm's nostrils flared, but he looked away from Nidor's gaze.

"Do you think," Nidor said more quietly, "we would let you compromise everything for some petty vengeance?"

"I am a Kanik warrior still."

"So you have demonstrated, regrettably. Change that."

Garm looked at his hands.

"Tomorrow morning," Nidor went on, "you will arrive officially in Yggdrasil, and after your initial assessments you will enter the Novice Training Program. You will find it pathetically simple, of course, and irrelevant. But you will pretend. You will pretend to be fascinated. You will pretend to like the empty-headed young people with whom you must associate. You will *pretend*! Start now, by pretending *not* to be a Kanik warrior! You will have duties here in Neffelheim in addition to whatever they give you, but your trips here must be made in utmost secrecy. We shall make those arrangements when the time comes. You will find full instructions waiting in your room. That's all."

Garm stood and crossed to the door.

"Power," Nidor said behind him. "That is why you are here. Remember, power lies in the mastery of emotion, not its expression. Remember!"

Garm hesitated. Then he opened the door and left without looking back.

Nidor discovered that he was trembling. When he had regained control of his voice, he called Val and made an appointment for 1300 hours.

He exhaled deeply.

Even the anticipation helped to relax him.

TEN

Asa moved among the Yulok villages, watching the arrivals and departures of hunters and fishermen, talking with everyone, telling stories to children who gradually overcame their shyness of this new Wanderer. Alone, he borrowed a canoe and paddled out to the village on Eyul, and was welcomed there. Alone, as Jared and Alva had done among the Alcheringians, he listened at the fringes of the Yulok councils, and worried about the fate of this people he had been assigned to protect. They were an outgoing and genial people, fond of bawdy humor, fond of laughter and strange stories that spiraled through one irony after another and ended almost, but not quite, where they began.

As the weeks passed, he saw more clearly the Yuloks' peril. They had all but abandoned their Codex and allowed themselves to become vassals of the sea traders from the south, who were richer, stronger, more daring. With the first trades for furs and whale oil the Yuloks' balance with their environment had been tipped, and with every subsequent trade they had drifted further into exploitation, into dependency on the traders' cloth and iron. Soon, they needed these commodities. Soon, they lacked the will to resist, despite the urging of their peregrini. Soon, what had begun as trade between equals became almost a form of tribute, and the arrival of the traders' lateen sails became an ominous event in Yulok. Merriment vanished. Women backed into their lodges. Fearful children scampered away. Agreements were sealed under the shadows of catapults on the black decks, and the traders smiled.

Who were they? Where did they come from? How was it that they had so swiftly attained supremacy over the Yuloks, for so many generations an independent people, secure in their heritage and their Codex? Asa knew the answers, but he asked these questions often in the four villages and received only evasive replies. They came from the south. Far to the south. No one knew how far, but farther than Yulok sailors had ever ventured. Their hold on the Yuloks had grown insidiously, step by tiny step, until at last no one dared oppose them. When Asa asked them why not, why they had not followed the advice of their peregrini, the young men hung their heads or looked glumly at the sea. They feared, some said, for the villages, for even if they took a stand against some of the traders, others would return, and the retaliation would be brutal and swift. The traders had made that clear.

Asa observed the traders from a distance. Since his arrival three of their ships had moored in the Yulok bay and swung on several tides while their crews gathered booty on shore. They were sleek, long ships, double-masted, lateen-rigged. Invariably their hulls were dark, their sails maroon or black. Even the longboats that moved incessantly between ship and villages, rowed by stalwart and swarthy oarsmen, were dark.

Asa had no contact with the men themselves, however, until late one afternoon when he was returning along the beach from a visit to the middle village. The day was sunny but groundfog moved restlessly off the sea and through the marshes behind the beach. Running, Asa was only a few yards from the traders' longboat before he saw it. It had been hastily beached. Two of the oars lay where they had been dropped. Incoming tide floated the stern, and the boat rocked. For a moment Asa thought that the boat might have drifted from the moored ship and stranded there, but then from behind the beach he heard guttural shouts, laughter, screams.

Breeze dispersed the fog, and he saw at once what had happened.

Yulok girls had been gathering berries in the rich meadows behind the beach, and the boat crew had surprised them, creeping up under cover of the dunes. Three of the women had fled. The fourth had been trapped. Four men surrounded her. As Asa watched, she made a desperate attempt to dash between two of them, but one tripped her and the other fell on her. The rest shouted with laughter.

Asa walked up the beach. He was only a few yards away when he spoke. "Get back," he said.

The sailors turned. The girl squirmed and half rose, still pinned by her captor's body. They saw a slight young man with long black hair and tranquil eyes. Old eyes. Eyes that had seen this all before, seen it all, and knew exactly what would happen next. He held a staff in his left hand, and on top of the staff was the emblem of a strange tree.

The burliest of the sailors grunted. "Go away, fool!"

"No. You go."

They looked at each other and smiled. Again the girl tried to rise and again the man holding her twisted her down. She cried in pain. The other three spread out. "Who tells us to go away?"

"I do. Asa."

"And I. Rell."

The seamen spun around. On the ridge behind them stood a second young man, a Yulok fisherman. He was squat, and neckless, and he was smiling a broad and homely smile that revealed missing teeth. In his right fist was a heavy piece of driftwood.

They hesitated. In that instant the woman kicked, broke free, and lunged snarling at the man holding her. He went down shrieking, her nails in his face. The second one attacked Rell. The other two came for Asa.

He could not have described the fight, only his feeling. He was exultantly happy. Happy beyond all thought, beyond all memory. He laughed. He was once again an

Alcheringian brave with the red hand of action on his face. He was once again a man outside time.

His staff slashed across the running shins of his first attacker and stabbed into the belly of the second. Both fell cursing, and both sprang up again, the first more quickly. Asa danced back, weaving, and when the man lunged, the staff snaked out again, harder this time, striking the man's right elbow. The first blow dislocated the joint and the second ripped the ligaments that held the arm together. The man dropped, howling. The second approached more warily, crouching and feinting, swinging an oar. Asa moved in fast, ducked under a swing, and stabbed for the throat. When the man fell there was a red instant when Asa almost dropped on him to crush out life. He froze. Seconds interposed. Snapshots. A human with bulging eyes pleading. A human fighting for breath. A human with legs twitching. A human.

Asa stepped back.

He turned to see the other two sailors on the ground. One was bawling that he was blind. One knelt, retching.

Asa and Rell moved together, touched hands. "It seems," the Yulok said, grinning, "that these traders are not indestructible."

The woman took Asa's hand in both of hers and bent to touch her forehead to it. She had startlingly clear, green, feline eyes. "Someday I shall repay this," she said quietly. "I promise you."

Together they watched the sailors float their boat and row it, with some difficulty, into the shifting fogs of the bay.

"You are very young to make oaths," Asa said to her when the boat had vanished. "What's your name?"

"Ruti."

Asa would have spoken to her further, but she bent to retrieve her pannier of berries and was gone among the dunes.

"She's from Middle Village," Rell said. "Half wild, like all those women there. Come. We shall walk together, you and I."

And they did that, laughing often, back to North Village.

* * *

The small house that the Yuloks kept for their Wanderer was set apart from the others on a hillside near a small waterfall. It was a low structure with a moss-covered roof and a little balcony looking down over the village and the sea. The two doorposts were carved with jovial Yulok images of greeting and hospitality. Inside, opposite the door, was the raised sleeping platform. A central hearth provided all heat and light. Plain mats covered the wooden floor, and the little dwelling was filled always with the mingling scents of sweet grass and cedar. Always, when Asa returned, a fire was burning and food and strong Yulok tea were laid ready.

Usually he would follow the little path that led to the edge of the stream and descend the steps into the eddying pool above the falls. He would bathe there in the darkness, gasping at the cold rush of the water, feeling the velvet on the rocks brush his skin, looking out across the bay below, all tranquil. Afterward he would dry himself, dress, and return to the bungalow to eat and sleep alone beside the fire.

One night shortly after the fight on the beach, he returned from the pool to find Alexis waiting for him. She was standing beside the steps with her hands folded in front of her, a tall, cool figure in the darkness.

He invited her in.

In the circling Yulok manner they talked about many things as they ate. She had an extraordinarily long and sinuous neck on which her small head swayed constantly as she talked.

"We have had many other Wanderers, but none like you, Asa. They all feared the sea traders. Feared what they saw in our future. They were nervous, like deer that have heard sounds others have not heard. They traveled on the land but were not of it. They were filled only with ideas, and with haste. You, you are not like them."

"We are many," Asa said. "We are different."

"But you . . ." Her head moved querulously.

"I am Alcheringian."

"Ahh. Of course. You are of the land, like us, although

you knew it differently. Perhaps you can help us, then, although the others could not."

"I don't know, Alexis."

"Come," she said, smiling, her head moving in the firelight, "you have power. You have knowledge that we do not have. Will you not use these to help us?"

"If I can, but I must know more. I must know everything."

She shrugged slightly. "You know our myths, or you would not have been sent among us."

"Tell me again."

She inclined her head, smiling. "Gaia first, then. Gaia is our goddess. We teach our children that it was she who created the Earth as a habitation for herself, and that she lives in it still, scorning the stars and the planets, and the other abodes of wrangling gods. She dreams in the Earth. She broods. She nurtures each plant, and every animal, bird, and insect. We teach our children that it is she who works the mysteries of love and birth, of disease and death. To go softly upon the Earth is to respect her, to love her. To violate the Earth is to violate Gaia. She is patient. She endures. She is slow to anger. For a time she may acquiesce in this violation, but in the end she will turn upon her tormentors and destroy them.

"Our legends tell of such a violation. Such a destruction. This is how we explain the dead cities of the Old Ones. This is how we explain the Waysts, scars on the face of Gaia, where she has suffered grievously and is healing. You know that here, at Yulok, as once at Alcheringia, the land and its creatures lived in harmony. Creatures and land, a seamless cloth. When that is true, as we want it to be again, Gaia smiles."

Alexis sipped her tea and was silent for several minutes before continuing.

"You know that this is why our law is called the Lex Gaiae, the Code of Gaia, and why in Yulok, although we live in one place, we do so only because Gaia suffers us. It is why we have many fables and funny stories for our children, all teaching the absurdity of the idea that *the land can be owned.*"

Asa smiled. "I know those tales."

"We hold all things in common, since all come from the Earth, and we teach our children that life is sharing the astonishing abundance of Earth. Nothing more."

"Nothing more?"

She shook her head.

"I have understood that the Yuloks, like the Alcheringians, found ways to celebrate that life and that abundance. Your totem poles, for instance, an accumulation of delights, one on top of another, reaching out of the earth as high as you can raise them. Are these not celebrations?"

She smiled and nodded.

"And your dances?"

She opened her hands.

"And your famed liberality with strangers?"

"The celebration is in the living," she said. "We all own all. We belong to each other.

"We believe, further, that women are the keepers of this knowledge. Women know it *beneath* knowledge. It is for this reason that the women in our fables are always large and disheveled, to suggest the burgeoning earth itself, but always shrewd also when it comes to striking bargains, and always insisting on limits which may not be transgressed. It is for this reason that they are always laughing, and their laughter is all one—delight, and astonishment, and scorn.

"In our stories, men come to women with a thousand schemes, to improve this or that about the Earth, and when they do so the women laugh. They laugh. And in a little while the men laugh also, and forget their schemes."

She paused. A breeze rose from the sea and rustled the leaves at the sides of the verandah. The stream murmured across cushioned stones.

"Our stories, all of them, teach the great danger that would befall mankind if ever again males rose to the ascendancy, and if ever women and the Earth became subservient to preposterous demands. We teach our children that men are but children themselves, but children eternally restless and inquiring, foolish, vain, greedy, intransigent and intolerant of mystery, incapable of foresight. We teach that men are dangerous because, though playful, *their games have purpose.* They play in packs. They strut and posture, and compare the size of their weapons, and shake them at each other. We teach our children to laugh such performances to scorn, to ridicule, but never to take them lightly, for men are capable of outrages beyond belief. Our definition of sanity is that it is what women use to defend themselves and the Earth from the foolishness of men. But now, now I fear we have made ourselves a people too soft. A people who cannot defend themselves."

Asa had listened through his fatigue, and had watched through the thin layers of smoke that rose between them, mesmerized by the slight, plaintive swaying of her head. "Your young men were at Alcheringia," he said.

"Yes. Oh yes, they were." She reached toward him, supplicating. "And even that was fear. A messenger had come to us. A Kanik. So strong. So sure."

"Garm."

"Garm, yes. He shamed them with his very speech, his very bearing. He told them that if they did not go they would be less than men. The Wanderer who was with us then said that he was right, gave reasons, justifications. They went, but came back sick at heart. Soiled. Diminished. Those who went said they would never fight again. Never."

"And now *you* are the victims."

She nodded. "And we do not know how to resist."

The fire had burned low. Asa dropped a fresh cedar root on it and it sprang to life again, lofting sparks through the roof opening toward the stars. "Call a council," Asa said. "And I will show you how."

It took more than a week to summon the people in. Runners went out beyond the Yulok Hills and into the Eastern Plain toward the country of the Montayners and the River Em, taking the message to hunting parties. Canoes skimmed out of the bay on fair winds, north and south along the coast, taking the message to sealers and whalers.

Asa spent this time mostly alone. He ate lightly. He slept beneath the stars. He spent hours listening to the voices of the sea. In evening calms he paddled along the

dusky shore of Eyul and gazed at the winding trunks of
great pine. He peered into cones and into the coils of new
ferns. He watched the eddies from his paddle. He peered
in wonder at the great dewy whorls of spider webs hanging
in the sunset. Out of the sea froth he picked little shells,
some broken, some intact, and he found that these cones
with their symmetrical chambers fascinated him still, as
they had when he was a child on the beaches of Alcheringia. In the detritus behind a remote beach he found a
broken walrus tusk, old and yellowed, and when he held
it to his eye he saw again the spiral of the pine. Gently
he opened the bud of a wild rose. For the first time he
saw the way a squirrel runs up a trunk, and the way bats,
startled, explode out of a cave in order, and the way a
hawk inspects a meadow, saw them as part of one of the
great patterns of growth and being. Quietly, in one of the
Yulok villages, he witnessed the birth of a child and afterward saw with amazement that same pattern in the fragile
strands that had linked life to life.

One evening Asa sat alone on a remote beach on the
outer side of Eyul. He had walked a mile or two in the
last of the afternoon, and had sat down on driftwood to
watch the sunset. When the spectacle had ended and the
afterglow began to fade, he stood up.

In that moment, something struck him. He reeled. For
one horrible instant he thought something had collapsed
in his mind, but then he knew the affected part was not
his head but his belly. The sensation was wholly visceral,
like quivering fear. Yet it was exultation, too, the sinking,
soaring turbulence he remembered as a child plunging
from bluffs into the river pools. It caused him to shout
like a child, first in surprise but then in jubilation; he knew
clearly what had happened.

He had been given an extraordinary gift: the key to
the Riddle of the Second Door.

He had not been thinking about it. He had not been
thinking about anything. But the riddle had moved sub-
consciously. *Circling, I am not a circle. Flat, I am not
straight. I give strength though I have none. Progressing,
I end where I begin. Single, I start life; double, I stand
in life's core; triple, I link life to life. Through me knowledge becomes wisdom. Through me time returns.*

It had blended with images, other memories, and then when he had least expected it, had offered a word.

"Helix," Asa said, laughing softly, raising both arms toward heaven. "Helix!" he shouted. He shook his head incredulously and then sat down suddenly, arms and legs slack as a child's doll. So obvious! All those years it had been so obvious!

He began at once to frame the message he would ask Vogh to relay to Jotunheim that night. But then he paused, and his laughter died. Jotunheim would test the key immediately. If it worked, all peregrini would be summoned in for the Opening. Under his oath, he could not refuse that summons. He would have to leave the Yuloks just at the very moment when they had begun to find the courage to set their limits. To desert them now, even briefly, might mean failure for his mission.

Besides, going back would postpone any possible journey to the east. To Persis.

Asa sat a long time in the fading light staring unseeing at the ebbing tide. When he stood up and brushed sand off his thighs he was in darkness.

He had decided.

He would wait.

After these years, he told himself, a few weeks would make little difference to Jotunheim...

The council was held at evening. All afternoon the Yuloks had gathered at the north village, coming by foot in little groups down the long beach and by canoe from the settlement on Eyul. The day was clear and hot. All afternoon they had laughed and feasted, and there was festivity in the air, for there was hope. Perhaps, just perhaps, this quiet and watchful young Wanderer who moved like a warrior through their villages could help them. So, at dusk, when the great fire had been lit and the council circle had been formed on the sloping beach, it was with a hush of expectancy and hope that they greeted Alexis' announcement that Asa would speak.

He stood with his back to the deep red and purple of the sunset, and as he spoke the sea rose gently to touch his feet.

"You know that you are in grave danger," he said, "and that is why you are here. You know that your law was a good law, and that you have broken it. You do not understand how you were induced to break it, but you know that you have done so. Your life has been worse since, more fearful and diminished, more harried and graceless. Even your myths have lost their meaning and become fairytales.

"Perhaps you wonder why the gods have not destroyed you for your folly, and I tell you that they have no need to do so, for you are destroying yourselves, and that in a generation, two generations, the Yuloks will be no more. Oh, you will have descendants, but they will be orphans in nature, uncomprehending, and the wilderness will be a menace to them."

Some of the young men shifted uneasily and murmured together. Asa waited.

"We have progressed," one of them said. "We have outgrown superstition."

"And we shall keep on," said another. "The sea traders will teach us to make iron, to make clothing as fine as theirs."

A third said quietly, "We can't go back."

"No," Asa said, "you can never go back. Not quite. You must grow. *But you must grow around a center*. Tell me, if you are growing now, where is that center that gives you strength? Where?"

He waited.

The young men looked at the sea, at each other, at the ground.

"Once," Asa went on, "that center was your knowledge that you were part of nature. Nature met your needs then. But now that you have grown greedy, where is nature? What has it become? Are you still contained by it? Or is it something outside, something you can *use*?"

Again he waited, but this time there was no talking, only silence, and wherever he looked, people dropped their gaze.

Finally, an old man, staring at the fire, beating his slack fist softly on the ground, said, "We are afraid. We are *afraid*. What shall we do?"

"Know the limits," Asa said. "Live within them."

Anguished cries of protest greeted this. "But we . . . never . . . we cannot . . . the traders . . . we need . . . we need . . ."

Asa held up his hand. "If you tell me this is impossible, I am not interested in hearing. If you decide to do it, I shall show you how. And I shall help you turn away the traders. If you do not decide to do this, I shall leave you. In three days. Three. You alone must decide."

He made the cut-off sign and walked away.

He returned to the little bungalow on the hillside, and he waited. He waited three days, while the council fire burned on the beach and the debate continued. On the third evening, coming back from bathing in the stream, he was met by a delegation on the path. They were four young men, representing each of the four villages.

Rell spoke. "We have decided. We are all agreed. We want to live again within the old boundaries designated by the gods. How shall we begin?"

"You have begun," Asa said. "The hardest is over. Now you must let your friends the traders know, so that nothing can happen by error or misunderstanding. What is the best way to do that?"

"Go to them," Rell said, grinning. "Take the message."

"Good. And who will do that?" He looked in turn into each of the four young faces.

"I will," Rell said, and the others added in a single voice, "and so will I!"

Asa smiled. "And so," he said, "will I."

They left the next morning for the south, borne by fair winds. They took Rell's open boat with its big square sail.

Yggdrasilian charts showed the contours of this coast, but in very little detail. For years Yggdrasilian patrols had reported few signs of life in those southern regions. South of the southern boundary of Merone, it was believed, coastal life had been largely extinguished by the Entropies. But now, from the prow of Rell's ship skirting the shore, Asa saw that the Yggdrasilians had been mistaken. His monitors signaled various dangers, but these were slight now, diminished by the passage of years, by benign rains, benevolent winds, sunlight cleansing and leaching away the poisons. Life had returned. The shore was green again. Asa smiled at the resiliency of nature and the determined thrust of life that had scattered its seeds in such profusion and with such blind confidence once more.

Sea birds wheeled above them. Eagles and ospreys perched among the crags. Smaller birds flitted through the branches of young trees. Deer gazed from the clifftops, tails twitching. Once, a wolf with its tongue lolling kept pace with them down a long beach. Once Asa was so sure he saw a man crouching among the boulders that he called out to him. Rell came about and sailed in for a closer look, but the man had vanished and drifting fog obscured the beach.

Rell shrugged. "We've seen them before, but they never come close to us. They're puny, frightened, but they seem to be a race. Not just freaks, like the Gerumbians."

A few miles farther they came to one of the dead cities of the Old Ones. It encircled a large bay, and Asa asked Rell to steer close, near what had been port facilities. Asa's monitors signaled safety, and Rell tacked in, giving a wide berth to skeletal superstructures that marked the graves of old ships. Fuel tanks lined the shore behind twisted docks, large fuel tanks, and Asa noted that although they were badly rusted they were still intact. He noted their location on his sketch of the coast.

South they went, past long beaches and towering palisades, until they came at last to a land that was fresh and green, where Asa's monitors showed no trace whatever of contamination.

A few miles farther they saw the first of the tall cairns built by the sea traders to mark the beginning of their territories. Soon after, one of the ships of the traders hoisted sail and put out to intercept them.

They hove to.

"Rell, you speak," Asa said quietly. "Leave the rest to me."

The other vessel also headed into the wind, her dark sails flapping. She was a low, sleek, fast warship. A catapult raised its ominous arm from her foredeck, and another from her poop. Midships stood a half-dozen archers with bows unslung. The master called across the distance with a megaphone. "Go home, Yulok! You have no business here. When we want to trade we shall tell you, and we shall come to you. Go home!"

Rell cupped his hands. "We have come to deliver a message, not to trade."

"So? What message can a Yulok give to me?"

"We are ending our trade with you," Rell called. "We are closing our boundaries. When you come north again, you shall see *our* cairn in the second bay south of the Great Promontory. If your business is trade, put to sea and sail past, beyond Eyul."

For a moment there was no reply from the dark ship. The archers in her waist muttered and laughed together, and gestured disparagingly at Rell's little craft. A few slipped arrows from their quivers.

Then the answer came. "The Yulok country is rich, my friend. We think we shall not abandon it so easily. But perhaps, as you say, the days of trade are at an end. Perhaps we shall simply take what we desire. What will you do then, Yuloks?"

"Say nothing," Asa said quietly. "Stand together."

The boats drifted closer.

"Well, Yulok? What? If you intend to resist, perhaps you should begin now, eh?"

"Say nothing," Asa said. The five men stood together, their shoulders almost touching.

"Perhaps, if their messenger did not return, the Yuloks would forget this foolishness. Well? If you have something to say, now is the time."

"We have given you our message," Rell said. "There is nothing else."

The master raised his arm and dropped it. Both catapults exploded at once, straddling Rell's craft with boulders. At the same moment a volley of arrows arched across the water, and two of the Yuloks fell groaning.

Asa drew his gun, sighted, fired. The movement was a single, calm action. The shot cropped off the foremast about eight feet above the deck, sending the spar and tangled rigging crashing into the sea. The dark ship heeled and swung toward them. Asa's second shot took the mizzenmast, slightly higher. The master collapsed under a tangle of canvas and cordage.

"Get underway!" Asa said to Rell. "Go!"

But before they could move, another volley came from the disabled craft, accompanied by howls of rage. Then another. Asa saw that they would be killed before they had drawn out of range. Reluctantly he took aim once more, and blew the stern off the ship. It sank almost instantly, leaving only a splotch of flotsam and the heads of stunned men bobbing on the sea.

The engagement had lasted three minutes.

Asa returned the weapon to his knapsack and stopped to attend to the wounded men. "Into the bay," he said to Rell, pointing to the port of the sea traders a mile away. "Go close."

Rell sailed in. They went unchallenged past the battlements, past the stunned docks and quiet ships with crews huddled on their decks. The *Y* of Yulok bulged on the gray squaresail.

"Tell them again," Asa said.

Rell stood by his tiller, cupped his hand to his mouth, and called toward the docks. "The days of trade have ended. Do not come to the Great Bay of Yulok. Sail past! Forever!"

They came about and tacked back again, and when there was still no response, Asa said, "I think we can go home."

ELEVEN

Early in the afternoon, a sudden and violent thunderstorm swept across Yggdrasil from the northwest. It bent trees on Jotunheim and whipped sea froth across the scholars' windows. It flattened Neffelheim's steam plume into a thin fan and howled across the tunnel entrances. It scattered strollers in the parks of Asgard, sending old people trotting with little steps back to the senarium.

In the Repository Access Building, Yida looked up, startled, as the first rain slashed across the skylights and the doors. She had been absorbed in deciphering a complex Spanish poem, and had not noticed the fretting gusts that were harbingers of the storm. Now it was upon them, a wet and furious animal.

She rose and crossed to the entrance. Beyond the streaming glass, trees swayed and trembled. Fingers of wind reached for her through the crack between the doors. Yida crossed her arms and peered out into this distorted world. Suddenly she was startled by a movement out of keeping with the berserk fury of the storm. It was a deliberate movement, measured and slow—the smooth cadence of a walking man.

He was coming toward her out of the storm, down the

156

center of the gravel path. He wore the pale green uniform
of an aborr novice. His hands were empty. His bare head
was lifted to the rain as to a lover, and was covered with
hair the color of bleached wheat. He squinted slightly
against the blasts of the storm. He was looking at the
doors, and through them.

Yida stepped back. One hand went to her throat.

The man had reached the bottom step.

She turned and walked quickly to the circular counter
behind which she worked, closing the waist-high door
behind her. She held her hand against it.

No one else was in the reading room.

The man reached the top flight of steps, and for an
instant he was but a humanoid shape, distorted by shadows and rivulets. Then the door opened and he came in
without breaking stride, coming directly toward her after
only a glance around the empty reading room, leaving a
track of wet footprints across the gleaming floor. She had
thought that she would have time to sit down at her console, to pretend busy-ness. But she did not have this time.
His pale gray eyes fixed her where she stood, so that she
did nothing but hold the little door shut and watch him
until he was close enough to fill her vision, until she could
hear water dripping from his clothes and read *Garm* on
his breast beneath the small Yggdrasilian tree. She watched
him, and she knew that what had galvanized her in his
stare was scorn, indifference, cool determination, and an
absolute chilling certainty about what would now happen
to them both.

"These," he said, producing a list from his breast pocket,
but not looking away from her as he did so.

It was the standard reading list for the third and final
stage of Novice Training. "I assume you want these in
the order listed," Yida said. Her mouth was dry.

"Do you?"

"Most novices take them one at a time, starting
with—"

"Do they?"

She laid the list on the counter between them. "Which
do you want?"

"All of them."

She tried to laugh, but produced only a foolish sound. "That's ridiculous! There are far more than you can read at one sitting."

"Are there?"

"If you want my opinion—"

"I don't. I want those." Garm pointed to the list.

She sat and tapped the call numbers into the machine, and in a few minutes the disks arrived—first one, then three together, then two. She arranged them in the order of listing, and he took them without a word. "Do you know how to operate the machines?"

Garm laughed and turned his back on her.

He worked for less than an hour, scarcely time enough for most researchers to begin properly. Then he was back, returning the disks, waiting.

"Is there something else I can do for you?"

He did not answer.

"I think you'd better go," Yida said suddenly. "I have to clean up now. I have to close now."

Garm did not move. His brow furrowed slightly, as if he were puzzled that something so obvious to him should not also be obvious to her.

Yida turned to the empty reading room. She looked at the blue button that would have summoned Asgardian security patrols. She did not press it. Instead, she touched the janitorial button, which brought the little clean-up robot trundling out of its closet. Programed to divide the floor into sections and to work on each section in turn, it would ordinarily have proceeded blithely with its routine chores. However, crossing in front of the doors it encountered Garm's wet footprints. It turned sharp right and began to vacuum them up. A moment later, silently, it bumped against Garm's legs.

Only aborrs moved so fast.

The little machine was already turning away automatically when Garm leaped and struck it with both feet. It toppled and spun across the floor, tiny wheels still trudging. In another instant he was upon it, swinging it over his head, hurling it down. It smashed, spilled parts, uttered a squeal, lay still.

Garm came back to the counter, opened the little door, and took Yida by the wrist. "Come," he said.

Later, she would remember stepping across nylon wheels and other little parts scattered like defunct insects. She would remember entering a night astonishingly still after the violence of the storm, a night washed clean, full of pine scent and the persimmon odor of the restive sea.

Because she was asleep she would not remember, much later, weeping, speaking a name that would cause Garm to rise, leave his apartment, and go alone into that still night.

TWELVE

Asa waited.

For the first month after the Yulok foray to the south, no sea traders came north. All day, every day, lookouts watched the horizon from the heights, but they saw no sails, only pods of whales passing far out; only, on the clearest days, the spume of steam that marked the Islands of the Gods.

Asa spent the month among the four villages. Everywhere he was thanked. He gave all credit to Rell and the others, but he knew that what he had done would be told and retold many times, and that as the months passed into years it would become the stuff of legend, part of that core around which the Yuloks would begin to build their society once again. Within a few generations he would have become a giant, and the blasts that destroyed the dark vessel would have sprung from his pointed hand. The ship itself would be not a single vessel, but a fleet.

Soon after their return he had crossed the Yulok Hills and made a full report to Peregrinus Control. The situation was stabilizing, he said, but if the sea traders launched a large-scale retaliatory raid he would need Yggdrasilian support. He specified helicopters with piezosonic oscillators, and was promised them.

He had met Fenris and Vogh at his checkpoint, and they greeted each other jovially. He had missed the two tough Wylders, and it seemed they had missed him. They had been moving constantly, traveling across the middle plain, past the country of the Montayners, over the Em, and as far as the Kanik Hills, but they had gone no farther. "No need," Fenris said. "No excuse. No maps."

When Asa asked if they would like to, they laughed. Of course they would.

He asked what they knew about the frontier and about what lay beyond.

"*In*teresting," Fenris said. "Ve-ry interesting. Some crews have been out there, farther south, farther north. Thing is, that frontier doesn't exist, except as a line on a map. Nobody polices it. You get people from the Outer Wyld moving across it, moving in. Question is, where do they come from? What kind of culture do they have? Nobody knows. You know, sir, once in a debriefing room I saw a map that was a little different from anything else I'd seen. Do you know what was marked there, all along that eastern border, down the whole Erthring? *The Interface*. The Interface! I ask myself, the interface with *what*?"

Asa asked about fuel to go beyond the normal patrol ranges, and again they laughed. "No problem, sir. We know where it is. If Yggdrasil won't give it to us, we'll find it informally, if you know what we mean." He winked. "Just give us a day or two notice."

Asa waited. He sent no message to Yggdrasil.

During the second month, the sails of two sea-trader ships coasted up from the south, but when they reached the Yuloks' new marker in the second bay south of the Great Promontory, they tacked seaward and gave all Yulok a wide berth.

That night there was much rejoicing. Fires burned in all the villages. Feasts occurred. Alexis came again to Asa's bungalow.

"You will be leaving soon," she said as they sat together beside the fire. Her head moved on the sinuous neck. "You will be going to her."

"To whom?"

"To her. She who haunts your dreams. She whose name you call sometimes in your sleep like a man dying. Persis, the woman you love."

"I don't know where she is, Alexis."

"But you believe she is alive?"

He looked up in surprise and nodded. He could not imagine her dead. He could not imagine her other than she had been. He could not think of her growing old, despite the passing years, growing gray and stooped. He could not imagine her maimed by accident or disease. He could not think of her toothless, like the crones who had haunted his boyhood. In his memory she was young, and they were together, and it was winter...

"If she is alive, then go to her, my friend. Go soon. You must do that at any cost." Her hand reached out and held his, and her eyes filled with ineffable remorse.

"I'll wait," Asa said quietly, "a little longer."

Still he had sent no message to Yggdrasil.

During the third month, the traders' ships kept far to windward, out to sea, and it grew clear that they had abandoned Yulok and were seeking other trading grounds farther north. The boundaries of Yulok had been reestablished, game was returning, and fish gathered in sufficient quantities once again. The councils in all four villages had meaning. Issues were hotly debated, and resolved.

Yulok was healing.

Once Asa mentioned the Islands of the Gods to Rell. He had half thought that this staunch Yulok might harbor a desire to go there. But Rell shook his head, laughing, and Asa let the matter drop.

Once he journeyed up to Middle Village specifically to find Ruti, the girl with the strange green eyes and the fearsome independence. She had grown, but not enough. Not yet. "I shall send for you," he had said. And she had answered, "I shall come."

At the beginning of the fourth month after the fight with the traders, Asa went east. He met Fenris and Vogh at the rendezvous. Except for helping to quell a small insurrection on the fringes of Gerumbia, they had had a dull year, and they were ready for a journey. They produced their charts of eastern Norriya and pored over them with their flashlights. They estimated that the run to the eastern frontier would take three days. Smiling, Fenris asked, "And then?"

"We'll see, Fenris." Asa tossed his pack into the cabin and began to climb in behind.

"Problem is, sir, if we're going beyond the frontier, into the Outer Wyld, we'll need fuel. If you want to keep this trip kind of, well, quiet, we'll have to make a stop at a place Vogh and I know about. We'll have to mount the extra tanks and fill 'em up."

Asa hesitated only a moment. "Do it," he said, and vanished into the hovercraft. He fell asleep as soon as they were underway, and did not waken until they were many miles to the south, passing east of Alcheringia across the path he and Kenet and his Nine had taken on their first raid against the Kaniks. In the distance he glimpsed the Larl, lead gray under a gray sky. Once he believed he saw the very bluffs where the graves of Alcheringian ancestors lay; once, to the south, spray rising from the falls where girls retreated at the onset of womanhood. Again he drowsed, restive with dreams and memories.

He awakened at dusk to find that they had halted somewhere in the Middle Wayst. Fenris and Vogh had fitted extra fuel tanks and were filling them. As far as he could see the landscape had a stunted and dreary sameness, but then . . .

"Spotlights," he said. "There!"

Fenris looked where he was pointing. "That's only an old Clinician bunker, sir. Hasn't been used for—"

"Please. Lights."

It was exactly as he remembered it. There was the ridge along which they had ridden after losing the stag. There was the place where Rusl had dismounted to go forward, and there, still visible under its slow overgrowth of moss and lichen, was the square hatch from which the silver creature rose. There was the place he had dismounted with his spear and run screaming at the thing.

And then . . . And then . . . But he could remember nothing else until he awoke far to the north, out of the Wayst.

"Thanks," he said. "I've seen enough."

The lights switched off. The doors banged shut. The vehicle picked up speed. Asa leaned back into the shadows of the cabin.

To the south, the city of the Old Ones gleamed like fractured teeth in the jaw of earth. It was a loathsome place, and yet it held a peculiar fascination for Asa, and he thought fleetingly that perhaps on their way home from the Outer Wyld they might visit it. As a peregrinus he needed no special reason to go there, provided the latent dangers from the Entropies had not been reactivated by earth tremors or other unpredictable events. Furthermore, in recent years all patrols, regular and irregular, had been issued standing orders to scavenge whenever possible, and all vehicles carried a list of items and materials in short supply in Yggdrasil. *Perhaps on the way back*, Asa thought as the gray buildings slipped into the distance and the darkness behind them.

He slept again.

In the late afternoon of the second day, they entered that area east of the Kanik Mountains where the maps grew vague. So far as they could tell, they were well within the Norriyan frontier, but the map was of little use, and they could not be certain they were following sanctioned routes. They were farther east than Asa had ever gone, miles past that point where, six years earlier, he had dropped to his knees and plunged Garm's arrow into the freezing ground.

They were proceeding slowly up a long valley when they saw the smoke. In the still air it rose like a delicate mushroom, a thin column with a bloom at the top.

"Stop here." Asa indicated an overhang to the right, and Fenris adroitly maneuvered the craft beneath it and cut the engines. "Come on, Vogh. You and I are going up there. Fenris, stay with the vehicle. If you don't see us coming back down that valley in three hours, come up and get us. And lean on the siren."

"Yes, sir."

Twenty minutes brought them to the fire. It was a single

campfire over which a young deer turned on a spit. Eleven people squatted around it, talking, laughing, prodding the meat with sharpened sticks. They had posted no guard. No horses stood tethered nearby, and the lodges among the trees were little more than brush lean-tos. The people themselves were so raggedly clothed that they seemed like dusky foliage.

When Asa called they looked up curiously. Those at the rear of the fire stood to peer around the smoke. None expressed alarm, only mild curiosity and amusement. Their eyes gleamed in the firelight, alert. Several answered his call, their voices high and fluting. Several laughed. Two old women nudged each other delightedly, and it was they who answered Asa's questions in a mocking sing-song. He had exchanged several remarks with them before he realized that only the upper parts of their bodies moved; they were Siamese twins, joined at the hip.

This was a family of migrants from the Outer Wyld. They called themselves "the people," and had no affiliation with any other tribes, though they spoke enough Kanik for Asa to understand. Vagabonds, they moved across the frontier as they wished, hunting and stealing, following the game. Sometimes Kaniks harassed them, sometimes Montayners. Sometimes they saw neither for weeks or months. East of the boundary, they competed with other similar groups for food and territory. Sometimes they clashed, sometimes they traded, sometimes they intermarried, always they moved. Whenever and whatever they could, they stole. They stole horses, children, women, and they traded them eastward.

Beyond these facts, Yggdrasil knew little about them.

"I am looking for a woman," Asa said.

The circle around the campfire exploded jovially. There was much elbowing and chuckling. What type of woman did the young man want?

"No type. A particular woman."

The gathering shrugged and smirked. "We see many women. Many. They pass through our hands. We take them east. Into the Wyld. Sometimes, when the Kaniks order them, we bring some here. Dozens. Hundreds. How would you expect us to remember any one of them?"

Asa described Persis.

The Siamese women murmured together, swaying, peering at Asa, squinting into memories conjured by the fire. "Dark hair."

"Yes."

"A Kanik, but taken from the Kaniks, long ago?"

"Yes."

"A scar? Here?"

Asa nodded.

"Big with child?"

"Perhaps. Do you remember her?"

Their two heads bobbed, their two torsos swayed apart, swayed together. "Gone," they whispered. "Gone."

"Gone—where?"

"There. There. To the east. Beyond us."

One of the men bent and consulted them. Then he turned to Asa. "They remember her well. They say we traded her to a band in the Wyld. And they say that perhaps she was traded again and again. She was a handsome woman. They remember her well. We had no difficulty selling her. She was much desired by men."

Asa sat, holding his knees.

"They say," the man went on, "that while she was with us she did not laugh, she did not weep, she did not speak."

The meat was cooked. They began to eat sloppily, tearing off hot chunks and carrying them away from the others. For a time there were no sounds in the camp but the chewing and rending of meat and the whining of half-starved dogs. No one offered anything to Asa or Vogh.

"Let's go, sir," Vogh said out of the side of his mouth, his eyes on the slashing knives of the eaters. "Let's get out of here. It's almost time."

"A minute," Asa said. He approached the leader, who had finished his meal and was wiping his hands on his thighs. "Tell me, my friend. If I were to travel to the east, what would I find there? What people? What places?"

There was a moment of incredulous silence, and then the camp erupted again in wild laughter. Those who had finished eating howled and slapped each other and pointed at Asa. Some spewed out strands of meat. The chief roared, and slapped his knees, and turned in little circles. "You hear?" he asked, tears streaming. "You hear what this one asks me? What places? What *people*?"

Asa stood unsmiling. Vogh stood behind him. Little by little the camp fell silent. The chief advanced, his laughter dying. He wiped his mouth with the back of his hand. He looked enviously at Asa's woven Yulok clothes. He looked with hatred at Asa's body, strong and straight and unmarred by deformities except the old scars of battle. "You? You want to know what *you* would find if you went farther east? I'll tell you." He thrust his hideous noseless face up at Asa's, so close that Asa was shrouded in the stench of rotting meat that rose from him. He choked. "*Death*," the man whispered. "That's what you would find, my young friend. *Death!*" Then he roared, and Asa gagged and turned away, causing even more merriment among them.

"Come on, sir," Vogh urged, taking his elbow. "This is no place for us, sir. Let's get back to the ship."

They went, chased by laughter. Once Asa paused and looked back, fingering the weapon concealed under his tunic. Vogh saw the gesture and his face brightened. "Sure! Why don't you do that, sir? Pack of brutes! Go ahead! Who's to know, eh?"

Asa shook his head. "Come on," he said.

"Two minutes," Fenris called as they approached. "That's how long before I started up there with fireworks."

"Fenris, are the two of you ready to take this ship east tomorrow?"

The Wylder massaged his belly, grinning. "Just give us the word, sir."

Asa looked at the night. It was clear and still, and promised good traveling weather in the morning. He thought of Yulok, and knew that his work was finished there. He thought of the promise Shem had made him, years before. He looked at the hovercraft, equipped and ready to go. He thought of Persis. There. Just there, perhaps ten miles beyond, perhaps a hundred, perhaps farther, but closer than she had ever been.

He nodded. "We go," he said. Fenris and Vogh slapped hands and cursed happily.

The radio in the hovercraft squawked.

"Don't answer it," Asa said.

Fenris shrugged and checked his watch. "Just routine, sir. We're half an hour late checking in, that's all. I'll give a false position, and from here on out we'll have reception problems." He winked and vanished into the cabin while Asa and Vogh stood together in the last of the sunset.

In a few minutes he was back, his face grim.

"What is it?" Vogh asked.

Fenris cursed softly. "They've issued a General Recall."

Asa spun around. *"What?"*

"Right. They're calling in all peregrini effective twenty-four hundred hours. Our orders are to tell you when you make contact tonight, and then to take you to the helicopter rendezvous. They want you back in Yggdrasil before dawn."

Asa shook his head. "No. We're going east."

"They're Master's orders, sir. Arborea orders."

"No."

"And there was a special message for you. From someone called Egon."

"Egon."

"Yes, sir. He says to tell you it's time to come back to Jotunheim."

"An Opening," Asa said. "They've had an Opening."

"Yes, sir. That's what it sounds like, all right. That's the only thing that'd bring the peregrini in. All of 'em. All over Norriya. All over the Erthring, I guess."

Asa sat down slowly, feeling behind him as an old man feels for a chair. "There'll be the briefings. All the new work. All the new knowledge." He swallowed. He stared unseeing at the tree symbol on the flank of the vehicle, faded and almost obscured by dust. A long time passed before Asa spoke again. "Well," he said. "Perhaps we should go back."

He did not look at the others.

Vogh turned away and spat.

Fenris said, "Whatever you say, sir. You want to go east, we'll go. You want to go back, we'll go. But if we don't go into that country tonight, you let us know when. Okay, sir?"

"Not long," Asa said. "Perhaps a month. When this work's finished . . ."

"Sure," Fenris said, turning away and following Vogh back through the darkness toward the ACV. "Okay. You let us know."

Asa stood and looked eastward to the dip in the hills that marked the pass to the Outer Wyld. "Soon," he said quietly. "I promise."

The engine roared. Headlights washed across his legs. A door swung open. He walked toward it.

THIRTEEN

THE CONDITION OF YGGDRASIL ALARMED HIM.

It had deteriorated badly in the months of his absence. Pipes were leaking, foundations were crumbling, rationing of many items had been imposed. More and more missions to the mainland were diverted from the Expedient and turned into foraging excursions. In fact, sections of the airport and the docking area had been set aside for receiving freight—raw materials from the cities of the Old Ones that were now safe for recycling. The Gaian Expedient was increasingly imperiled. In his first briefing sessions, Asa heard stories of rebellious tribes in all five districts. Worse, from Merone, from the Center, and from the Underlakes came reports of increased menace from the tribes of the Outer Wylds.

Listening to these reports, talking with other peregrini who had come in for the Opening, Asa realized what a comparatively easy assignment he had had in Yulok. It had been isolated and neat. He had had only one tribe to contend with, and not several. Other peregrini raised their eyebrows enviously when they heard about it. For them, maintaining the Expedient had grown much more difficult. All hoped fervently that this new Opening would provide reserves of knowledge to simplify their task infinitely. Perhaps, behind that enigmatic door would lie the final answers that would make even the Expedient obsolete. They asked each other, "Are we wise enough now? Will we do it? Have we arrived?"

Process, Asa knew, was all. Only questions counted. Questions led to questions, and so on to infinity, blossoms of surprise opening forever. Not answers. Answers killed. Answers led to progress. Answers reduced joy to satisfaction, divine stasis to human restlessness. The great problems were not those capable of solution, but those that swelled to greater problems.

And yet, Asa knew, we must act. We must have answers as the belly must have food, or we die. He thought again of the hawk circling on the updraft, and of the stately winding of the pine, and of the frail double strands winding around their axis, trembling with the knowledge of all life, and he was sure that these would give the answer to this door, as surely as Earth spirals through space and time on its endless journey with the sun. But what greater knowledge lay beyond?

Even more disturbing than the erosion of the Gaian Expedient were rumors of a deep schism within the Arborea.

"What's happening?" Asa asked Shem.

"More of the same. The solution proposed by Rees and Bret is simply to eradicate five border tribes. They say they are five fractious and troublesome tribes. They argue that if they don't do this the problems will infect the whole Erthring to the point where the Expedient will crumble. This time, Joell may vote with them."

"That would make three. Three masters of six."

"Yes." Shem rose and hobbled to his window, placing his lumpish foot carefully. He had grown more lame, more bent, more careworn. "But it goes deeper even than that. Rees and Bret are arguing for what they call a 'reassessment.'" Shem spoke the word as if it left a bad taste in his mouth. "They're saying that perhaps the Old Ones erred. That perhaps the assumptions on which they founded Yggdrasil were foolish, mistaken. Perhaps the whole work of the Project is a sham. Perhaps, whatever man may be, he is forever separated from nature. Profoundly separated, and forever."

"No."

"That's what they're claiming. Separate from nature and above it. They say we must learn to control nature."

"No!" Asa was on his feet. "That's what caused the Entropies, that attitude! They *know* that! They know what it cost the Old Ones to give us this last chance!"

Shem opened his hands. "I know. You know. Nevertheless, here is the idea again. In the Arborea. For the moment, because of the Opening, they're quiet. They're waiting to see what will come from behind the door. But believe me, the issue isn't dead. It's a matter of time. Only a matter of time." He looked at Asa from under ashen brows, out of a profound fatigue.

What if they failed? Later, returning to his apartment, Asa asked himself this question. What if the Project failed, all time used up? The tribes would go their separate ways. New societies would evolve, all containing the same old tensions, the same flowerings of human arrogance and dread. Eventually the Entropies would recur. And so again through the cycle, until at last the Earth had had enough of the human experiment, and ended it. Asa looked at the lights of Jotunheim on one side and Neffelheim on the other. He imagined them winking out one by one until the islands lay in darkness. He imagined the first cautious canoes from the mainland, creeping close . . .

For three days before the ceremony, peregrini arrived from throughout the Erthring. Helicopters brought them, and submarines, and sometimes jump-jets that pounced like dragonflies on the landing pads. They came with the dusts of far wildernesses upon them, in the finery of the tribes. They moved to the debriefing rooms and hence through the hallways and meeting rooms of Asgard like men and women accustomed to space, to silences as profound as time, to the tastes of all weathers on their lips. Asa reveled in their feral presences.

Of them all, he wanted most to meet Aleaha, peregrinus to the Kaniks. Several times during his period with the Yuloks they had exchanged dispatches, although they had no chance to discuss personal matters. Asa was sure she knew who he was and would seek him out. He waited. On the evening before the ceremony she found him.

He had left a gathering in the banquet hall and gone by himself into the coolness on the terrace. Scudding clouds hid the mainland and the moon. He breathed deeply for several minutes and he was about to return inside when he sensed that someone had joined him in the darkness.

He waited.

Aleaha laughed. It was the scraping of a crab's shell on dry cobbles. "So," she said. "The last of the Alcheringians."

He had seen her photograph, but the ugliness of her still shocked him. It was an ugliness deeper than disfigurements of face and body, deeper than the foul skins that covered her. Aleaha's ugliness was an ugliness of the soul.

"You have no right to be alive, Alcheringian. Tell me, why did you not die?"

"I was saved," Asa said.

"Shem!" She spat into the grass at her feet.

Asa stood with his hands resting lightly on his hips. "Tell me the truth, Aleaha. Why did you hate us so much?"

"Young fool! What is this thing you speak of, *the truth*? Do you think there is a single truth, and that it can be told so easily?"

"I think some part can always be told. Always. I have asked you about a part."

She nodded slowly. "Here is a part, then. I hated you because you laughed so much, you Alcheringians! I hated you because there was joy in your lives. I hated you because you were *beautiful*!" She spat the word so violently that Asa at first did not understand what she had said. Then again her laughter came, a bleak croaking of loss, agony, endings. "Cold," she said suddenly, rubbing her hands and shivering. "Cold. Cold." She whined, and hunched against the evening breeze, and peered fretfully into the darkness looming above the beach.

Fleetingly, when she had cursed at him, Asa had imagined springing upon her, his Alcheringian war ax splitting her skull like a melon. But now he was touched by pity. She was a pathetic crone, a bit of human detritus, wizened, old, and befuddled.

"Cold," she whimpered.

He drew his cloak around her shoulders and took her into the shelter of a wall. "Aleaha, let us let the past die, you and I. I have questions."

She mumbled something incomprehensible.

"They are questions about a woman. A woman who was brought back to the Kaniks after the destruction of Alcheringia. Her name is Persis."

"Garm's woman," she said. "But she is no longer with him. Taking her was part of his pride. Only that."

"Where is she?"

"Beyond." She lifted her chin eastward. "I don't know, Alcheringian."

"What can you tell me?"

"Who her father and mother were. How old she was when you took her from Garm and humiliated him. And I can tell you that from the time he returned with her after the destruction of Alcheringia she did not speak, did not laugh, ate only enough to live, reluctantly, like one who was kept from death only to nourish some small knowledge within. The following winter she ran away twice, and would have perished had Garm not brought her back."

"In which direction did she go?"

Aleaha flung out her arm. "Toward the sea. He brought her back, but before spring he had grown tired of her, and in the first of his April journeys to the east he traded her to the people from the Outer Wylds, for the hides of five deer." She laughed. "Women! Women and Garm! Sometimes days, sometimes weeks. They are objects to him. His eyes are beyond. Even now. Even here." She squinted into the darkness toward the sea.

Behind them, the hum of conversation spilled through a door suddenly opened. Behind them, people smiled, and exchanged pleasantries, and discussed the prospects for the Opening.

"Here?" Asa asked, surprised at the levelness of his voice. "Here?"

She grunted. Her claw plucked at Asa's sleeve, drawing him to the edge of light, to the screen of trees through which, a few hundreds yards away, moonlight glinted on a lip of sea curling over the beach. *"He sent me,"* Aleaha hissed. "He said the time had come for you to meet."

A dark figure waited at the edge of the sea. His hair gleamed silver in the moonlight. Moonlight brimmed in his tracks and in the froth that washed across them.

A flight of stone steps wound down from the terrace to the beach. Asa did not recall descending them. He did not recall kicking off his shoes, but he must have done so, for when he reached the bottom he stepped barefoot onto the beach. The wet sand was cold.

He recalled only Garm. Garm waiting. Garm at the edge of the sea.

Asa crossed the beach. Garm's hands moved slowly out from his sides. Perhaps he was preparing to fight. Perhaps he was showing that he had no weapons. Asa stopped a few feet away.

"Garm."

"Hello, Alcheringian."

"I won't fight you," Asa said. "Not this way."

"So? What have you lost? Your manhood?"

"My childhood," Asa said.

Garm smiled.

"Why are you here?"

"A test," Garm said, touching the pale green uniform of the aborr novice.

"Have you passed it?"

"Yes. I haven't killed you."

Asa gestured toward the long beach. "It seems we are going in the same direction. Perhaps we can walk together."

"Perhaps."

"First, let us say the worst that can be said. Then, when we walk, we shall leave those things behind forever."

Garm's chin rose. His face moved back and forth across the breeze, like a wary animal's. Then he nodded. "Speak."

Asa said, "You killed my people. You took Persis." Going out of him, the statements bore away all passion, and left him calm. He would never forget, he would never forgive, but he had gone past hatred.

Garm waited until he was sure there was no more. And then he said very softly, "You shamed me."

"Well," Asa said, when the necessary silence had passed. "Let's go on now."

They took the first few steps. Then more.

Behind, the sea rose, and smoothed the place where they had stood.

FOURTEEN

At noon the next day, the peregrini, dream masters and masters, all the hierarchy of Yggdrasil, gathered in the Assembly Hall surrounding the Central Chamber in Jotunheim. The six masters sat closest to the great stone wall and to the open First Door. Through it, through the chamber behind it, the Second Door waited, unlocked but not yet opened.

Behind the masters sat the dream masters, and behind them the peregrini in their Yggdrasilian uniforms. To the right sat the scholars in their umber robes. Egon smiled and nodded when he saw Asa.

Precisely at the time appointed, the Colm rose and began the speech required by law. He summarized the events surrounding the first Opening long before. He outlined the information that had been gained from it. He restated the worrisome riddle of the Second Door:

"Circling, I am not a circle. Flat, I am not straight. I give strength though I have none. Progressing, I end where I begin..."

He gave credit to those scholars who had worked so diligently on this problem, in some cases giving several years. He used an analogy from one of the strange sports of the Old Ones, and said that they were like a team of triumphant mountaineers, all of whom had been essential, although only one had reached the peak. That one was a pale young linguist-biologist, Seweryn, who had effectively used the analytical capacity of SKULD. When he was ready, he had come down to the chamber alone and tapped his answer into the coded panel. The bolts of the lock, immobile for 165 years, squeaked open.

Seweryn had reported to his supervisor at once, as protocol required. The supervisor had notifed Colm, and the time had now arrived for the actual Opening. Colm introduced Seweryn, who stood blushing with pleasure and embarrassment and received the applause. All knew what his answer had been. "Helix," said Asa, smiling, applauding with the rest.

"Now," said Colm when the audience had settled, "we shall have the silence required by the General Instructions. Remember that this is the last opportunity you will have to show just cause why the door should not be opened. You are required to search your minds and consciences; for knowledge, once freed, stays free."

The Colm sat down, and a hush fell over the assembly.

Asa thought again of all the warnings of the Old Ones against the acquisition of knowledge—stories upon which Yggdrasilian ethnographers had constructed innumerable derivative myths for use among the tribes of the Erthring. He thought of Prometheus, of Pandora, of Eve, of Bluebeard's wife and Lot's wife, and finally of the one that haunted him most poignantly, Orpheus and Eurydice.

The two minutes passed. Asa stayed silent. So did the rest.

"Very well," said the Colm, rising. "The time has come." He crossed to the door and pressed the button that released all the seals with a pneumatic hiss and the crackling of old rubber.

The door swung open. A catch clicked into place and held it. Lights flickered on. Old air, fragrant with cedar and a musk of flowers, rolled into the outer chamber and through the crowd.

From the crowd came a languorous sigh of relief and disappointment. What lay before them was obviously not the final repository, for another identical door stood waiting inside the vault. Three large stainless-steel boxes, each the size of a large suitcase, sat on a low bench.

Colm was stepping toward these boxes when he was halted by a voice. It was the reedy and mischievous voice of an old man, perhaps a schoolmaster. It came from inside the chamber.

"PLEASE SIT DOWN."

Colm sat.

"While I have your attention, there are several things I would like to say. I won't take more than ten minutes, I promise, and then you can go to work on all this lovely new material we've left for you.

"First of all, I'm Teperman. The others elected me to speak to you on this splended occasion of the opening of the second door, and they join me in congratulating you on your progress. We hope that things are well in Yggdrasil, and that time is not running out too fast. Your familiarity with the ubiquitous but subtle helix is an obvious sign of good health. We chose it for the riddle of the second door because we want to suggest that perhaps there is such a thing as a helical way of thought, a way of entering a mystery as an auger enters wood, or a corkscrew cork—

"Well, onward.

"This first box contains much information that will be helpful in maintaining Yggdrasil more efficiently. In fact, it should lengthen your time remaining quite considerably if you apply it well.

"The second box contains information on a specialized technical project into which we hope you will consider diverting energy when you have heard the rest of what I have to tell you.

"The third box contains all the information we can leave you on a people whose existence you have not suspected hitherto. They are called Xtaplacians. If you consult the map

*provided you will see that they are south of you. Far south.
In fact, on a different continent. They are a second Erthring."*

The speaker went silent.

A hubbub of astonished voices rose in the Assembly
Hall and only slowly subsided into silence.

"Yes. We thought that would interest you.

*"Now, Xtaplacia ought to exist. Whether or not it does
depends first on the accuracy with which we predicted the
manner and sequence of events which destroyed us and,
second, on how closely the Xtaplacians followed our original
instructions. If they have been as dutiful in their quest as
you, they should be at approximately the same stage of
development. They will have solved comparable problems
and they will be encountering similar difficulties and frustra-
tions in maintaining their form of the Gaian Expedient. You
both will have reached a critical point, at which you would
benefit from cooperation.*

"We recommend that you contact them.

*"The second box contains all the technical information
you will need for this enterprise. Your scholars and scientists
have encountered many references to various satellite programs initiated by us during the decades immediately before
our departure. We attached great prestige to our moon flights,
our interplanetary flights, and our space stations, but these
were all horrendously arrogant and wasteful programs that
brought us few returns. As technological exercises they were
a great success; in all other respects they were a disastrous
failure except that they gave us an opportunity—too late,
alas!—to see the Earth whole, from the outside.*

*"Most of the payloads on the ends of our rockets were
not headed for deep space but remained near the Earth. We
sent aloft over twenty thousand satellites. Launchings became so routine that the press stopped reporting them. Being
what we were—paranoid, jingoistic, and xenophobic—we
designed most of our satellites for spying and for hastening
our destruction. A few, however, we built for peaceful communication. It is these you must use to reach Xtaplacia.*

*"We have no way of knowing which of them will have
survived, if any. If certain types of explosions occurred in
the final convulsions of our civilization, it is possible that the*

communications systems of most satellites will have been hopelessly scrambled. Much depends on their positions at the time of the blasts. By the time you listen to this recording, several more will have deteriorated to the point of uselessness, or spun into erratic orbits beyond retrieval.

"One group, however, may have survived intact. These are the geostationary or synchronous ones. They are located twenty-two thousand three hundred miles from Earth, directly above the equator. Each orbits the Earth once every twenty-four hours, traveling at eleven thousand feet per second. Each is clothed in solar cells that should be capable of generating energy indefinitely. Each can communicate with the others, provided they were sent aloft by compatible nations and were not destroyed by renegade killer satellites that various madmen may have hurled up toward the end. Three of these synchronous satellites, equidistant from each other, can relay messages anyplace on Earth. Since gravitational force decreases with distance, all will have been subjected to very little stress.

"We think that some will have survived in working order. You must use the information we have given you to discover which ones. You can identify them by their size, their call signs, and their broadcast bands. All will receive in the six-gigahertz band and transmit in the four-gigahertz band.

"Included in the material in the second box are full instructions for the building of the microwave transmitter you will require.

"On disks in the third box is a full dictionary and grammar of Xtaplacian as it is spoken at present. Your scholars will recognize its essential elements as Japanese, Spanish, and Tahitian, with an admixture of Indian dialects. We have no way of knowing what changes it will have undergone, but it will likely not have altered so much that communication between you will fail for that reason alone. The Xtaplacians, similarly, have access to the fundamentals of your language. We recommend to you both that in the preliminary stages you attempt communication by some means other than spoken language, thereby eleiminating as far as possible the margin for error and misunderstanding. You might try the elementary arithmetical forms of Freudenthal's Lincos, a beautiful system fully described on Disk Three, Box Three. Or perhaps some form of Ivan Bell's interplanetary message, described on the same disk. Or perhaps something else.

Eventually, of course, you will have to venture into language if you wish to establish any significant relationship, and at that point you are on your own. A caution: The Xtaplacians are likely to be more sensitive than you to nuance and connotation. Your linguists and diplomats should proceed delicately.

"*Proving your ability to cooperate with people different from yourselves is crucial at this stage in your development. If you do not succeed in this, you will make no further progress. We have provided for your mutual assistance by giving the Xtaplacians the key to the problem of your next door. Similarly, you have the information that they will need to open theirs. If all has gone as planned, you are both now aware of this fact. The keys can be discovered only through tolerance, generosity, audacity, cooperation, and even friendship. With these, you will succeed. Without them, you will make no further progress and your third doors will stay closed.*

"*Good-bye.*"

The recording ended with an exuberant burst of ghostly laughter—Teperman's, and the others' as well. The assembled throng could imagine them patting him on the back, raising their glasses to him.

When all was silent once again, Colm rose and hesitantly entered the inner chamber. He bent, peered at the inscription on the third door, and read it aloud as the General Instructions required: "*When a stag runs out of the clearing to the edge of the abyss, his horns and his head and his hoofs all pass through. Why can't his tail pass, also?*"

Utter silence greeted this.

"What?" said Colm, squinting, pushing his glasses up onto the bridge of his nose. "*What?*"

FIFTEEN

Early next morning, the Arborea met in extraordinary session.

Harrower was in the Chair. Pale, tense, he called the meeting to order. He did not need to announce the purpose; obviously it was to decide on a course of action.

Rees spoke first. He was very red, and he launched immediately into a tirade. "It should be clear that these Old Ones, Teperman and the rest, are simply making fools of us, Mr. Chairman. Look at this absurd new inscription! Look at this even more absurd suggestion that we fly off somewhere and meet people who may or may not exist! They're mocking us even from the grave. I say we go no further in this preposterous scheme. I say we consider and adapt at this meeting a plan that Bret and I—"

"You have made two proposals," Harrower said drily. "Would you care to put one into a motion?"

"Very well. I move that no mission be sent to Xtaplacia and that no attempt whatever be made to determine whether Xtaplacia exists."

"I second," Bret said.

Rees pressed a button on his console, and the screen slid out of the ceiling. On it appeared a neat graph. "Here is an estimate of the cost of building the microwave installation described. It is the equivalent of roughly one-third of one year of Yggdrasil's time remaining. Graph Two, here, is SKULD's estimate of the cost of making one journey to Xtaplacia, assuming it exists where the Old Ones' maps show it. As you can see, it would require an inordinate amount of fuel." Rees paused and let his listeners absorb the significance of what he was saying. "Here, now, we are about to make one of the most significant decisions since the Entropies. Perhaps *the* most significant decision. If we pursue this venture we shall seriously lower the Time Remaining Quotient, with no guarantee of success. Even if Xtaplacia still exists, even if it is possible to make contact with them, even if we send a mission to them, we risk sacrificing much for nothing. On the other hand, if we forget this mad scheme, we conserve much and sacrifice nothing."

"On the contrary," Froele interrupted. The others were startled to hear her speak. She had been half lying in her chair with her eyes closed, and she did not open them now to make her comment. She was ghastly pale. "We shall lose...the chance to risk...to...enlarge ourselves..."

Rees paused respectfully, in case the sick woman wished to say more. She did not. Rees cleared his throat. "With respect, my dear Froele, I believe we have taken risks enough. If we continue as we are, maintaining the Expedient, buying time for Jotunheim, we have only thirty-five years left at most. As those years pass our options dwindle. Should time run out without any breakthrough from Jotunheim, then Yggdrasil will simply decay. It is a gamble in which the odds-against increase with every year.

"I propose that we gamble no longer.

"If this assembly rejects the Xtaplacian nonsense, then Bret and I have an alternative plan ready to place before you, a plan on which we have collaborated with several others, both here in Asgard and on Neffelheim. We believe—"

"First," Harrower interrupted, "the Xtaplacian proposal. Shem."

"I'll be brief," Shem said. He leaned forward over his

folded hands. "We are in the business of life here. Not death. That is why we have rejected—so far—suggestions that we destroy the aborr bands menacing our boundaries. Alcheringia has left a red scar on our memory. Is this not so?" He looked from one to the other around the table, and none could meet his gaze. Froele nodded wearily. "So," Shem went on. "We have learned, perhaps. We are in the business of life. And what does that mean? I'll tell you. It means to risk, as Froele says. To reach out. To explore. To grope. Above all, it means *to stay vulnerable*!

"So, we must take the risk to go to the Xtaplacians. It is not, after all, a very large risk. There is no question that they are alive and anxious to meet us. You know that. You have all heard the recordings of their music."

"We're not sure—" Bret began, but Shem waved him to silence.

"Of course we're sure! Who else could it be? No, we *must* go."

"But the *practical* problems," Rees insisted. "The fuel!"

"Fuel can be found. There are depots to the south. Location H-295. On the coast. North of the sea traders."

A murmur of surprise ran around the table. Rees leaned forward. "How do you know that?"

"A peregrinus."

"Reliable?"

"Absolutely. We've confirmed the reports."

"Why haven't the patrols discovered this before?"

"Because the depots are beyond normal operational range." Shem touched buttons on his console. The map descended and a small cursor of light slipped down the coast. "There," Shem said. "And there. And there."

"Who *is* this peregrinus?"

"Asa."

Rees cleared his throat. "If this is true, Mr. Chairman, if we can indeed send a mission to the Xtaplacians at low cost, then I would withdraw my motion."

"Thank you," Harrower said.

"However, should this mission fail . . ."

"I understand." Harrower closed his eyes and raised

a hand. "But for the moment can we agree that the mission will proceed?"

Heads nodded around the table.

"Good. We'll need someone to prepare it. Lay out the timeline. Choose personnel. See to logistics. So on. Time is crucial, of course. Who will take this on?"

Bret and Rees were suddenly engaged in intense conversation, with Joell listening. Froele smiled wanly and turned her face toward the windows, letting her hand trail down into the sunlight.

"I'll do it," Shem said.

SIXTEEN

Alone on the beach, Asa made his plans.

The Opening had elated him. Like the others, he had felt a pang of mingled disappointment and delight at the revelation of yet another door. With them, he had listened enthralled to Teperman's voice and his announcement of the Second Erthring, Xtaplacia. Later, talking with Egon again in one of the lookouts of Jotunheim, he had felt the lure of that place stronger than ever before. How good it would be to stay! To work on the Project! To drop out of time into that amniotic world of knowledge! How good it would be to watch the syntheses as the material from behind the second door was absorbed!

But, just as time was running out for Yggdrasil, it was running out for Asa, too. He was no longer young. He had served Yggdrasil impeccably. Both his missions had been successful. And he saw behind him, in the ranks of the novices and peregrini, many able young men and women who could carry on...

And Persis was waiting. Somewhere. There. Behind the Kanik Mountains...

The next morning he would tell Shem that he was leaving. He would notify Fenris and Vogh and give them rendezvous instructions. And then they would go. Together. East. Into the Outer Wyld...

Slouched in his chair in the twilight, his grotesque foot on a stool, Shem summarized the short debate in the Arborea. Asa congratulated him on his victory, but he laughed bitterly and shook his head. "'We've scotch'd the snake, not killed it,'" he said. "'She'll close and be herself.' No, Asa, it's only temporary. Only a respite. You know that. We've won a little time, that's all. Time enough to reach the Xtaplacians. Exchange information. If what they have isn't valuable to us, if we don't open that next door quickly, then we'll face these challenges again."

His intercom beeped and he flicked the switch. "Yes?"

"Yggdrasil Control, sir. We're receiving that signal as usual. Loud and clear."

"Can you relay it?"

"I think so, sir. Hang on."

Shem heaved himself to his feet to face the speaker. "It comes at different times," he said. "Usually just after sunset."

There was silence, then a high-pitched whine, then static. And then, through the static but gradually prevailing over it, sounds such as Asa had heard only during that period of his novitiate when they had studied the eighteenth century of the Old Ones, mellifluous sounds passing through measured cadences with the sublime confidence of dancers who know that though others might replace them, the dance would go on, forever. "Music," Asa said.

Shem held up his hand. He smiled. "Mozart. The G-Minor Symphony. Listen."

The music swelled and faded and swelled up again, passing through vast distances of time and space. The ghostly voices of those long dead wove through it, uttering information that would never be used, commands that would never be obeyed. They faded, these voices, and the music prevailed above them. It spoke of the human soul at the mercy of caprice and ignorance. A soul watching gulfs open where solid ground had been. A soul terrified by a universe sublimely indifferent to it. A vulnerable soul, but one raising a fist, and laughing.

"The Andante," Shem said. "The second movement. Listen."

They did.

The stately counterpoint of strings worked itself out and ended. Then a hollow period returned when the voices of the long dead joined again in their ghostly cacophony of threats and recriminations before fading out for good.

"That's all, sir," the controller said. "I'll call if there's more later."

"Thank you." Shem switched off the speaker. "Extraordinary! Those last three symphonies in three months! Do you know what he said, Mozart? He said, 'I write as a sow piddles.'"

"That was Xtaplacia?"

"Yes. It could be no one else." He struck his palm into his fist and laughed. "What a people they must be! Imagine it! For all they know, they are totally alone in all the universe, and *every night they broadcast Mozart into heaven*! What a people!"

"Shem, I've come to tell you—"

"Wise. Cultured. How can it be, Asa, that two peoples whose backgrounds are the same, who have had access to the same information, can behave so differently? They try to reach us through music, whereas our first impulse is to send them code! Numbers! Mathematics! Extraordinary!"

"Shem—"

"I know why you've come. I'm sorry. The answer is no." Shem's face was like a cadaver's in the pale light. "You're going on a mission. One more."

"To—"

"If I could," Shem said, "I'd go myself. Instead, I'm sending you."

"Others could—"

"No. You."

Asa's hands and feet had gone numb, as if he were dying and those extremities had congealed. Yet, in his center, a white-hot point of anticipation burned. He wetted his lips. "Who—who else?"

"Egon. And someone from Neffelheim. And Yida, to translate."

"This isn't a job for a peregrinus."

"Yes it is. For this peregrinus. I need you, Asa. Once again, I need you. Please. Do it."

The music slipped into the room, a footman, beckoning. Beyond lay a new world, bright with promise.

"After—"

"Afterward, go east. Go to Persis."

Asa tried to speak, but no words came. He nodded.

PART THREE

THE
LAST
JOURNEY

ONE

—HELLO, YGGDRASIL, THIS IS HUGIN ONE. OVER . . .
Hello, Yggdrasil, are you receiving me? Over . . .

—Hello, Hugin One. You are very faint. What is your position?

—Ten miles south of H-295.

—Have you refueled?

—Positive, Yggdrasil.

—Do you have contact with Xtaplacia?

—Positive, Yggdrasil. ETA Xtaplacia eighteen hundred.

—Notify on arrival, Munin One. Out.

The aircraft rose through a clear sky. Below, green sea and gray cliffs fused along a white seam. Inland, far away at the edge of desert, one of the sepulchral cities gleamed like cracked enamel.

Asa did not consult his map to find the Old Ones' name for that place. All that mattered now was the sinuous ccastline unrolling under them, leading them toward Xtaplacia. All that mattered was that the fuel they had found was uncontaminated, just as the scouts had reported. That fuel now lifted the old aircraft on the last leg of its journey.

The *Hugin One* was a powerful seaplane, as old as

Yggdrasil. It had been tenderly stored through the decades, and never used. Manuals covering its maintenance and operation were included with those for other vehicles in the General Instructions, and it had been maintained scrupulously. It was ready for the journey, therefore, and the two handpicked pilots, Kai and Yosser, had needed only a few weeks to learn its peculiarities. They and the plane had been prepared to leave as soon as the orders came.

Building the satellite dish and establishing clear communications with the Xtaplacians had taken five months. Long before it was finished, Shem had finished choosing the delegation. It consisted of four emissaries. Egon would lead. From Asgard came Asa, who would serve as historian, and Yida, who had become the best of Yggdrasil's linguists. From Neffelheim came a young biological engineer named Temothy, who would inspect and record all the technical aspects of Xtaplacian society.

One by one, Asa looked at his companions now. All were sleeping or drifting into sleep. Egon slept like an effigy, long hands folded in his lap. During the months of intense preparation, Asa had grown to know Egon very well, and his respect for him had soared. Shem had chosen his leader well, for behind Egon's curiosity was a towering intellect tempered by tolerance, compassion, and an ironic appreciation of man's need for the irrational. In Asa's opinion, he represented the best principles of the Arborea.

Across the aisle, Temothy slumbered serenely. Asa knew him mainly by reputation as a bright young scientist who had already made several important discoveries, yet he had noted a contradiction in him. On the one hand, Temothy acted decisively and confidently, as if the frail systems of physics and mathematics actually described the realities of Earth. On the other hand, there was a touching vulnerability about Temothy. He was like one of those knights of the Old Ones—gleaming armor on the outside, soft flesh within.

Of the three, Asa knew Yida best. She had once told him that she loved him, and she had helped to sustain him through a time of profound loneliness when he first arrived in Yggdrasil. He wished he could have repaid her with something kinder than the harsh knowledge of his abiding love for Persis. But he could not. He had remained fond of her. They were, he thought, good friends. He regretted that she had been hurt yet again, by Garm, and it had not surprised him that she had taken final refuge in scholarship, quickly rising to the top through the ranks of linguists. Even in sleep she suppressed all emotion. Her lips were pressed tight together.

Asa looked away, over the lush green canopy of forest, and soon he slept also.

He was awakened several hours later by a change in direction and in the pitch of the engines. He went forward. Kai pointed ahead to a brilliant patch of white in the jungle. "Xtaplacia," he said. "We've been in touch for three hours."

A great bay lay before them. From its center a river, a silver snake, wound as far as Asa could see into the green and purple flatlands of the interior. At the northern end of this bay rose a steep-sided plateau about two miles in diameter. On this plateau stood Xtaplacia.

Asa gasped. Often he had imagined the cities of the Old Ones as they must have been before the Entropies, imagined them resplendent with lights, throbbing with energy, euphonious with the sounds of human celebration. Sometimes he had imagined what Yggdrasil itself would have looked like had it possessed unlimited resources and had its designers conceived not a bunker, but an architectural hymn. It was such a vision he now beheld.

The aircraft circled, spiraling lower. He looked down upon the spires and minarets rising from lush gardens, upon glimmering pools and white spumes of fountains, upon terraces, patios, and balconies on which people had begun to appear, waving. Broad avenues linked the spacious squares and circles of the city, and all was glowing and brilliant in the setting sun. Xtaplacia was an extravagant civil bloom set in the profligate monotony of the jungle.

Kai banked right and prepared for a landing on the tranquil bay so transparent that they could see the shadows of great fish passing across the white sand of its bottom. Yosser switched on the cabin speakers.

—Hello, Yggdrasil aircraft. Come in, please.

—Hello, Xtaplacia.

—Ah, Yggdrasil! Welcome! Welcome! You will find a sheltered cove at the north end of the bay. Come there. We shall have a crew to assist with the mooring.

—Thank you, Xtaplacia.

And so they arrived. Kai landed smoothly. The aircraft settled like a complacent duck, taxied around the point and into the small cove, where it was safely moored. The Xtaplacians greeted them effusively, raising both arms above their heads as the plane's doors opened.

They were taller than the Yggdrasilians, and browner. They took the hands of their guests so earnestly that the Yggdrasilians, used to masking their emotions, were embarrassed. Never before had Asa experienced such a welcome, such a sense that he was regarded with interest and respect and even adoration, and yet, somehow, with no *authenticity*, as if he were no more than a passing dream in the life of Xtaplacia.

Yida translated while officials welcomed them graciously. Then they walked together up a broad road leading from the port to the high city. Porters followed, bearing their luggage and equipment, and on both sides Xtaplacians welcomed them with smiles, and light applause, and calls in their soft, lilting language.

The city was naturally fortified. The plateau on which it stood had been uplifted by some geological anomaly for several hundred feet. Scaling the cliffs to reach it would have been unthinkable. The road entered at the base, passed a heavy gate, went along a short tunnel, and ended in a huge man-made cavern cunningly lit and ventilated with auxiliary shafts.

They rose in an elevator of glass. Pallid sunlight filtered right to the bottom, but as they neared the top the walls of the shaft grew damper and moss-covered. Luxurious vines trailed down, brushing against the elevator.

They emerged into a lush garden, abundant with exotic flowers and so beautiful that Yida cried out in delight. Her cry mingled with the murmuring of long-feathered birds.

A short walk through this garden brought them to the

pavilion reserved for them, where their attendants showed each of them to a sumptuous apartment with a bath and a spacious balcony overlooking the city and the jungle beyond.

That evening they joined their hosts for dinner in the garden and met Muan, the chairman of the Xtaplacian Arborea. He was a small, gnomelike person whose mobile face was marked by the open ingenuity of a child. His eyes were extraordinarily large, like those of a nocturnal animal, and his ears, also, seemed too large for his head. He laughed often and gleefully, rubbing his hands together. Like all Xtaplacians, he seemed easily amused.

"Tomorrow, my friends," he said, "we shall tour Xtaplacia together, but tonight we have much to talk about." He clapped his hands and music infused the garden, music so sinuous and subtle that it was at first indistinguishable from the natural sounds of the night.

"Our time is yours," Egon said.

Muan's brow creased in puzzlement, and then he slapped his knees. "Time! Oh yes. It is a word often mentioned in your communications. Our scholars have given me a report on it." He raised a finger and smiled mischievously. "Time is that which can be defined only in retrospect. Correct? Do I understand?" He laughed high-pitched laughter.

"Do you mean—"

"That we have no time? Yes. That is precisely what I mean. You see, our sole aim here in Xtaplacia is to perfect ourselves through music, to make ourselves finally into a sublime piece of music. And that is something quite at odds with your objective in Yggdrasil, which, as I understand it, is *to manufacture time*."

"But my dear friend . . ." Egon leaned forward. "Did you say your *sole* aim?"

"Yes."

"But—how is that possible? If you are interested only in the perfecting of your society, how can you maintain the Project? Or the Gaian Expedient?"

Muan laughed merrily, slapping his knees. "But we don't! We don't."

"But didn't the Old Ones leave you a problem, a puzzle, the solution to which allowed you to open your First Door?"

"Yes. Of course. In that we are alike."

"And inside, besides the new information you found there, wasn't there a second door, a second puzzle?"

"Yes. And when we found the solution to that problem we opened the second door as well and found, among other things, the knowledge that Yggdrasil existed."

"And information, also, on how to maintain your Erthring? Information on the Gaian Expedient?"

"Oh yes, yes. We found all of that. But, my dear fellow, what differences there are between us! Apparently you have attempted actually *to follow* those instructions of the Old Ones, whereas we selected what we would attempt and what we would ignore. Do you mean to tell me that you've tried to do *everything* the Old Ones asked? All those regions? Those tribes? Those elaborate communication and transportation systems?"

"Well, yes," Egon said.

"And you have taken *literally* the injunctions of the Old Ones to find the key to evolving a new man? Undestructive? Part of nature?"

Again Egon nodded.

"Good heavens!" Muan said, his eyes wide in astonishment.

"You have not?"

Muan raised his hands, palms out, as if refusing an offer. "Never! You see, we decided at the beginning that our chances of succeeding, where the Old Ones had failed with all their knowledge and advantages, were very slim, especially when it became clear that they had decided to play games with us by keeping knowledge back, releasing it piecemeal. So we conserved our energies and directed them into our own form of what you call 'the Project.'"

"So," Egon said. "That explains why you have no aircraft. No submarines. No cars."

"Precisely."

"You've isolated yourselves here on this hilltop. Pursued your own goals."

"Yes."

"And what has become of the tribes around you, those people who would have formed your Erthring?"

Muan opened his hands with the slightest shrug. His expression hinted at neither remorse, nor concern, nor interest. "We have no idea. Oh, there are occasional encounters with them, of course. Sometimes hunting parties come close enough for us to see their fires in the jungle, and once or twice a year some of their young men fall to their deaths attempting to scale the cliffs, but in fact we know virtually nothing about them and we care less. Presumably they have worked out their own quarrels, followed their own paths as chance dictated. They don't concern us. You see, the fundamental decision that our ancestors took was *to limit their responsibility*. They simply admitted—as yours apparently did not—that they could not be responsible for the world."

"And so," Egon said after a moment, "everyone here in Xtaplacia is descended from the original Inheritors? You've brought in no one else?"

"Intermarriage? Unthinkable! We are quite pure."

Asa laughed, and then quickly apologized.

"And this modification of the Project," Egon asked. "What is it, exactly?"

Muan smiled. "The premise of the Old Ones was that the next evolutionary step for man would be to develop and transmit restraints on his own activities. Otherwise, they said, in his greed, ambition, stupidity, confusion, and petty animosities, he would ultimately destroy the planet. Is that correct?"

Egon nodded.

"But you must see the irony in that, my friends! They assumed that somewhere they had simply taken a misstep. They assumed that, given time and intelligence, the error could be corrected and mankind guided onto a safer path. Even the most perspicacious of them, even Gonzalez, saw most things mechanistically or—or—what was their word?"

"Technologically."

"Yes. As if everything, the inestimable intricacy of the animal body, the ineluctable delicacies of ecosystems, the subtly myriad balances of the Earth and its multifarious creatures, even the galactic profundities of the universe itself—as if all of these were simply machines that could be *adjusted* as required, understood, all their mysteries solved!" Muan laughed abruptly, eyes wide. "What an assumption! What a responsibility! It is incredible to us that such a gigantic trick had been played on man, that he could be so deluded about his capacities! Even the best of them believed that man could reintegrate himself and control his environment simply through the exercise of *intelligence*. Like a mechanic! Adjusting here and there, eliminating this troublesome factor and creating this helpful one. Why, it is like allowing a monkey to pilot your aircraft because he nods and grins when you ask if he can do it!

"Yet, to the very end, even as their civilization crumbled around them, the Old Ones simply refused to acknowledge the inadequacy of their intelligence. They refused to acknowledge that mystery opened into mystery, and that no matter what trifling problems man might solve there would be always, beyond, the Incomprehensible."

Muan smiled sadly and sighed. "They committed all their energies to a straight line, you see. They established *goals*, and they believed so pathetically in those goals that they grew willing to shatter and debase any beauty and mystery to attain them. And they did. That's why we see them as ailing creatures even at the last. Especially at the last. We believe that anything they designed, including the Project, would be tainted with the seed of destruction. *It would have a purpose*, you see." Muan fell silent, eyes wide, smiling companionably.

Egon returned his smile. "Assuming you're right, you still haven't told us how your version of the Project differs from theirs. From ours."

"Celebration. There you have it in a word. We start from different premises, do we not? You control and search; we celebrate. Forgive me, but we feel that we understand the absurdity of mind contemplating itself, while you do not. We understand the impossibility of man's defining man. We know that because the ultimate consequences are ever unknowable, all human purposes are artificial and all action directed toward them is absurd. The only exceptions are endeavors intended to celebrate mystery. Therefore, we celebrate. And in forms that least intrude upon that mystery." Muan gestured toward the soniferous garden. "Like music. After opening the first doors, we realized that whether we followed the ends of the Old Ones or our own would matter little in the short term and not at all in the long term. The only difference would be that if we did what seemed sensible to *us* we could maintain ourselves somewhat longer and spend the time more happily. So, as I said, we took control of our own destiny. In place of the Old Ones' Project we substituted our own, based on the premise that life should be joyful—joyful in spite of mystery. Joyful *because* of mystery."

While Muan had been speaking, Temothy had been very uncomfortable, and finally he could contain himself no longer. "But that's hedonism!" he said. "Responsibility abandoned for pleasure!"

"Ah, not quite, my young friend. Not quite as you imagine. For we hold that the greatest good for man is not the pleasure of the body (although we don't deny that pleasure) but the pleasure of the soul. Gratification greater than pleasure. Joy from the creation of beauty, through either the emulation or the transcendence of nature. Yes, the *transcendence*, although I see that the notion shocks you. We believe that the essence of humanity lies in art, and that the work of art does transcend nature and rival it, and we believe further that in making this choice we are wiser than you, wiser than the Old Ones, for we have eliminated all chance of committing some irreparable blunder.

"As you will see, we work hard at what we do, but all our actions will have no effect whatever on the world. Absolutely none." Muan paused and allowed his audience to hear the silence of the Xtaplacian night, a silence relieved only by the harmonious sounds of the garden in which they sat—the splash of water on rocks, the random cheeps and raspings of the insects of the night, the whisper of the music among the leaves. "None," he said again. "And yet we are human, are we not?"

"Time..." Temothy began.

"A word," said Muan. "As I have told you, it denotes nothing here. If you speak to us of change or transmutation we shall understand. But time? No. We have outgrown it. Bypassed it. We have no more need of it because we have no longer any need to marshal people, to compel them to conform to some ideal, perform some task. We live in an eternal present."

"But a present that will end!" Temothy exclaimed.

"Yes. Of course. But that is true of all things, is it not? Your Yggdrasil, too, will end, will it not? And sooner than Xtaplacia, I'm afraid."

"You're just deluding yourselves! You're tricking yourselves with words!"

"Temothy!"

Muan smiled. "No, Egon, let him speak. It is important not to kill thought, for it might lead to a new thing of beauty." He turned to Temothy. "Delusion? Oh, I hope not. The beauty is so palpable, you see. Tomorrow I shall show you, and I shall ask you then, How can this be a delusion, this music, these buildings, these gardens, this laughter of children?"

Temothy struck his thigh with his fist. "I won't believe that all those years of civilization, all that sorrow and striving was for only *this*, that a few could live in luxury for a little while."

"Oh? Would you prefer to believe that it was *for* nothing at all? In fact, that is the truth. If not this, then what? For the life of the savage, skulking with animals? No, no, my young friend. Look upon all that has gone before as the blind groping of a plant. Look upon us as the blossom."

"You have no...*responsibility*! To the future!"

"There you're quite right. We have none of that at all. Posterity will just have to look after itself." Smiling, Muan rose. "But forgive me. You are tired after your long journey and I have talked too much. I'll leave you now and let you rest. Call your attendants if there is anything you need. Tomorrow we shall continue our talk, and tour the city."

Soon after he had gone, they went to their apartments.

Asa fell asleep easily, listening to the harmonious sounds of the nocturnal city—laughter, and bells, and gentle wind harps sighing in the gardens. Deeper, farther, softer, came the sounds of the jungle where large-eyed animals drifted among the trees, and strange birds murmured to one another, and unknown men and women, survivors, huddled together against the perils of the night, and slept, and dreamed of warm dawns...

Next day, the Yggdrasilian delegation began their tour of Xtaplacia. They walked. Spacious streets curved around the contours of the plateau, and they followed them, passing easily from one to another through the cool shade of great trees. Nature dictated the scale everywhere. No building was taller than the tallest tree, and the whole community had a sense of shelter and seclusion, enfolded by the forest as it was. Yet this forest was not the wilderness, or even the sprawling and unpredictable copses of the Yggdrasilian islands. It was the domesticated symmetry of the garden, carefully planted and nurtured, carefully fertilized and pruned. Evidence of the shaping hand of man was everywhere.

Egon asked about the place of the garden in Xtaplacian thought.

"Ah," Muan replied. "You have perceived one of the paradoxes with which we choose to live. If you recall our first principle, that man's art transcends nature, you should not be surprised that the garden is our paradigm of the correct relationship between the two. It is the result of man's shaping of nature to his own aesthetic requirements. Yet, obviously, we do not *control*. At intervals around the periphery of our plateau we have built lookouts where our citizens may contemplate the burgeoning wilderness, true nature, stretching as far as they can see in all directions. Surrounding them. Containing them. Gazing upon that is for us an exercise in humility, a reminder that we must have no illusions about control. Never. In this little place, and for a time that is only the blink of an eye, we participate and cause a human beauty."

"Madness!" Temothy said softly.

Muan turned to him. "Do not be afraid."

"Afraid! I'm not—"

"Yes. Yes, you are. It is your fear of the new and the different that leads you to cling to what you know, and to judge us so quickly. But I ask you, Is life a delusion because it ends in death? Because a child will grow old and die, is that reason never to give it birth? So with cultures. As I told you, look on us as a beautiful flower that will wither and pass back into the elements. Enjoy. Come. Life is short." He grasped Temothy's shoulder and shook him gently.

"The garden," Muan went on. "What are its requirements? First, that from it should emanate the essential sounds of nature—the splash and gurgle of water, the whisper of breezes among the leaves, birdsong, the hum of insects. Since delight in the garden consists largely for us in the spontaneous meeting of order and chance, some of these elements we orchestrate, some we do not. Consider: Two hundred years ago there was nothing here. At Gonzalez' suggestion, the Old Ones planned the irrigation system for this plateau, planned buildings, planted trees. We have maintained their plan, but altered it. Our greatest pleasure occurs when chance participates in our endeavor—when, for example, rain disrupts our plans, or birds arrive uninvited. Why? Simply because we enjoy being surprised and reminded that we are not omnipotent. The signs of life are also *momenti mori*, reminders of our mortality and of the fact that when we are gone, when the wilderness has rolled across our bones, such birds will still sing among their branches and the world will continue to unravel utterly indifferent to the fact that we existed." Muan laughed, clapping his hands softly as he walked. His laughter was like the calling of a fragile insect in the heat. "So, you see, finally, all our endeavors will be but a moment of birdsong in infinity—unheard, inconsequential, but human! And beautiful!"

Wherever they walked, Xtaplacians came out to greet them, stretching both hands in welcome, laughing. Touching the Yggdrasilians seemed important to them, and they did so often, and innocently. Both sexes wore flowing garments made of some gossamer material that frankly revealed their bodies and flowed around them. Their delight in the strangers was simple and childlike, and the

Yggdrasilians were infected by it. Even Temothy, at last, began to smile.

They were never out of gardens. Everywhere mottled sunlight played across water. There were fountains, and falls, ponds and rivulets. All were softly musical, and all added their notes to the rhythmic undulance of the Xtaplacian day. Streams turned waterwheels cunningly designed with tubular buckets that tapped out intricate rhythms as they fell, dipped, and began their circle once again. In some gardens, waterfalls of various heights and volumes, falling into tuned receptacles, all combined in a sonorous chord that harmonized with others. So, as they walked, the Yggdrasilians passed through subtly shifting resonances, a long exhalation as if the Earth itself were sighing in the pleasurable depths of sleep. Above the melody rose the tintinnabulation of innumerable chimes and the euphonious hum of wind harps in the trees.

"Sound," Muan said, "is the most important aspect of our environment, although we do not neglect the other arts. Our architecture, for example, attempts to emulate the shapes and textures of nature and to blend into its background rather than to command it. So, you will see a variety of styles—spheres against the globular masses of shade trees, there; layered dwellings against the strata of cliffs, there; slim columns there, where erosion has left an assemblage of pillars; and cantilevered terraces, there, where the plateau juts out above the jungle. Inside each of those buildings you will see the same scrupulous homage to harmony. If you find our buildings restful, and if you feel yourselves often inclined to laughter in them, then we have achieved the equilibrium for which we searched. Scent, too, we control as far as we are able, and then we are pleased to leave the rest to chance. We have one workshop, there on the hill, given entirely to the careful blending of aromas. We need never be afflicted with odors, stenches. We even choose carefully the types of wood we use for cooking."

During the morning, Muan gave the Yggdrasilians a tour of about a quarter of Xtaplacia. Everywhere they were surrounded by music. Everywhere they heard the poetic lilt of the Xtaplacian tongue. Everywhere people came out to smile and touch them.

The days that followed were similar.

"An amiable people," Egon said at the end of their first two days. "A cultivated, sad, beautiful, and most amiable people!"

Temothy scoffed. "A depraved and self-indulgent people! We shouldn't stay here, Egon. We should go home. Now. Immediately."

"Why? What do you fear?"

"Fear? Nothing. What should be feared? What is there to fear, here? These are *soft* people, without discipline, without principle. Why... why—they have no objectives! No plans! How can they claim to be human and *give up* so easily?"

"Their question to us," Egon replied, "although they have been too polite to ask it, is: How can we think of ourselves as human and yet be so earnest and *responsible*?"

"Well, I for one," Temothy said, "want nothing to do with them. I've seen enough. We have nothing to learn from them. Again, I recommend strongly that we go home." He glanced at Yida, and she nodded slow agreement. She was gazing past them all, through the open windows and into the mesmerizing gardens.

"We've come to learn, Temothy. We haven't properly begun yet. Why, we haven't even met with their Arborea to discuss this strange riddle the Old Ones have left for us. And you haven't spent any time in consultation with their engineers, their doctors, their biologists. Isn't that what you came to do?"

"Their point of view—"

"Is different from yours. Very well, record that fact. Record all the interesting differences you can find. And do it, Temothy, dispassionately. Without prejudice. That's normal scientific procedure, isn't it? Hm?"

"Yes, sir."

"Certainly. Now, why don't you list your requests, so Muan can begin to arrange the necessary appointments for you."

TWO

When Garm took the oath as Dream Master of South Merone, only a few were present. His appointment had been confirmed perfunctorily by the Arborea, which had been preoccupied by more important matters. There were few questions; the young man had, after all, passed all tests and was clearly gifted. One question was raised about Garm's spectacular success as peregrinus to Eastern Underlakes. That region had been so tranquil since his appointment that there was some interest in the means of pacification he had used. Bret had explained that Garm had acted resolutely from the beginning, and had used the full range of devices available, including frequent transportation of key aborrs to Yggdrasil for treatment in Val. If the Masters would care to see the records...

They did not. Other matters were pressing, and they had hurried on.

Garm was confirmed as dream master the following afternoon. Bret administered the oath and Garm repeated it coolly after him: "I hereby renounce all pleasures of the soul and the flesh. I give my life wholly, hereafter until I die, to the principles of the Old Ones, to the furthering of the Project, and to the maintenance of the Gaian

Expedient. I shall always act to teach these principles, for the good of Earth."

Words, Garm thought, *are wind*.

The glances of Nidor and Moran met across the room. Moran smiled. Nidor's expression did not change. It was the detached look of a scientist completing an interesting experiment.

THREE

For three weeks, the Xtaplacians arranged all the interviews and tours that the Yggdrasilians requested. No one was ever too busy to talk to them. No one was too preoccupied to take them where they wished to go.

Asa noted that the guide assigned to Temothy was a spirited woman physician of his own age, and that as the days passed he began to spend more and more time in her company, and to laugh more often. He stopped suggesting that they hurry back to Yggdrasil. Yida's guide was a young musician, and she soon began to fill her evenings as well as her days with activities that required his presence.

Asa stayed with Egon and Muan.

They moved through bowers and gardens, along trellised porticos and through buildings so light and airy that they seemed less structures than simple changes in atmosphere. They had the transitory and insubstantial quality of all Xtaplacian art, like laughter caught for an instant in stone, in paint, in the fluidity of dance. Everywhere the message was the same: Life is short, too short to be anything but beautiful.

The Xtaplacian system of doors was similar to that in

Yggdrasil. They had moved more swiftly in opening their first two, and now they confronted the third. Muan showed Egon and Asa the inscription: *I am endless; will you direct me to an end? I am useless; will you force me to a use? I am motionless; will you make me move? I am perfect; will you diminish me?*

Asa contemplated the inscription. He smiled. He asked Muan, "How important is it for you to open this door?"

"Only as important as a game," the old man replied. "For what will it matter to us in the long run? Of course we are curious. Of course we would like to see what lies behind the door. But unlike you we do not believe that whatever knowledge we acquire will significantly affect the course of Earth. We are more concerned with not causing harm."

"But," Asa persisted, "is it enough simply not to damage the Earth?"

Muan stopped walking and stared at him in surprise. "Enough? Why, what do you mean? What could be more important? Surely that was the principal instruction of the Old Ones—*find the means to cease to abuse the Earth*. We have done that, you see. Not only that, but we have created a life full of grace and beauty. What more could there be?"

"But you have done it for yourselves only."

"Of course. Do you expect—"

"Yes," Asa said. "I do expect that."

"But, my idealistic young man, it is no small thing to be responsible for oneself. Most people are not. And you would have us assume responsibility *for the world*?"

"That is what the Gaian Expedient means," Asa said quietly. "We must try."

"And that is why we abandoned the Expedient, because it was doomed."

"Perhaps." Asa walked away in silence. Then he said, "But even if that is true, we must behave as if it were not. I think that is what being human means."

Muan shook his head sadly. "So you will destroy yourselves with that delusion. Believing you can do the impossible. Striving to achieve it while Yggdrasil wears out, wears down, to the bitter end. Well, we have no such

delusions. We know that we shall die. We have infinite
hope for Earth, little for man's place in it. And as for
Xtaplacia, all of this, well, the jungle shall pass across it
as if it had never been. We accept that. We no longer
have nightmares about savages lighting fires on the floors
of our concert chambers, because we know that it will
happen. We have substituted certainty, you see, for the
agonized uncertainty in which you live. That frees us. To
enjoy. To celebrate."

They walked in silence. Four years earlier, filled with
fervor for the Project, Asa might have been disgusted with
this old man and his self-indulgent society. But now he
was just saddened, saddened not by the Xtaplacians who
were like the inhabitants of a grand castle singing and
dancing through a last night while the besiegers crept
close, but by the squandering of the opportunity won at
such cost by the Old Ones—the opportunity to make man
what he might have been, *the responsible animal*.

"Responsible to whom?" Muan asked, reading his
thought. "Responsible to what beyond the Earth? Beyond
posterity?"

"That doesn't matter," Asa said.

"Oh, but it does. For unless there is some meaning
drifting there among the stars, hidden in the conversations
of your genes, then all your striving is absurd. Far, far
more absurd than our acquiescence. As for posterity, keep
in mind that *this* is the legacy of the Old Ones." His arm
swept out across the endless darkening jungle. "And it
will be yours, too. It will come to this always, no matter
what you do."

"Perhaps not."

"Well." Muan sighed. "Come. You have been very
patient with us and with our frivolity. Tonight we shall
have a feast in your honor. An Xtaplacian feast. And I
promise that however you describe us on your return to
Yggdrasil—epicurean, soft, immoral, pleasure-seeking,
irresponsible, even corrupt—tonight you will enjoy yourself. I promise." And he laughed his shrill laughter, like
the cry of a flamboyant bird.

The banquet was indeed extravagant, offering all the
indulgences that the Val of Yggdrasil had made obsolete.

Instead of the calm, clinical atmosphere of Val, the pavilions of Xtaplacia shimmered with revelry and excitement. Instead of the precise analysis that every visitor to Val received, here was chance and randomness. Instead of the controlled dreams of Val, designed to purge the tremors of uncertainty and fear, guaranteed to soothe so that the dreamer would emerge from them as refreshed and invigorated as from a plunge into the deep currents of a river—instead of that triumph of human management, the Xtaplacians resorted still to the archaic comforts of wine and food, laughter and sensuality. And, of course, music. Always, everywhere, there was music.

Passing through the pavilions, Asa felt that he had reentered the last days of the Old Ones. He felt that he was seeing them when they knew that they were doomed and had lost irretrievably the means to save themselves. For the first time he was able to imagine what that orgy of consumption must have been like—the lights burning always; the machines frenziedly running; the shops overflowing with silken baubles, while in the slums women stitched rodents' hides for their children's clothes; food, extravagant food left to rot on the tables, while the wretched millions of the Earth moved through their darknesses toward the pools of light. He imagined the behemoth vehicles laboring through clogged streets, and he imagined other machines striving futilely to clean away the poisons with which man had befouled the Earth...

In the pleasure gardens of Xtaplacia that festive night, people laughed and danced, and swam, and drank the sweet Xtaplacian wine. Asa imagined it, finally, as a god might see it and hear it, passing above—a glowing jewel set in the darkness of sea and jungle, uttering a long chant that was at once a dirge and a hymn of celebration.

Asa dined with the others, with Muan and the Xtaplacian Arborea. As they feasted, Muan said, "You tell us, my friends, that you must leave us tomorrow. We have decided, therefore, not to wait until the morning, but to give you now our comments on the puzzle of your third door." He and his colleagues nodded, smiling eagerly. "What a lovely puzzle it is! 'When a stag runs out of the clearing to the edge of the abyss, his horns and his head and his hoofs all pass through. Why can't his tail pass, also?' It has given us many hours of pleasure. Unfortunately, it has also presented us with an insoluble dilemma. We know the answer, you see, but we cannot put it into words. Any attempt to do so would make it obscure and destroy forever your opportunity to perceive it. Therefore, we can tell you only that the answer will not be found by thinking positively." Muan smiled and opened his hands. "We know that will sound perverse to you, but it is, believe us, the best we can do."

Asa blinked in astonishment.

He thought first Muan was making some elaborate joke. But as the moments passed and the old man kept smiling benignly, Asa's surprise turned to anger. It simmered deep in him, that anger. It was the same old resentment he had felt as an Alcheringian warrior against the restraints of the gods and their smug holding-back of knowledge. Once it had driven him to demand answers from Jared and Alva; now it drove him to demand answers again, from this old man with the bland and patronizing smile that said *Not yet; you're not ready yet.*

"By what right—" Asa began. But he was stopped by the touch of Egon's hand on his arm.

"My friends," Egon said quietly, "ours has been a long journey."

Muan inclined his head.

"The cost has been great."

"Indubitably," Muan said.

"Considerations of a"—Egon pursed his lips—"delicate nature at home make it important, critically important, that we return from this trip with the key to our problem."

"Your young companions have described those difficulties to us. We understand and sympathize."

"And yet you will not help us."

"We cannot," Muan said.

Asa's voice was cold when he spoke. "You know, but will not tell."

"Cannot," Muan repeated. The gnomic smile had vanished and he looked infinitely old and full of sadness. "I have told you. What you seek is inexpressible. It is beyond all words. It will not be acquired. You may perceive it but you will not comprehend it. Never. That is why we cannot help. Because there is, finally, no key to pass to you. You must make your own."

"And so," Asa said, "our journey has been in vain."

"Oh, I hope not! I hope that, if nothing else, your journey to Xtaplacia has taught you that language, the most human, is the least of all the ways of knowing." Muan smiled once more.

"Obviously," Egon said after a moment, "there is no point in pursuing this. But, my friends, we have been giving thought to your problem also. And although you cannot help us, we believe that we can help *you*."

He took from his pocket four circular pieces of wood, all carved round with small holes in their centers. He joined two of them with a short stick. Then the other pair. He laid a little platform on these axles and secured it. Then he rolled the toy cart across the table to Muan. "The answer is the wheel," he said.

The Xtaplacians looked solemnly at this object. None touched it. "Truly," said one, "it is like turning perfection into a straight line."

"It is a child's toy," said another. "Nothing more. It must *never* be anything more."

"Imagine," said a third. "The havoc!"

They sat in silence for several minutes, staring in horror at the little cart.

"My friend Egon," Muan said at last, drawing a deep breath. "What you have shown us is a device very simple and yet inestimable in its consequences. It is a thing of uncontrollable power. Therefore, if you are correct in your analysis of our problem, as we believe you might be, we are being presented a question behind a question. The deeper question is: *Are you interested in such power?* If our answer is yes, then of course we would use your key to open the door. If the answer is no, then we will not. I think I can tell you now, decisively, that our answer is no. Therefore, we will never try this key. We will never open our third door."

Sighs of relief from the Xtaplacian elders greeted this announcement. Egon opened his hands and inclined his head. "As you wish," he said. The little cart was carried away and dropped into a brazier by a servant who held it at arm's length.

Wine flowed again. Musicians played.

As soon as he could, Asa excused himself and went down to the nearest terrace that looked out over the forest. Temothy and Yida were nowhere to be seen, but at the balustrade he found the two pilots, Kai and Yosser, standing glumly together.

"Not enjoying yourselves?"

"When're we going home, sir?"

"Tomorrow. Xtaplacia not to your taste?"

Both shook their heads. "We miss the north, sir. We miss Yggdrasil. Things are harder there, but . . . well . . . they're cleaner, if you know what I mean."

"I know," Asa said.

"Tell me, sir," Kai went on, "do you think we'll ever come back here—Yggdrasilians, I mean?"

Asa shook his head.

"Never?"

"Never," Asa said.

Temothy and Yida did not appear all evening, but next morning, as Asa and Egon were preparing to leave, both came back to their apartments. They were dressed in Xtaplacian clothes, and they were flushed with excitement, but nervous. They had no luggage. Temothy handed Egon several folders of drawings, notes, and photographs that he had made during their stay. "These are yours," he said. "I've done what I came to do. But I'm not going back. I'm staying here."

Asa looked at Yida. Her lip was trembling, and she shook her head slowly. "I'm not either," she said.

"Ah. As I feared," Egon said. He smiled sadly. "But you were sent on a mission of trust. The Project—"

Temothy interrupted with an angry sweep of his hand. "Whatever we owe to the Project we've discharged. We've done what we came to do, both of us. We're sick of the Project, and the Expedient, and Yggdrasil with all its worry, and pressure, and silly haste."

"And besides?"

"Besides, we've fallen in love with Xtaplacians."

"And it is more important than anything else, that love?"

Yida nodded, but she did not look at Asa. She looked at the ground.

"Yes!" Temothy said. "It is! But how would you know anything about that? Either of you!"

Egon offered his hand to each of them. "Good-bye," he said simply. "I wish you well." Then he went out through the pavilion to the group of Xtaplacian officials who had gathered to see them off.

Asa shook hands with Temothy, but when he turned to Yida she shrank away. Her eyes were wet. She said, "Don't touch me, Asa. Please."

He followed Egon into the heat and sunlight, and they went together down the long path to the harbor. He embraced Muan and said farewell. The little Xtaplacian was smiling genially, as he had been when they arrived. "All is well," he said. "All is as it should be."

Kai started the engines. They taxied out, turned into the wind, and rose above the bay. Asa watched Xtaplacia grow small and smaller as they circled and set their course for the north. Clouds intervened—first wisps, then strands, then solid, thickening banks. Only then did Asa allow himself to think about Temothy's remark.

What, indeed, did he know about love?

Only that it was not the property of mankind alone, for he remembered the stately rage of a great goose flailing the attackers of its mate, charging upon them to its own certain death in the sand.

Only that it was something beyond curiosity or desire or habit.

Only that it could last a lifetime.

Only that it was both part of the mystery and part of the key to the mystery.

Only that he too, because of love, would abandon Yggdrasil.

Soon. No, now.

FOUR

THEY RETURNED TO A TROUBLED YGGDRASIL.

Shortages had grown more acute, breakdowns more frequent, morale more depressed. The failure of the Xtaplacian mission added to the general despondency and gave fresh ammunition to Bret and Rees in their drive to terminate the Project.

To make matters worse, Froele had died. Two of the six candidates to replace her as Master of Esterholme had passed the initial tests, tests devised by the Arborea and administered in such secrecy that often the candidates themselves did not know what they had been. A final test was now being arranged.

Grim, Shem told Asa who the candidates were: Alva and Nidor.

"Wha— Does Alva want this?"

"No, but she will do it."

"And Nidor?"

Shem grunted. "He wants it very much. It means power, of course. He could tip the balance in the Arborea if he wins, and I fear that he might win. I fear it very much."

"But they'd never appoint Nidor! He's a technician with no experience—"

"A technician who controls great power in Neffelheim. There are those who would like to use that power."

Asa shook his head. "The tests," he said. "I have watched the tests whenever they've been known, and always they've been designed to reveal some weakness that is also a great strength. A paradox. Nidor has no such weakness."

"Perhaps," said Shem. He smiled. "Perhaps there's something that hasn't been revealed yet. Or perhaps invulnerability is itself a weakness. Do you think?"

No one knew what tests were devised, or what debates in the Arborea preceded the final selection, but within a week Asa returned to his apartment one evening to find an announcement waiting on his VDT:

2100 HRS 14 JULY 167 P.E.
APPOINTMENTS/ARBOREA: ALVA/MASTER ESTER-HOLME.

Asa was with Alva when Nidor came to congratulate her. The bitterness shone in his face, although he smiled. He did not offer his hand to take the paw that rested concealed in her tunic. "The troubles will spread north," he said. "As you know. Esterholme will be affected soon. Quite seriously. If I can help . . ."

Alva inclined her head and said nothing.

"Liquidate them!" Nidor said suddenly. "Liquidate the tribes on the border. Stabilize the rest. Then progress can be made."

Slowly Alva drew her paw out of her tunic. Her paw: the awful reminder of other violent solutions. Nidor stared at it. Slowly, to his horror, she reached up and laid it on his neck and shook him gently in a way that Asa remembered very well. "Your advice, Nidor, is well known to me. And if I want the kind of help that you can give me, I shall certainly ask for it."

"Gerumbian," he said evenly, "it is only a matter of time before you beg for help from me!" He drew back out of her grasp and strode away.

"You know," she said to Asa when Nidor had gone, "what my appointment means for you. It means that you will be a dream master. You will be Dream Master of West Norriya. In my place."

"No."

She nodded grimly. "Yes!"

"I don't want that, Alva."

"Ah, but what you want and what is necessary are two different things."

"I'm going to Persis," he said.

She sat beside him on the couch and they looked together through the eastern windows. The sun was high, the day clear. They could see the Gerumbian Hills. Alva sighed. "We have come a long way together, you and I. Do you remember what you said to me when you came for me, to bring me back to this place? To take me from the man I loved and the life I had grown to be content with? You told me that you believed that without the Project we had no hope. That is what you said. I believed that. I believe it now, or I wouldn't be here. And you believe it, too. Don't you? *Don't you*?" Her paw seized his neck, shook him.

"Yes."

"Of course! In spite of everything. *Because* of everything. So now you must help again. We need you, Asa. We need you now more than ever."

"I owe—"

"You owe me."

Only a few attended the confirmation ceremony of the new Dream Master of West Norriya. The Arborea had approved Asa's appointment quite perfunctorily, concerned as they were with a welter of emergencies in Yggdrasil and throughout the Erthring. Moran came, and Harrower, and Alva. Egon came from Jotunheim, more bent than ever under the weight of the Xtaplacian failure and yet, somehow, more amused also. Shem administered the oath, and Asa repeated it after him: "I hereby renounce all pleasures of the soul and the flesh. I give my life wholly, hereafter until I die, to the principles of the Old Ones, to the furthering of the Project, and to the maintenance of the Gaian Expedient. I shall act always to teach these principles, for the good of Earth."

Promise, Asa thought, *is debt.*

And yet there was a small stubborn part of him that refused to hear that promise, a homunculus with its fists clenched and its eyes shut tight. He could not have said, as he swore to give himself utterly to the Project and the Expedient, whether that small part was his betrayer or his savior.

Moran shook his hand and smiled. "We shall get on well together. One hand washes the other, eh?"

Shem embraced Asa, but said nothing.

At the first of the monthly meetings of the dream masters after Asa's induction, Garm rose to offer a brief speech of welcome. He and Asa were old enemies, he said, who had dispelled their enmity with reason. Fools quarreled, Garm said, but wise men agreed.

The other dream masters applauded briskly before turning to the urgent business of the Expedient. Several glanced at their watches.

Asa's first year in his new job was filled with problems, all of them serious, all of them urgent. Attacks from the east increased, and in order to relieve Moran and give more support to the Kaniks and Abibones, Shem repartitioned Norriya and reassigned the responsibility for Montayn to Asa.

On top of Gerumbia and Yulok, Montayn was a heavy extra load. Montayners were reclusive, living sequestered lives in the labyrinthine mountains that only they knew well. Peregrini among them encountered formidable difficulties in transportation and communication.

Free of the sea traders, the Yuloks had remained relatively stable, but the Gerumbians were increasingly troublesome, and their notorious unpredictability had turned that region into a seething cauldron of feuds and vendettas. Several peregrini had recently died violent deaths there.

Among the Kaniks, Aleaha had complicated matters even further—with Moran's tacit approval, Asa suspected. She had allowed them to take liberties with their Regulae yet again, bending the code to permit raids on those Gerumbians who had settled in marginal land between the Waysts. Many Gerumbians had been killed for sport, for there was a clause in the Regulae that permitted the eradication of morphs, although it had previously been applied to plant life only. This wantonness had provoked unity among the Gerumbians, and despite all efforts of their peregrinus to restrain them, despite even low-level helicopter sweeps, they had three times swarmed eastward through the marshy headwaters of the Larl and wiped out Kanik encampments.

So Norriya was all friction and turbulence, but it was not yet assailed along its entire eastern boundary by the tribes from the Outer Wylds, as the Center was, as the Underlakes and Merone were. The raids on the Kaniks and Abibones, however, were growing more frequent and more destructive.

"That's how it begins," Moran said in one of the meetings of the Norriyan triumvirate, his eyes shifting from Shem to Asa. "Predictable, of course. Bit by bit. Foot in the door, eh? Soon you're in the same predicament as the Center or Merone. On the run. On the defensive."

"What's your proposal?" Shem asked.

Moran shrugged. "Only one thing to do, of course. Perfectly obvious." He drew a finger across his throat.

Shem turned to Asa. "And yours?"

Asa was looking at the three-rooted symbol of Yggdrasil on the wall of the conference room. Not at Shem. Not at Moran. "It occurs to me," he said, "that we know nothing about those people. We've assumed that they're enemies and acted accordingly. We haven't tried to cooperate with them."

"Coop— Haven't you seen the reports?" Moran asked. "Why, these people—"

"We could include them," Asa said. "We could extend the boundary of Norriya."

Moran shook with incredulous laughter. "Include— Oh no, my dear fellow. Oh no, no, no. Quite out of the question. Why, we can't maintain what we've got. Those boundaries should be drawn in, not expanded."

"At least let's make some contact with them," Asa said. "Let's find out about them."

"What do you propose?" Shem asked.

"A special unit of peregrini. Specially trained. Specially equipped. Send them out there."

"Withdraw them from regular duties?"

"Temporarily, yes. Say a few months. By then we should know enough to make some decisions."

Shem thought, stroking his beard. "I like the idea," he said. "Let's do it. I'll get the necessary clearance from the Arborea. Get started, Asa. Let me have estimates as soon as possible."

By the end of that year, the new units began to move east. There were two of them, specially equipped hovercraft with specially trained crews. They were called Pioneers. Their standing orders called for them to reconnoiter the territories east of the Norriyan frontier and to make peaceful contact with the inhabitants.

Peregrini along the routes leading east were ordered to reinforce the old taboos with fresh recitations of the myths, to discourage the more daring youths of the Kaniks and the Montayners from venturing out into the rights-of-way. So the big ACVs droned safely east, and the hunting parties at the edges of the plains and on the plateaus of the mountains heard them in the night, or saw the dust clouds by day, and trembled, and kept away.

They went east to the boundary of Norriya, and then beyond. They passed with their great engines laboring under the weight of armaments and special monitoring equipment, the crisp pennant of the Norriyan Pioneers fluttering from whip antennae. Mission by mission as the months passed they expanded Yggdrasilian knowledge of what lay beyond the eastern frontiers, and when the crews returned, their eyes full of strangeness, full of distance, Asa and a special staff debriefed them in one of the cool rooms of Mission Center. He asked them about topography, levels of poison, quality of forest cover, quality of water, and so on, gradually filling in the map whose rough outlines aerial photography had already established. Then he would ask about inhabitants. Had there been contacts? What were they like, those people? What was their dress, behavior, and so on?

The crews brought photographs.

Beyond the immediate frontier, where renegades

roamed, the people of the Outer Wyld seemed free and fearless. This was true especially in the north. The men were lithe, the women comely. Strong children looked at the Pioneers' cameras with frank eyes. They showed little possessiveness of the land, but welcomed the Norriyans hospitably, provided fresh meat, fresh water, fresh berries and tubers. But their languages proved difficult even for those Pioneers with special linguistic training. Listening to tapes of their speech, hearing its haunting rhythms, Asa had the eerie feeling that these were the voices of another time, sounds from the bright beginnings of mankind, some noble era long before the Entropies, long before the Old Ones and their sad millennia.

Alone in his office, he would turn off the machine and cross to the eastern windows. Across the strait, the enigmatic mainland stretched away. What was he doing? Was he perpetrating some enormity? Twice that second year he had come close to ordering the ACVs back to their hangars and disbanding the Pioneer units. At those moments they seemed to him malignant probes swollen with the bacilli of incalculable disease. Perhaps Muan had been right, after all. Perhaps the Xtaplacians were right. Perhaps it would be better to leave those tribes to whatever fates might be waiting to shape their destinies, for surely those fates were more benevolent than the attentions of Yggdrasil would prove to be.

Yes, perhaps they were right, the Xtaplacians. Perhaps the Gaian Expedient was a farce, a hoax, a bitter trick played by Teperman and those warped old men. Perhaps it was unmanageable. And perhaps the Project also was a joke, for how could there be a natural center in man, that wily and infinitely adaptable animal? Perhaps they were simply wasting the last few years of their time, as they had wasted the first.

So, instead of spending one's short life in a futile search for what did not exist, would it not be better simply to drop away and let oneself be carried back into the wilderness again as a canoe is borne downstream on a friendly current? How much easier that would be! How much easier simply to shake off this duty that tied him to the past and to the most forlorn of man's dreams of conquest, simply abandon it and follow the route east, and there, somewhere in that green land fresh as it had been in the first dawn, find Persis.

Images and dreams of her were vivid still, despite the eroded time: the liquid movements of her body; her hair cowling both their faces; her laughter in the cold days, the ermine of her parka fringed with breath; her tears pleading with him not to make that last descent to Alcheringia. And he could recall her voice as well, her laughter, the intonations of her tenderness. She had lapsed into profound silence, Garm had told him once, when Asa had found the way of asking. She had spoken only in reply to direct questions, and in monosyllables—

Sometimes Asa was struck by a memory like a blow. He never knew when this would happen. He had no warning, as he had of the onslaught of a seizure. Sometimes walking alone, sometimes in meetings, sometimes in conversation about other things it would happen. He would speak her name. Those who knew him well simply looked away when that happened, as they might from a man convulsed by a fit of coughing.

Yet, he had not gone. There was his oath. There were the problems of Yggdrasil, like a vortex drawing him down. There were the daily crises to prevent him.

During the third year, Asa quietly began the second phase of the Pioneer program. Light reconnaisance vehicles began to skim eastward through the Waysts and through the Kanik passes, probing into the Outer Wyld beyond range of the heavily armored Pioneer ACVs. They were crewed by a new breed of Wylders trained by Fenris and Vogh and others like them. These were exceptional young men and women, capable of vanishing into the wilderness, alone, for several weeks at a time. Debriefing them, Asa could hear the laughter of rivers in their talk and see endless vistas behind their eyes. In the pungency of their clothing he smelled wild smoke and the fragrance of balsam forests.

"Contacts?"

"Yes, sir. More than contact."

"You lived with a group? Traveled with them?"

"Yes, sir."

"Show me. Where?"

"Here, in these hills. And southward into this plain. But mainly in the hills. Everything they need is there, so they go down into the plains only for the rendezvous, twice a year."

"Group Two hunter-gatherers?"

"Basically, sir, but with variations."

Other questions would follow, questions drawing out the kind of detail that would fill in the picture of a people as a careful map fleshes out the face of the land.

"I assume you want to be reassigned out there?"

"Yes, sir. Very much."

Unlike the fliers and technicians on routine duty, these young peregrini rarely had need for Val, for the ministrations of its doctors and the solace of its fabricated dreams. They required no readjustment; but as soon as possible they went back to the land again. Some defected, but there was nothing new in that. That had always been a hazard with peregrini from the tribes, beguiled by mists and timelessness. Usually it was a specific image that tipped the balance in their memories: a copse of alder or birch across a dark hillside at a bend in a river; wind in prairie grass under the belly of a strong horse; a beloved island glimpsed through fog; a column of smoke on a cold night above some mountain pass. Yggdrasil took a calculated risk that men and women would be drawn by such simple things out of the life of order.

Others died on their tours of duty and left their bones in forests and plains, in caves and riverbanks. Their names dropped out of communiques. New peregrini took their places.

The Pioneer Corps had been closely watched by the masters of the other districts, and its success led to the establishment of similar units along the whole boundary of Erthring and the Outer Wyld. Shem and Alva urged the annexation of that eastern area, arguing in the Arborea that the people living freely there were healthier and more vital than those within the Erthring. Somehow, a truer social fabric had survived among them, and there was much to be learned from them.

Bret, Rees, and Joell disagreed with this point of view,

however, and the quickening deterioration of Yggdrasil lent force to their argument for what they called "simplifications."

Then it would happen. The helicopters would be fitted with the special tanks that the engineers of Neffelheim had designed. The special nozzles would be attached. The noxious fluids would be pumped in, carefully. The tanks would be pressurized. And then the aircraft would go. Brightly, beautifully, they would lift off into the eastern sunshine like delicate dragonflies. When they returned, the forests of the Outer Wylds, all along the boundaries of Merone and the Underlakes and the Center, would sicken and fall away, leaving only black fingers reaching for heaven. Rivers would seethe with poison. Earth would fall sterile. Animals would crawl into holes to die. No birds would sing. People, those who survived, would be slain by Yggdrasilian volunteers or by raiders from other districts with old grudges to settle.

And that would end it.

When Bret, and Rees, and Joell spoke of this prospect, they did so with profound sorrow but also with a bright expectancy that turned Asa cold. They wanted *to clean up the world*! They had forgotten the principles of Yggdrasil, abandoned its hope. Even they! Even Masters!

Asa was horrified at this acquiescence and fatalism so insidiously creeping among them. In the monthly meetings of the dream masters, under Garm's cool stare, he argued vehmently for that diversity in which he knew the strength of nature lay, argued for the myriad checks and balances, for the compromises and accommodations through which the sinewy processes of life grew, and changed, and subtly celebrated one another. He argued for cooperation. It didn't matter, he said, that the people in the Outer Wyld lay beyond what had been Yggdrasil's sphere of influence; he pointed out that the General Instructions actually used the phrase "adjustable at the discretion of the Arborea" in speaking of the boundaries of the Erthring. Nor did it matter that blood had been spilled already, for wounds could be healed with time and patience. What mattered was that force not be used again, not ever. There were many reasons for that, Asa said, but among them was the fact that if massacres occurred outside the Erthring they could occur inside also.

Everyone knew that. Only the Alcheringian said it.

FIVE

During Asa's fifth year as Dream Master, two new regions east of what had previously been the frontier were annexed to Norriya. New peregrini were trained and dispatched to them. New information, exciting to the scholars, flowed from them. Friction with East Norriya ceased. And all of this had been accomplished peacefully.

Much more, however, remained to be done.

Beyond these newly annexed regions was a band of desolated country inhabited by formidable warriors. Little was known of them except that they moved swiftly and furtively, they attacked when least expected, and they were never captured alive. Their neighbors called them Drils. Asa had seen photographs of their corpses—small, wiry men with skin burnished leather-smooth by desert sands, snarling their defiance even in death.

Beyond the territory of the Drils the land grew gently green again, rolling out into fertile plains and gathering into ranges of hills dotted with upland lakes. Migrant horsemen moved there, following the game.

Several of the Pioneers had penetrated to that region, and a few had skirmished with those horsemen. Two units had passed beyond, toward the Far Mountains, but they had turned back after three days. Only one of the Pioneers had reached those mountains, and she had done so on foot.

Her name was Ruti. She was a Yulok. She was that same Ruti who told Asa once that she was indebted to him and that one day she would repay the debt. New Yulok peregrini had taken note of her, and two years after Asa's departure she had been brought to Yggdrasil. In the years that followed she had become the best of the Pioneers, the toughest, the brightest, the most intrepid. She preferred to travel alone, and no mission really began for her until she had left the vehicle behind. Often she would pass beyond all contact for weeks at a time, and then she would reappear with reports and photographs of new lands, new peoples. Her descriptions were always laconic, especially if she had been attacked. At those moments in her narrative, as she recounted it to Asa, her face would cloud momentarily. Then she would shrug and pass on. *I'm alive*, her gesture said. *Those who attacked me are not*. Always, at the end of the briefing, she would shake her head in answer to Asa's unasked question. "Not yet. But I will find her. I will."

In the late summer of that year, Ruti returned to Yggdrasil with exciting news. She had traveled alone beyond the range of any Yggdrasilian land vehicle, past the foothills and into the Far Mountains. The journey had taken many weeks. High among the passes she had seen the tracks of hunters, and a few days later she had seen the people themselves. They had moved parallel to her at a distance, shadowy figures among the snow squalls and the evening trees, taking care to be seen. She had slowed, stopped, waited. And one evening they had simply materialized soundlessly on the other side of her campfire. One minute there were whirling sparks, and smoke, and darkness; the next, two fur-clad women and three men. She had motioned for them to sit, and they did, first making a sign that she interpreted as a gesture of peace. They offered her fresh meat, and she took it, spitted it, began to roast it. They were all large and well fed. Their faces were deeply tanned; their hair, when they drew back their hoods, flaxen. They laughed much, showing white teeth.

Their language was unintelligible to her, but by signs and drawings in the dust they made her understand that their village was three days' journey to the east, beyond the passes. She felt no threat from them whatever. Indeed, she felt (she told Asa) that they were members of a culture that had acquired sanity in that wilderness far, far beyond the Gaian Expedient; acquired it and preserved it.

One of the group was younger, a boy on the watchful edge of manhood. He was slighter than the others, and his long hair was black, not blond. He listened silently to everything that was said, and he watched her intently, hanging back a little from the others.

Then (when she told Asa this she reached across the table and laid her hand on his), when they had eaten, this youth had risen and come round to her side of the fire, and knelt on one knee beside her. He touched his breast and said, "Tanus." He looked at her with an unsettling intensity as if (she said) he had sought to look through her and beyond her, into all the places she had been. With a gesture he indicated that she should open her fur jacket. She realized only then that she had already loosened it in the heat of the fire, and that it had partially revealed the Yggdrasilian tunic she wore underneath, with the tree symbol on the breast. It was this symbol that Tanus wanted to examine, and when he had done so he smiled and spoke a name.

"What name?" Asa asked, feeling his hands go numb.

"Yours," Ruti said. *"Asa."*

"And . . . then?"

"Then," she said, taking her dream master's hands in both of hers, "he said another name."

He formed it with his lips. He did not speak it.

Ruti nodded, her own lips pressed tightly together. "He—he pointed east. He drew a map on the ground and divided it into three sections with a sun above each section. Three days."

"Did you . . . go?"

She shook her head. "I will if you send me. But I came back, instead. I wanted you to know. I promised you."

* * *

"You've found her." Shem was looking not at Asa's face but at a spot on his chest. He seemed mildly curious, but Asa knew that he was listening intently, through whispers of mortality. He had been growing steadily weaker, and now the thing that was destroying him had turned patches of his skin a ghastly bluish gray.

"Yes."

"Where is she?" Alva asked.

Asa crossed the room and pointed to that portion of the map that the work of his Pioneers had added to Norriya. His finger touched the eastern edge.

"The Far Mountains," Alva said, her lips pursed.

"Your oath," Shem said.

"Two weeks," Asa answered. He held up two fingers.

"No. You know the importance of this meeting. How can you even ask? No. Not even for that long."

Alva stood, her paw buried in the folds of her tunic. She cradled it in her right hand. "Of course, there is an alternative. Bring them here. Both Persis and the boy."

"The thought had crossed my mind." Asa smiled. He looked at Shem.

"Have you someone who could do it?"

Asa nodded.

"It would need to be quite secret, of course. Can you provide a cover?"

"Certainly."

Shem nodded slowly. Then he inhaled in a long, shuddering breath and his frail hands struck the arms of his chair. "Do it," he said.

Alva made a small, guttural sound. She was standing with her back to them in front of the open window. Drapes billowed like sails beside her.

Ruti asked for twelve hours' sleep and six hours to prepare.

The next night, Asa stood with her in a darkened corner

of the airport while the helicopter with special fuel tanks and special clearances warmed up nearby. He placed in her hand a little bracelet of black hair and tiny obsidian beads. "Please," he said.

She reached up and laid a hand on his face. Then she turned, and went.

SIX

Rees' motion was simple: that the Erthring's eastern and southern boundaries be clearly established and defended, and that a buffer zone at least five miles wide be established against the tribes from the Outer Wylds. It was seconded by Bret.

"You've all seen the latest projections from SKULD," Rees said. "They contain no surprises, of course. We have less than thirty years remaining, even with the most stringent conservation measures." He paused and gazed with pursed lips at the set of charts that had been projected on the screen. "I wish I could tell you that I still have faith in Jotunheim, in the Project. I wish I could even *pretend* to have faith. But I have none left, my friends. None. I despair when I listen to the debates of the scholars. I despair when I seek advice from them and they can give no answers to my questions. I despair when I see simple matters grow so complex under their examination that they open to infinity. I despair when they tell me that nothing is irrelevant, and that in true scholarship there is, finally, no system."

The scholar-observers in the gallery grumbled, and their umber robes shimmered in indignation.

"Oh, I haven't given up all hope, of course. One never does, not quite. I know that thirty years is still a long time, and that we might still break through to that understanding we've sought so long. Yet I believe that we would be foolhardy to approach the end with no contingency plans whatsoever."

"Excuse me," Harrower interrupted. "We do in fact have a contingency plan for the dismantling and abandonment of Yggdrasil, if it comes to that. The plan is detailed in the General Instructions."

"Yes, of course," Rees said quietly. "But what I am proposing as part of this motion is an alternative. A better alternative."

"But there *is* no practical alternative," Harrower said. "If we run out of time, Yggdrasil will simply stop. We've always known that. There's no way to keep it going. We haven't the necessary resources and we've no way of getting them."

"You're wrong," Rees said. "We have both the resources and the means. All we require is the will." When he said this he looked infinitely sad, his eyes deep and dark under the disheveled abundance of white hair. Silence filled the council chamber. "We know where the necessary ores and minerals lie in the Earth. Our prospectors, our scouts, our pioneers—they've located them for us as a matter of routine for many years. We have the inventory."

"But we can't extract them!" Harrower interrupted, exasperated. "You know that, Rees! We've considered everything and the task is impossible. It would require a radical restructuring of energies, and even then—"

"Unless we use the tribes."

The long silence was broken finally by a single whispered word from Harrower: "Impossible!"

"No. It is not impossible. It would require mass reconditioning, but we have the means to do that, also. Neffelheim—"

"So," Shem said softly. "Neffelheim!"

"Nidor," Rees continued, closing his eyes wearily, "has prepared a dossier on this proposal, complete with alternatives and full projections for each scenario." Rees nod-

ded to his assistant and she briskly distributed copies
around the table. The dark blue lettering on the light blue
cover read: THE TRANSFORMATION: A PROPOSAL FOR THE
INDEFINITE MAINTENANCE OF YGGDRASIL.

"I suggest," Rees concluded, "that we plan a session
as soon as possible to consider all aspects of this plan and
that my motion be shelved until the implications are clear."
He sat.

Shem had been leaning forward with his hands in his
lap, listening closely to his colleague. "I suspect," he said
now, "that the implications are quite clear and that no
later meeting will be necessary. But let me be sure that
I understand the essence of what you are proposing. First,
you suggest that the boundaries of the Erthring be defended with force."

Rees nodded, his eyes closed.

"Second, that we abandon the Gaian Expedient. Is that
correct?"

"Yes."

"Third, that we 'retrain' the people of the Five Districts
to do our will. That we make them laborers. Serfs."

"That's a very negative way of putting it. You know—"

"Is that what you propose?"

"Well, yes, but only temporarily. If you read—"

"Fourth, that Yggdrasil be perpetuated but changed
radically. Consolidated in a new power."

Rees nodded.

"Like Xtaplacia. Light and luxury for a few, for a little
while. The darkness and the cold for most."

Rees began to protest but Shem waved him to silence,
at the same time rising with difficulty.

"No, Mr. Chairman, I don't think we need another
meeting to consider this proposal. I think we all understand it very well. What my friend is suggesting is the
substitution of certainty for uncertainty. It is a very tempt-
ing proposal, but I must ask him this: For whose benefit?"

"Posterity, of course," Rees said.

"Of course. But my dear fellow, there will be a posterity no matter what we do. Posterity will always look
after itself, somehow. That, as your friend Nidor says, is
its function. People will be born, will live, will love, will

die, even if we fail dismally with the Project. Whatever strands of nucleic acid link humanity to life will simply continue on. *That* is posterity. Raw posterity. It may not be what *you* would like, but it will be posterity." Shem was smiling, but his eyes were bright and cold. "As for myself, I would prefer that to this thing that you propose, this thing that asserts power and safety over everything. That is what you're interested in, Rees. You, and Bret, and Joell, and Nidor and the others. Power! Power and safety! And why? Because you're frightened!"

"I have made my terms with death," Rees said, flushing. "So have we all."

"Oh yes. But it isn't death that frightens you most. It's failure. You cannot bear the prospect that Yggdrasil will end, and that the last chance for the kind of posterity the Old Ones envisioned will end, will pass beyond your control, beyond mine, beyond anyone's. You have dedicated your life to the Project, as we all have, and instead of letting it go when that time comes, *you would substitute an enormity!*" In the shocked silence Shem said the word again. *"Enormity.* You would impose this plan, your *will*, on life and growth for as long as you possibly can. You would do away with—"

"I don't—"

"—exploration. And chance. And vulnerability. For all of these you would substitute mere power."

"Don't be naive, Shem! The Gaian Expedient itself is power, is a means of control. It's never been anything else."

"Oh yes it has! It's been much else—a way of preserving benchmarks, for instance. Standards. If you do away with it, Rees, how will you ever know that you are doing the right thing? When you have cut yourself adrift from the wild, what standards will you have, besides the pathetic little tests of pragmatism, always shifting, always blind?" Shem lifted his copy of the blue dossier. "Of course this is possible. Of course it will work. So might a dozen other schemes. But if we fail in the Project then we have failed posterity no matter what else we do. Yggdrasil should be abandoned then, according to the Instructions. That is the only alternative that leaves control in the hands of nature. It is the only alternative that is, truly, vital."

"Death," Bret said quietly.

"The death of Yggdrasil, yes. But not the death of death. Remember the Entropies. Remember how close we came. Remember!" Shem paused. His face was ashen, but his eyes searched all their faces intently, and his jaw was set like granite behind the graying beard. "We have lived all our lives in these islands as if there has been hope. We must continue to do that, for if Yggdrasil is not hope it is nothing. We must behave as if tomorrow, or next week, or next year, we will make a discovery, have a revelation, be given a gift. Who knows? Perhaps it is *that close*.

"So, Mr. Chairman, that is why I shall be voting against Rees' motion. Because we were formed in faith. We are an act of faith. Perhaps our problems, some of them, result from faith, but without faith we will not solve them."

Slowly, leaning heavily on the arms of his chair, Shem sat.

No one spoke. The sea wind whispered at the window sills and in the branches of the great tree.

"Question," Alva said, and they voted.

For the proposal: Bret and Rees.

Against: Shem and Alva.

Then, slowly, just when the others thought he might have decided to abstain, Joell raised his hand: against.

"Neffelheim," Bret said, looking at Joell, "won't like this decision."

"Neffelheim," Harrower replied, "is not in charge. We are." He rapped his gavel. "Adjourned!"

SEVEN

SHE STANDS AT THE EDGE OF A FOREST WITH ARMS OUT-stretched, and her shadow mingles with the long shadows of firs on the snow. She bends at a fire. Beyond the lodge, faint in the crystalline night, a wolf howls and is answered by another. She brushes back her hair, comes to lie beside him on the bed of boughs. She runs on the summer beach at Alcheringia, and he believes that she is laughing. He tries to go to her, but is held back. She is standing on the edge of a lake calling to him, calling his name with one hand at her mouth, one hand beckoning, but when he tries to move toward her—

"Hugin Control, sir... Control, sir... Sir..."

"*What?*"

"Control here, sir. You asked to be notified when the chopper with your peregrinus arrived. It's landing now."

Asa found the green digits of his clock. 1430. He sat up. "How many passengers?"

"We don't know, sir. They've had a radio failure."

"Assign them to Briefing Room Four."

"Yes, sir."

"And notify Garm. Ask him to meet me there."

"Very good, sir."

Asa pressed the buttons that brought his monitor to life. A dusky helicopter rocked gently on the tarmack with its rotor feathering down. Ruti, filthy and bent with fatigue, dropped out of it and came toward the camera.

She did not look back. She did not look ahead, toward the entrance to the hallway which would lead her to her meeting with Asa. She looked at the ground.

She was alone.

Asa dressed, blindly.

"Hugin Control, sir. You asked to be told when Ruti—"

"Yes," Shem said.

"Now, sir. She's just arriving."

"Asa's been notified?"

"Yes, sir. And Garm."

"Which room?"

"Four, sir."

"Notify the others, please. We'll meet in the viewing room adjoining Room Four."

"Very good, sir."

Garm met him in the corridor. "I was in a meeting," Garm said.

"This won't take long. It's about Persis. You should be here. I want you here."

They went in together.

Ruti embraced Asa, her head against his chest. "Bad," she whispered. "Very bad. I'm not sure I can go out again."

He held her, surprised that she was weeping, for he had never known Ruti to cry, even after the most terrible missions.

Garm had sat down at the table. He glanced at his watch.

"You reached the village?" Asa asked, when at last she had turned away and rummaged for a pack of photographs in her knapsack.

She nodded. She laid prints on the table. They had been taken from various positions, but all showed a spacious scattering of wooden dwellings on an alpine meadow. A path meandered through the center and out of sight beyond a ridge. A few fences criss-crossed the meadows. Blue in the distance was a thickly wooded slope, and rising above were the jagged peaks of mountains. Snow lay on the heights.

Other photos followed. All showed a young man with long black hair and wide-spaced, watchful eyes looking at the camera. Deep, deep beneath wariness and sadness, he seemed amused.

Asa had trouble breathing.

Garm picked up one photograph by the corner and examined it idly. "An aborr," he said. "You brought me here to look at pictures of an *aborr*?"

"The Outer Wyld," Asa said.

"Ah!" Garm looked with fresh interest.

"And there is something else."

"What?"

"His name is Tanus. He is Persis' son." Asa had not anticipated how Garm would react. He guessed that perhaps he might be indifferent. Perhaps angry. Perhaps mildly curious. But he was not prepared for what happened.

Garm laughed.

Garm laughed, but not the cold, mocking laughter that Asa had heard many times. This laughter was surprised, even pleased, and for an instant the Kanik glanced at Asa with something almost like warmth. He reached out, perhaps to touch the other man on the shoulder. But then he hesitated. The laughter faded. The screen moved again across the gray eyes, like ice-fog on a winter sea. "So," he said. "You are close to the end of your long search, then."

Asa said nothing.

Garm nodded. "Let us assume that his parentage is as you want it to be. That would please me, too. I have no time for children. During a life, one has many women. Sometimes these women produce children, sometimes not. Sometimes the children know their fathers, sometimes not. It matters little." He shrugged and turned to open the door. "I cannot imagine, Alcheringian, anything more mawkish and debasing than meeting this young man on the possibility that he might be my son. You have business with him, perhaps, but I do not. I have other matters to attend to."

"Persis," Asa said. "There are no pictures."

"She wouldn't allow it," Ruti said.

"But—you saw her?"

She nodded.

"She's—"

"Oh, Asa. She's dying. That's why she couldn't come. That's why Tanus wouldn't."

Garm had opened the door and he hesitated for only a moment, holding it. Then he said, "Women die," and the door hissed shut behind him.

"She sent this," Ruti said, looking not at Asa but at the little bracelet of dark hair and obsidian beads that lay curled in her hand.

"Did she— Was there—"

Ruti nodded. "One word."

"What?"

"Hurry!"

EIGHT

"Promises," Shem said, "are good intentions. They can't always be kept. Circumstances sometimes—"

"I'll go without your promise. In spite of circumstances."

"I can't authorize a helicopter, of course."

"No matter."

"You'll break my orders. And your oath."

"Yes," Asa said. "I will."

Shem sat perfectly still, grim and white. Only a few strands of color remained in the once-fiery beard. Slowly he raised his arm, and Asa thought for one macabre moment that he was going to curse him. "Help me up. I want to walk to that window. There's something else you should know before you decide. Look! How blue the sea is! And the sun! You can see the mountains all the way to the north, almost to Gerumbia!"

"Almost to the Great Bay," Asa said. "To the city of the Old Ones."

"You've passed many tests," Shem said, leaning heavily on Asa's shoulder. "What you do not know is that you are facing the greatest test of all. The greatest of your career."

"I have no career. I live. I work. I do what appears to be right."

Shem shook his head impatiently. "No quibbles. I have no time for that. What you do not know is that I am dying. It seems that this abominable weakness is more than just senility. The doctors tell me it is something quite specific. Something that will take me back to those blue hills, quite soon. Oh yes." He smiled at Asa's surprised glance. "Those are the arrangements I've made. I want to be scattered there. With your mother. You know, it's strange, but it really doesn't *hurt* much. Nothing compared to this foot I've lived with all my life. But it makes me so *weak*! Like a baby!

"Well, in any case, if you go this will be one of the last times we shall speak together. I tell you this not to blackmail you with emotions, not to bully you, but for a good reason. My colleagues in the Arborea know fully what is happening. Soon Norriya will need a new master." Shem inclined his head toward the couch. They turned from the window and very slowly crossed the room. He sank with relief into the cushions.

"Norriya will find a new master," Asa said. "There are—"

"Let me finish! I have made all the plans I can make. So has the Arborea. Unfortunately, they are not the same plans. If the appointment were my decision, you would be the new master the day after my death. The Arborea, however, is not convinced. They perceive uncertainty in you. Doubt. Some call it softness. They feel they might prefer someone more...reliable. Someone capable of taking strong measures, especially if this"—he waved his hand as if to disperse a bad smell—"this *plan* of Rees and the others goes ahead in the near future, as it well might. They believe they have found such a person. His name is Garm."

Asa sat down slowly. "They wouldn't *do* that! Moran—"

"Yes. Oh yes, they would. They will. Unless you prove yourself a worthier candidate. As for Moran, he is far too old. Too old, too weak, too discredited. Even if he had a philosophy, an idea, even an *attitude* underneath all those proverbs! No, Asa. It will be either you or Garm. And what you do now will decide it."

"More tests."

"Yes, tests always. We never escape them, I'm afraid."

"I've made the decision," Asa said. "I'm going east."

"Asa—"

"No."

"Listen! *Please!* Please. If you were in the Arborea there might at least be a chance that they would stay with the plan of the Old Ones, and the scholars, for better or worse, would be given their full time. With Garm, they will have no chance. No chance at all. You know that. It must be you. It *must!*"

Asa shook his head. He looked at his hands, and then at the blue hills. "No," he said. "I'm going."

Shem sighed heavily, but he was smiling. "Go, then." He held out his arm.

Asa embraced him. How frail he had become! How had he found energy to fight those long battles in the Arborea, to delay and delay, and still administer Norriya? "I'm sorry," Asa said. "I'm disappointing you."

"Never!" Shem whispered. "Including now! *Go!*"

Later, Alva grasped his neck with her paw. "Let me understand this. You are saying that a little time with her, perhaps only hours, is worth more to you than all we have worked for here. All of Yggdrasil. All the plans of the Old Ones. Is that what you are saying?"

"Yes."

"Then go!" She pushed him roughly away, her face contorted. For an instant before she turned from him, Asa thought that she was smiling.

NINE

H E KNEW WHERE VOGH AND FENRIS WOULD BE. HE
found them in the sun in the park between the Repository
Access Building and the senarium. They were grizzled
and a little stooped, but with the sinewy strength of the
Wylders in them still.

"We're going," Asa said.

They said nothing. They stood up, ready, as if the quiet
years in Yggdrasil, the years of waiting and of training
others had been but an hour's interlude. Fenris pushed
back against his hips, stretching his shoulders, right, left.
Vogh polished his glasses.

"Can we get the old ship?" Fenris asked.

"Yes. I've arranged a rendezvous at five hundred hours.
Tomorrow."

"Weapons," Vogh said. "I'll need—"

"Whatever you want," Asa said. "You have a meeting
with the armorers at fourteen hundred. Come on. We're
going to take a look at the route."

Ruti briefed them. She had prepared well. Using slides,
she showed them where the rendezvous would be made
next morning and where they could refuel at the Pioneer
stations behind the frontier. After that, she said, the fast-

est way east was not straight out from Norriya and through the passes of the Kanik Hills, but south across the vast plains of The Center and then into the desert where the Drils moved in darkness, moved in storms, and were rarely seen. Passage through this territory was dangerous, Ruti said, but it was not the worst. Worse lay to the east, where marauding horsemen roamed amid a huge network of streams, lakes, and rivers. The worst lay beyond them, for in the foothills of the Far Mountains were tribes that lived for war, lived for killing. In the Far Mountains Asa would find Persis and her son. Ruti pointed out the location. To Fenris and Vogh she gave compass bearings, indicated landmarks, and outlined local problems with the terrain.

The briefing took several hours.

"Why not a chopper?" Fenris asked when it was over.

"This is unauthorized," Asa said. "We're going illegally."

"Good for you!" Fenris laughed, drawing on his thin gloves.

Vogh smiled behind his glasses.

They left at dawn. By noon they were skirting the eastern boundary of Yulok, following one of the broad riverbeds that swept out of Esterholme, wound through the passes of the Ester Mountains and out through the foothills onto the great plains of The Center. Asa had seen to it that their route had been cleared all the way. Until evening they maintained radio contact with patrol vehicles from other districts and answered new call signals as they passed out of one region into another.

At dusk, picking up speed as they reached the plain at the outer boundary of The Center, they held their final conversation with a Pioneer patrol. When they signed off there was no sound in the cabin except for the whine and rumble of aging engines. No one spoke. The plains of the Outer Wylds stretched ahead as far as they could see, purple, and pale blue, and pink in the last of the sun.

At dark, Fenris stopped. They stepped out into a cold evening, hearing the rotor whine down to a growl, to a hum, to a dying flutter of blades. Motors completed their tasks and shut down automatically. Circulating fluids settled. Fenris flicked off the headlights, the running lights, the blue and green lights of the instrument panel. Then he came to the front of the machine and stood with Vogh and Asa.

Night rose around them. It was so thick, so black, that they seemed to be in a towering forest, with the stars mere pinpricks in a solid canopy of leaves. West, above a ribbon of afterglow, the minute lights of an aircraft moved steadily toward Yggdrasil. Overhead, parts of the last rockets hurled aloft by the Old Ones tumbled serenely through their orbits, sunlight glinting off their flanks. North, the aurora shimmered like translucent silk. From it and from the stars, enough light spilled to earth that Asa saw they had come to rest in an enormous bowl. He heard only the blood surging across the membranes of his ears. In the chill embrace of that night, he felt again the sublime indifference of the universe to all the deeds of men, to all paltry human hope and accomplishment, to all joy and love. He knew absolutely that time, the most ludicrous of man's creations, would cease at last, and all history curl into a wisp of dust. When that happened, *this* would remain, utterly unchanged by the human spasm. And against that certainty, Asa raised his fist.

They were not attacked that night.

Nothing moved on the plain.

Wind rose with the sunrise. Wind and scudding clouds swept down from behind them at the first tremor of sun. For half a day they traveled in an ominous twilight, through wind that whipped loose sand into swirling and enveloping clouds. Three times Fenris had to stop in the scanty protection of knolls, and he and Vogh, shouting to be heard above the wind, went out to empty the filters of the air ducts and secure the dust covers on other parts of the machine.

Progress was slow. They were following one of the old highways, a once-broad asphalt strip now buckled and broken. Sometimes they saw remnants of white strips of paint, but more often they groped from one tilted section to the next, unsure whether they were still on the roadway or whether they were angling off into the trackless expanses of the plain.

"Only good thing," Fenris said, hunched close to his windshield, "if we can't see them, they can't see us, either. Anyway, not even aborrs'd want to go out in *this*."

Asa was less sure. Perhaps worry, and tension, and fatigue had brought on hallucinations, but three times he believed he had glimpsed figures amid the storm, figures like none he had seen, even in Gerumbia. Shrouded, gesticulating, frozen in such distorted attitudes that they could as easily have been grotesque trees as men, they appeared for a moment and vanished again into the folds of the storm. Asa said nothing. He peered close to the glass. For an hour he saw nothing but swirling sand.

When Fenris stopped again to clean the filters, Asa did not think it was necessary to give a warning. He had concluded by then that what he had seen were creatures of his imagination, and that nothing could survive in that storm, let alone keep pace with the ACV.

So, he inspected maps while Fenris and Vogh did what was necessary outside. He was aware of their shouting over the roar of the storm. He was aware of Fenris' climbing back into the pilot's seat and slamming the door behind him. Then, glancing up from his map, he was aware of Vogh frozen in the right doorway of the cockpit. One hand held the door. The other, two fingers spread, pressed his throat. It gleamed red, this hand. Between the fingers protruded a perfect steel arrowhead the size of a thumbnail.

Asa lunged forward, grabbing Vogh's jacket. "Get in!" he shouted, knowing it was useless, absurd. The look of gentle wonderment in the man's eyes glazed even as Asa reached him. His knees buckled, he slumped forward into the doorway, and the last of his life gushed out over the skirt of the vehicle. Asa fell across the seat, grabbing the man's jacket, reaching past the trimly feathered little shaft that protruded from the back of his neck. Another arrow grazed Asa's shoulder and embedded itself in the instrument panel. Another thumped into Vogh's back even as Asa held him. Asa felt the life shudder away, and he dropped him, stretching to slam the door, shouting to Fenris, "Go! Go! Go!"

Fenris was shouting, too, shouting something unintelligible, a long snarling howl of rage and fear that blended into the scream of the engines as he accelerated and swung the craft in a vicious sweep to the right. And he was still shouting as Asa managed to seal the door and the craft roared through the tatters of the storm into humanoid shapes crouched on a little ridge, grinding one under the edge of its skirt, sucking another into the rotor, scattering the rest. Fenris spun the machine wildly, searching, pounding the heel of his hand into the red rubber button that sent jolts of 300-decibel piezosonic agony into anything within five hundred yards.

"Who were they? Who were they?"

"Drils," Asa said. "Go! Go! Get out!" He was sitting in the copilot's seat with his arms braced against the instrument panel and his head hanging between them. For a moment he had feared that he might suffer a spell and prove useless. But it was all right now. He had driven it back, and although that spell might return later like a stern creditor, now he felt only the profound disgust at failure and futility that he had always felt in the presence of violent death.

Fenris was beating the controls and cursing softly like a defeated child. His face was wet. "Dumb dumb dumb," he said. "Dumb dumb."

"It always is," Asa said.

They went on. The storm wore itself out. Winds lifted above them and trailed away to the east. Behind, the setting sun broke out of the clouds. Ahead and around them, the great plain stretched away, all purple, as far as they could see. The first foothills of the Far Mountains lay against the horizon, so faint that they were almost indistinguishable from the fleecy underbelly of heaven.

The highway had leveled out. Fewer upheaved and tumbled sections obstructed their passage, and Fenris was able to accelerate to high speed for an hour in the last of the light.

At dusk, they stopped in a flat and desolate section to inspect the vehicle. Dril arrows had caused only slight damage—various dents and a couple of broken lights. One of the steel points, cunningly fashioned from the alloys of the Old Ones, had penetrated the outer skin, the insulation, and the inner skin as well, decompressing the cockpit. They took time to seal this hole.

More serious was the steady grumbling that had developed in the main bearings. Fenris feared that despite the frequent cleaning of the filters, grit had sifted through the innermost parts of the machine. "Old," he kept saying, circling his craft, caressing it, checking and rechecking its vulnerable parts, its vulnerable patches. "Poor old girl. Worn out. All these years we've had her, sir. Same ship. The three of us, we've covered a lot of country in our time. Vogh, he used to say he figured we'd all go together. One blaze of glory at the end, he used to say. Against the aborrs. No wasting away. No wearing out. Just a last, bright light." Fenris snorted and kicked a place where dust and dried blood had congealed on the neoprene skirt. "And look what happened to him! Never had a chance. Never had time even to *think* about what was happening to him. You know, sir, it's almost funny."

"It often is," Asa said. "Death. Sometimes people laugh. Sometimes they don't."

Fenris came up beside him and peered into the evening. "How much farther, do you think?"

"Those hills are about halfway. Will the machine make it?"

"Hard to say. I can't do anything more for it."

Asa lowered the glasses and looked suddenly at the other man. "You could go back," he said.

Fenris scratched his chin. "Well, yes, sir, I guess I could."

"You'd make it, Fenris. Take the machine. It would be much safer than going on."

Fenris nodded.

"Well," Asa asked after a moment, "what do you think? Do you want to?"

The man peered into the dusk, rubbing his belly, not looking at Asa. "A part of me wants to, sir. I can't deny that."

"You know this is unofficial. It won't help Yggdrasil a bit. It won't help the Project."

"Well, as for that—"

"This is for me, Fenris. Only me."

"To find a woman. Right, sir?"

"Yes."

"An aborr. Dying."

"Yes," Asa said.

"Even if we make it, sir, it doesn't seem likely that we'll come back, does it?"

Asa shook his head.

Fenris unzipped his coveralls and scratched his chest reflectively. "You know, sir, I'm Yggdrasilian born and bred. So was Vogh, though some said his father was an aborr. Worked for the Expedient all our lives. Gone on patrols, gone on missions. Dull stuff, mostly. We'd go out, do the job, come back, take our leave, go out again. Spent all our lives in and around machines. Sometimes, evenings like this, we'd look out on the wilderness, *feel* a little bit of it, maybe, but we'd never be *in* it, if you know what I mean. We'd talk sometimes about how it might be out there beyond the Erthring, how the aborrs could get along by themselves without Yggdrasil to keep them going. Thing is, sir, we never really took any *risks*, if you know what I mean. We were always enclosed, safe, either in Yggdrasil, or in the ship, or just in all the answers Yggdrasil gave us. You gave us the chance to go outside, beyond all that." Fenris shivered and zipped up his suit. It was almost dark. "As for the woman, well, sir, I never felt that way about any woman—not that I'd risk my life for her. If you feel that way, I guess that's good enough. I guess we'll just go on." He turned away abruptly and began to set up the little stove over which they would cook supper.

Next morning, they were attacked at the first pass in the hills. Rocks crashed on the roof and Asa shouted, "Back! Back!" seeing movement along the ridge, an instant before an avalanche thundered down, filling the place where they had been, shrouding them in dust. Fenris spun the machine, cursing, hitting the piezosound button, and they roared back down the valley. Once again they hadn't seen their attackers except as spindly shapes gesticulating on the skyline, but the aborrs had obviously been watching the ACV approach across the plain, and the ambush had been well prepared. Detouring around them and through another pass took a day and a half. Random rocks had inflicted only minor damage, but the grumbling of the bearings had grown much louder and the machine trembled constantly. "Not long," Fenris said grimly.

The end came at noon next day. They had been following the graveled shore of a broad river that, according to the map Ruti had given them, led through a network of smaller tributaries and into the heart of the hills. They went slowly, partly because of the shuddering of the craft, partly out of caution, although all seemed safe enough. The shallows of the river danced under a warm sun, the generous shores spread like welcoming arms, the trees shifted like feathers as the breezes moved across them. Asa knew that if they stopped, if he got out and inhaled deeply, he would smell evergreen warmed in a summer sun. He would smell sweetly decaying humus and the green life springing out of it. He knew that if he walked across the bank and into the twilight under the boughs he would sink ankle-deep into damp mosses, and find the dusky plumage of mushrooms near the boles of trees. If he—

The forest trembled. In a little spasm, a part of it separated and rolled toward them.

Men on horses came out of the trees. The horses were short and stocky and strong, and they ran fast, despite the terror-stricken white eyes they rolled at the vehicle. The men were small, too, clinging like monkeys to their mounts. They shook fists in the air. Some gripped spears and bows. Some bore the ancient guns of the Old Ones.

"Left!" Asa shouted: "Across the river!"

Fenris was already accelerating and swinging toward the river, hitting the sound button at the same time. Asa saw the charge collapse into a melee at the sudden blast of noise. Horses reared. Men cursed, howled, clamped hands over their ears. Some fell and buried their heads in their arms. Some reeled for the protection of the forest. Many would be deafened permanently. Many would endure the rest of their lives the banshee wail of this monster that attacked them even as it gave ground. The violence sickened Asa, but it was better than killing. Better than Vogh's guns, which he had not even uncovered.

The ACV labored to midstream before it died. It gave a mighty shudder, tipped up, and settled into the shallow water. "That's it!" Fenris shouted, switching off the motors, closing down all circuits except the one that kept the sound blasting. "We walk from here."

They clamped on ear protectors, snatched up the emergency kits that lay ready under the seats, and dropped into the knee-deep icy stream. They splashed to the deserted north bank and scrambled gasping up the gravel into the protection of the forest. Nothing moved. Behind, the river lay serenely in the sun, with the defunct ACV squatted like a dying tortoise blaring defiance. They had two hours before the batteries ran down and the screaming dwindled to a querulous whine. Then the most daring of those hominids would creep close through the trees to watch for signs of life. They would hurl stones, test for life with a probing shot or two, and fall with avenging fury on the carcass of the ACV.

Fenris and Asa would have a day at most. It was a good head start, but it would mean little unless they could reach terrain impassable to horses. That meant going high.

They started. For three days they saw no one, saw no signs that they were being followed. For three days they slept in daylight and traveled by night, keeping to the cover of the forest. On the fourth day they heard shouts from ahead, echoing down a valley, and on the fifth day they saw laughing hunters, well fed and dressed, bring down a deer in a clearing below them. It was a classic kill, executed so efficiently that Asa almost strode out of his hiding place to give the old Alcheringian cry of triumph.

On the sixth day they ran out of rations. The high-energy foods that had enabled them to travel fast and light were gone, and they began to hunt as they traveled, using the silent charges of their weapons sparingly until at last they had only five rounds each remaining. They would keep these for emergencies.

Asa made a spear.

He made a bow and several types of arrows.

In his hands the wood and stone and sinew came alive. The feathers shimmered as he fitted them. He had forgotten nothing, although the crafting of the weapons took longer than it had once. Despite the sorrow that enveloped him, despite the sick urgency of his mission, he smiled as he worked. The weapons were elegantly simple. Hand and brain, he was part of them once again.

On the seventh day Asa gave his handgun and the last of his charges to Fenris. He made his emergency pack into a quiver. The tattered Yggdrasilian coveralls he cut into a loose shirt and breechclout. That day he felled a small stag after a perfect stalk. He would have liked to use the hide but he had no time to tan it, so he left it with the rest of the carcass to scavengers.

On the eighth day Fenris died. He died as he had lived, hard.

They had separated to hunt, and a quarter mile of low ridge and forest lay between them. At noon Fenris did not keep the rendezvous, and Asa began to circle back. He found him by the gibbering shouts of hominid warriors, whom he never saw alive. He found him with his throat slit and more stab wounds in his body than Asa cared to count. He was smiling. Around him lay the bodies of six of his attackers.

Asa buried him and said over his grave the Alcheringian prayer of the dead, which came back to him easily although he thought he had long since forgotten it. Then he took what little was useful from the bodies of the aborrs and headed east again, traveling fast.

He saw no one else until the eleventh day. He was in the Far Mountains by then and the peaks rose around him, sublime and indifferent, wrapped in clouds. He was cold. He believed he had entered the last valley, and that the village of the mountain people, where he would find Persis, lay less than a day's journey ahead. Early in the afternoon he knew he was being watched. Cover was sparse, and he had no alternative but to move in the open, keeping well clear of any copses or boulders. It was not long before he saw his pursuer. In fact, the man was not pursuing so much as accompanying, traveling in the same direction as Asa and keeping pace with him several hundred yards up a slope to the right. He made no attempt to conceal himself. He moved easily, with a hunter's grace.

He was wrapped in bulky furs. A fur cap engulfed his
head and much of his face. From it, a blond beard protruded. He gave no sign that he was aware of Asa, and
yet whenever Asa changed his course slightly and angled
up the slope, the man also angled away, keeping the same
few hundred yards between them.

He was, it seemed, a scout.

Soon, other figures appeared on the slopes, until Asa
counted seven. Like the scout, they were traveling parallel to him and a little ahead. All were clothed in the
same ample furs.

At dusk Asa stopped by a small stream and built a fire,
roasting a little venison that remained from a kill two days
earlier. He ate slowly, his face turned to the fire, his eyes
watching the edge of the forest. He waited.

They came suddenly, as he knew they would. There
had been no sound, no warning movement at the edge of
the forest. They simply materialized. Three of them. Asa
stood, raised a hand in welcome, and they came forward
close to the fire, drawing back their hoods. They were all
large men with broad brows and open, alert expressions.
All were bearded. Only the two at the sides bore weapons,
and these they carried slung across their backs. Their
hands were empty. The man in the center carried a suit
of fur garments, which he held out to Asa. "Take," he
said, using the Kanik word.

Asa put them on gratefully. He was thoroughly chilled,
and the soft fur against his skin felt luxurious. He smiled
and nodded his thanks. He offered them meat, which they
accepted, sitting across the fire and eating slowly, atten-
tive to the food. When they had finished they cleaned
their hands and beards with snow. The one in the middle
gestured to Asa, smiling fleetingly. "Come," he said. "We
must hurry."

They moved. Beneath his anxiety there was a part of
Asa that exulted in the speed, and the ease, and the silence. For a little time Alcheringia lived again in him. For
a little time he was a hunter again in a correct and vital
world, a world with its mysteries intact. And he was going
home. To Persis. Yggdrasil was but a bad dream, and he
would move with these hunters now ever deeper into

wilderness and life, until he had lost forever all memory of those dying islands.

They reached the village at first light. Its smoke slipped down the mountainside to them in the cool drafts of morning. A rooster crowed. Dogs barked as they reached the first houses, and then they were in the village center and the hunters who had brought him there were handing him a bowl of something warm that a woman had brought from one of the houses, drawing a shawl around her shoulders. Others emerged, too, strong people with broad and sympathetic faces who spoke quietly in a language Asa could not understand. He held the bowl in both hands, and sipped the warm broth it contained, and through its steam saw a very old man hobbling forward through the crowd, which parted to let him pass. A young man with long black hair followed him, watching Asa warily. His eyes were red. Tanus.

"She's been hoping," the old man said in halting Kanik. "She waited until last night. She said that if you came, even now—"

"Persis."

"There." The old man nodded toward the mountains, to the north. "You may not be too late—"

But Asa was already moving up the narrow trail that led behind the village. He was already singling out from the other tracks the ones he knew were hers, and when, two miles up the trail, they separated from the others and continued alone toward the crags, he followed. The steps had grown shorter, and were clearly made with great difficulty. Several times she had fallen to her knees, and once he came upon the full imprint of her body.

He found her at sunrise, a small, fur-wrapped figure, sitting in the shelter of an outcrop, facing east. She did not move at his approach, and for a moment he feared that he had come too late. But when he fell to his knees beside her and embraced her, and said her name, then her eyes opened.

Her arms reached for him.

She was very frail. Her hair was almost white.

"Persis," he said to her. "My love."

"Asa."

"My love." His tears fell on her neck. He held her.

"I had given up," she said. "Almost." She could no longer move her legs, and she raised her hand to touch his face only with great difficulty. It seemed that the outermost parts of her body had already died, and only the center of her remained alive. She whispered. She strove to keep her gaze on him. She drew his face down and kissed him.

The sun rose in a clear sky, and all the world was white, except for the lowest valleys beneath the mist. All the world was silent.

"Do you remember our winters?"

"Everything," he said.

"They were the best times. Only the two of us."

"Yes," he nodded. "Yes."

"It's like that again. As if we were young again."

He held her. He opened his fur jacket and drew her into it. The tiny bracelet of hair and beads slipped easily over her gaunt hand. "I love you," he said. "I have always loved you. I always will."

She gave no sign that she had heard him, except that her fist, clenched against his chest, unfolded above his heart. There was a long stillness, and then she said so softly that he almost failed to hear, "He is your son."

"Yes. I know." He held her. He wanted to give her all his warmth. All his life.

Quietly she sang the death chant he had heard many years before:

> From darkness we are born to light;
> In light we bear joy and sorrow;
> In light we bear memories.
> Be kind to my memories, O gods,
> For they are orphans.
> Be kind to me, O gods,
> For I am an infant again,
> Newborn into darkness.

The sun warmed the ledge above them. Snow melted and formed a crystalline droplet, perfect in the clear day. It hung, trembled on a tiny spur of granite. And then it fell.

* * *

Later, perhaps two days later, perhaps three, Asa returned to the village that lay in a saddle of the mountains, above the great valleys, looking both east and west. He was very weak. He wanted only to sleep. He had not thought beyond that sleep, and yet random images came to him—not thoughts but offerings from other portions of himself—images of long and timeless days, of far rivers and forests forever green, of the warmth of the fire, the joy of the hunt, the hiss of northern lights. Only the sounds and the solace of the wild were in those images.

There was nothing in them of Yggdrasil.

So it was that when he became aware that he was looking at the insignia of the great tree of Yggdrasil, a dormant part of him awoke. A warning part. He stopped walking. His brow creased. He shook his head slowly, a dazed animal.

The emblem was clearly there, in front of him. It shone on the flank of a small helicopter waiting at the edge of the village. It was the type of machine used for reconnaissance and long-range missions. From its antenna fluttered a two-tone blue pennant with a white *N* emblazoned on it.

A small group waited beside it: Tanus, and the three hunters who had brought him the last miles to that place, and the pilot sitting on the step of his machine.

And Alva.

Alva.

Even at that distance she was unmistakable.

Asa turned around. He looked at the mountains. He looked down the great valleys to those green places where, far in the distance, fresh rivers ran. He looked at the untroubled sky.

Slowly he turned around once more and went forward, trying not to stumble.

Alva came to meet him. She embraced him. Her grotesque bear's paw patted his back. "Dear man," she said. "My dear, dear man."

"Alva. Why are you here, Alva?"

"To take you home."

"I am home."

"To Yggdrasil."

"No." He shook his head. "No," he said again.

She drew back, and to his surprise he saw that her face was wet. He had known her to weep only twice before, and both times because of a great loss. He looked down, but she lifted his chin with her paw, forcing his gaze to hers. "Shem's gone," she said.

His eyes closed.

But she left her paw on his face. She held him. "More," she whispered, grimacing in pity. "Worse. *You are the Master of Norriya!*"

"No!" He drew back from her, back toward the mountains. "I don't want it!"

"Asa, you must."

"Moran."

"No. Unsuitable."

"Garm, then. Give it to Garm," he said. "Let Garm have it."

"There was a test," Alva said. "Garm didn't pass. You did."

He laughed bitterly. "Test? What test?"

"Going to Persis," she said.

Behind her, above the little group gathered at the side of the helicopter, the blue-and-white pennant beckoned. The pilot stood up and stretched. He reached inside the craft and found dark glasses, which he put on. He drew thin black gloves over his fingers. He looked at his watch.

ABOUT THE AUTHOR

Wayland Drew was born in Oshawa, Ontario, and received his early education there. He began to write seriously in high school and continued while studying English Language and Literature at the University of Toronto. Since graduation he has combined high school teaching and writing. He and his wife, Gwendolyn, live in Bracebridge, Ontario, where he has taught English for ten years at Bracebridge and Muskoka Lakes Secondary School. They have four children.

The Gaian Expedient is the second novel in *The Erthring Cycle*, a trilogy that began with *The Memoirs of Alcheringia*.